Chasing Light Fantastic

Paul Morris

Copyright © 2019 Paul Morris

All rights reserved

ISBN 978-1-0886-9622-4

First published in Great Britain in 2019

This paperback edition first published in 2019

Paul Morris has asserted his right under
the Copyright Design and Patents Act 1988
to be identified as the author of this work.

Every effort has been made to obtain the necessary permissions
with reference to copyright material as quoted.
The author apologises for any omissions in this respect and will
be pleased to make the appropriate acknowledgements
in any future editions.

Dedicated to the memory of
all the talented bands
that entertained teenagers
at Venturers Youth Centre
in Wolverhampton in the late sixties;

to all the Wolves players who made many
sixties Saturday afternoons so special;

and to the music of the time.
There will never be a more eclectic soundtrack
to go through such formative teenage years.

And to the late Keith Farley,
whose inspirational work,
on documenting the music scene
in the Black Country,
made me write this novel instead of
attempting the hopeless task of
improving on his work.

Contents

		Page
	Introduction	1
1	Another Saturday Night	5
2	Flowers In The Rain	32
3	Hello Goodbye	59
4	Bend Me, Shape Me	85
5	Time Of The Season	111
6	Last Time Around	138
7	The Urban Spaceman	166
8	Surround Yourself With Sorrow	194
9	Tears In The Wind	222
10	She Is Still A Mystery	250
11	Suite: Judy Blue Eyes	285
	Acknowledgements	322

Introduction

There is a now an oft-quoted maxim – "If you can remember anything about the sixties, you weren't really there". Well, I know I was there, and I know exactly where I was in the latter years of that decade of change, adventure, exploration, revolution and innovation – I was in Wolverhampton.

As a teenager in the Black Country, growing up in the sixties was full of strange and wonderful experiences, whether as a supporter of a football team who often failed to match their efforts on the pitch with the steadfast support that came from the many thousands of fans on the terraces, or as a devotee to the era's musical backdrop, that began with bland 'Moon and June' crooners, and ended up with psychedelia and prog rock.

Nations were venturing into space and families began going abroad for their holidays. Television could now be watched in colour and BBC radio changed from the staid Light and Third programmes to Radios 1, 2 and 3, with the Home service becoming Radio 4.

Was it the 'swinging sixties' in Wolverhampton? Somewhere in the vicinity maybe but that description was more at home in London, Manchester and Liverpool than in the Black Country. But that's not to say there weren't matters from our local area that defined that era.

Over half the population owned their own homes and manufacturing was on the rise in the Midlands, especially cars and white goods. Employment was a given to most people. Apprenticeships taught good, steady trades, and many families enjoyed a much better standard of living than in the post-war years. And Enoch Powell was our MP.

It was also a time when things were not so immediately available as nowadays and you needed to bide your time before you could buy them. Teenagers relied on generous relatives and godparents to supply the record tokens to buy LPs or they would take Saturday jobs or paper rounds in order to supplement their weekly pocket money.

However, there was one important thing that was accessible to teenagers at that time – music – and dancing – at youth clubs, right across the town, from Codsall to Penn, Fallings Park to Warstones, and Compton to Wednesfield.

On most Saturday evenings, the music was provided by musicians – teenagers themselves often – who dreamt of becoming the next Beatles, Stones, Who or Kinks. Some of them went on to find fame and fortune, others didn't. Some made a decent living in the music business, and some never gained the accolades that many local fans thought they deserved. They were all highly talented entertainers and musicians who could ably reproduce the hits of the day for those many youngsters just out to enjoy themselves at the weekend.

Of course, fifty years on, no one can be expected to remember everything exactly as it happened and so, by writing my experiences as a semi-biographical novel, I can be somewhat economical with the truth and perhaps it is a smidgen more sugar-coated than it really was.

Some names have been changed, some haven't. Some things actually happened, and some didn't. I never did a paper round, but I was in the choir. We did set up a choir football team (and we did lose our first game 17-3!) and much of our family life was centred around a mission church in the Penn area of Wolverhampton.

We spent holidays in South Wales (great) and North Devon (not so great). Family visits were to Emsworth and there were tiresome days in Chesterfield, although that is where I discovered the joys of the wireless!

Each chapter has three main features. First – a Wolverhampton Wanderers football match, illustrating the 'religious' way in which supporters attend matches, through thick and thin, and then moan, praise or rant on matters over which they actually have no influence whatsoever.

Second – it's about the music of the time and those years – 1967 to 1969 – which, to me, were probably the most eclectic time in popular music. By featuring an LP in each chapter (that I would save up to buy) I hope it will strike a note (pun intended) with many of a similar age.

Third – an evening's entertainment, usually on a Saturday, provided by the local bands of that era who are rightly and deliberately celebrated in this novel for providing so much joy and pleasure.

All the groups featured in this novel played at the Venturers youth club in Warstones, but not necessarily on the dates as written. The setlist for each band's gig includes the hit songs around at the time, chosen to suit their styles together with some of the tracks that I am aware the bands released as singles.

As a teenager, it was very much a time when football and pop music just seemed more important than life itself although, when attending an all-boys grammar school which may have been excellent for your education, and getting on in life, most lads were left spluttering at the prospect of even talking to a girl, never mind asking her out for a date.

Some say, "Nostalgia isn't what it used to be" and they could be right. There is nostalgia aplenty in this novel, whether it's about space travel and the moon landing, or the comics and toys of the era, or fashion, new technology or food, or what was changing in the town – shopping centres, the demise of the trolley bus, or shops that are no more.

Please enjoy it for what it is – fond memories of originality, fun, pleasure and the delights that come from family, friends and growing up in a decade when so much seemed imaginable, especially when you had such a brilliant musical soundtrack to accompany it.

Paul Morris, 2019

Chapter 1 - Another Saturday Night

The bathwater was just going cold. It had been a pretty good Saturday. No more Saturday morning school. Two terms now with a double lie-in at the weekend. The Wolves had won again, even if it was only against lowly Rotherham United, and that win had kept them on top of division 2, just a point above the Sky Blues. And Saturday evening was still to come.

Phil lifted himself from the bath and reached for the towel. The weather looked likely to remain clement, so he wouldn't have to ask Dad for a lift. Not that Dad minded, but a walk down to Warstones Road would be welcome, as Phil had stood for over two hours on the South Bank Stand at Molineux that afternoon. But he would still need to take a coat or jacket on this early spring evening, not for the saunter down to the youth club but the walk home tonight could be a mite chilly.

That April afternoon Derek Dougan – the Doog to the Wolves faithful – hadn't been able to repeat his debut hat-trick, scored a fortnight before in the game at home to Hull, but he'd got the first goal and Ernie Hunt had tapped in the second to secure the win and keep the crowd chipper.

Over 32,000 were at the game, cheering their team's eighth win in just over two months since a bleak January when the Wolves could muster only two goals and two points from four games. They now looked certainties for promotion, back into division 1, being ten points ahead of third place. Phil was convinced that he would be watching Spurs, Liverpool, and Chelsea next season, as well as making sure he kept well clear of any Nottingham Forest and Leeds supporters.

Phil dried himself and, as he decided whether to wear the paisley shirt or the purple one with the broad club collar, he wondered which band might have been booked this weekend at the youth club. Last week, like most Saturday evenings, the music had again been fabulous, even though there had been a DJ rather than a band.

The DJs, booked at the youth club, were mostly local although sometimes there would be guest spots for some of the lesser names from the remaining pirate radio stations. They would all play great records, a mix of the current chart hits together with some fantastic soul tracks, mainly Stax, Atlantic and Tamla tunes. It was a youth club where the audience never stood around if the music necessitated that the dance floor should be full.

And who would be there this Saturday? Coops, Spud and Angie would often make their way across town from Wednesfield, unless Spud's band had a booking. And now that Brian and Martin were on the youth club committee, it was one of their responsibilities to get the very best acts each weekend.

And Joe and Adrian? Well maybe, if the TV wasn't up to much, then they would shuffle in, but they never danced. They had no real excuse, but Adrian and Joe usually managed to avoid moving much most Saturday evenings.

As the bathwater finished disappearing down the plughole, the Methodist church hall, two-thirds of the way down Warstones Road, stood unlit and quiet. In an hour's time, that would change as the doors opened, the cloakroom hooks began to fill up with parkas, anoraks and the occasional Crombie, and the committee would probably be on their first cuppa of the evening.

The band for that evening may have even arrived, with their roadie, if they had one, lugging cables, microphone stands, Vox or Marshall amps, guitar cases and drums onto the stage, into what was the most modern youth and community centre in Wolverhampton. Although it had yet to be officially opened, Venturers Youth Club had already gained a reputation for the place to be on Saturday evenings, for all youngsters, not just in the Penn and Warstones areas, but right across the town.

Week by week, more and more came to hear the finest music, played by some of the best local bands and DJs, all booked by the teenagers who made up the Youth Club Management Committee, at the Springdale Methodist Church.

It would be very different from last Thursday evening, when Phil had boarded the number 11 bus into town, meeting Adrian, Joe, and Martin, to go to a concert at the Gaumont Cinema, situated on the junction of Snow Hill and St. George's Parade. Not that Phil had told his parents he was going to a pop concert, particularly one with the guitar legend Jimi Hendrix on the bill.

Maybe if he had told them that the guest artist was Engelbert Humperdinck, then that might have been just about acceptable but, like most parents, any pop concert was an unsuitable evening's outing for most fifteen-year-olds, especially those with rather important O-level examinations in a few months' time.

The Gaumont was one of the most impressive buildings in the centre of Wolverhampton and, although it functioned primarily as a cinema, an audience of just under two thousand could be seated for live events. It had an impressive stage, eight dressing rooms, its own restaurant, and had become one of the top entertainment spots in Wolverhampton over the past few years.

From the late fifties, it had become a regular venue on the rock 'n' roll national circuits, hosting Bill Haley, Chuck Berry, the Everly Brothers, Gene Pitney, the Rolling Stones, and even the Beatles twice, back in their early days, but this Thursday's line-up was such a diverse array of stars that there really was something for everyone.

There were two shows that evening and the boys had decided that the early 6:30 performance was a better bet than the 8:40 start, as they could then get buses back home by around 9:30, and so continue the pretence that they were all involved in getting together to help each other with homework and, of course, the all-important exam revision.

Martin and Joe were already massive Hendrix fans, raving about his guitar playing on his two recent chart hits, 'Hey Joe' and 'Purple Haze'. They also saw this as a real chance to be the cat's whiskers with their classmates, at school the following day, thinking that it was unlikely that many of them would be there that evening.

Adrian rarely raved about any band or singer, often going along with whoever was 'in' at the time. Phil thought he would enjoy all the artists on the bill – except Mr Humperdinck – and was interested in seeing the 'fabulous' Walker Brothers, whose hits had mimicked the Phil Spector 'wall of sound' style of production, from a few years back.

He had also championed teenage singer-songwriter Cat Stevens who had had a recent big hit with 'Matthew and Son', with Phil telling everyone, who might listen, that songs with good storylines would always sell better than those that sounded like modern nursery rhymes.

Joe and Adrian had recently begun to grow their hair long, and Martin always looked older than most, so they strolled through the Gaumont foyer without a second thought. Phil was very conscious that he was the youngest of the quartet by over six months, and was worried he wouldn't be allowed in.

He shouldn't have. Most of the fans were around the same age and, whilst the management could have enforced their 'eighteen and over' rule, these days they rarely did. They found their seats in the rear stalls just before the MC, Nick Jones, came on stage. They had all saved up for many weeks to buy their tickets at seven shillings and sixpence. Fifteen bob, for front seats up in the gods, was well out of their reach, but they listened attentively as he introduced the first act, a band called the Quotations.

Joe and Adrian shook their heads.

"Never heard of them," said Martin, who read both the *New Musical Express* and *Melody Maker* on a weekly basis.

"Isn't the guitarist Johnny Gustafson from the Big Three who played at the Cavern before the Beatles?" said Phil.

"Unlikely," said Martin, but Phil was right. They played good, faithful covers of recent hits from the Kinks, the Who, and the Merseybeats, and their strong Liverpool vocals convinced Phil that he was correct.

Then it was the turn of the local band, the Californians.

"They'm great," said Joe and, as always, Adrian nodded in agreement.

Phil had seen them at Codsall Youth Club some months back and they did songs from the same set, mostly harmony tracks – their own versions of hit songs by the Fortunes, Ivy League, the Four Seasons, the Beach Boys, Jan & Dean, and the Tremeloes.

Phil had saved enough money to buy a concert programme. He would later store it away, with the ticket stub, and inside it, he found a brief biography of the band.

> "The Californians were formed in June 1966 and quickly became extremely popular. Their happiness, good looks, and talent all helped to promote their success in the early stages.
>
> They have now had their first record released entitled 'Golden Apples' which came out on March 24th, and this should help increase their popularity, along with all their other assets.
>
> Their favourite groups are the Beach Boys, the Four Seasons, and the Freshmen, and it is slightly apparent they base their own sound on their favourites.
>
> They are all under 21. Their names: John O'Hara (Lead vocals); Keith Evans (Drums); Mick Brookes (Lead guitar) and Peter Habberley (Bass guitar)."

They went down a storm with all the local fans at the Gaumont, and Phil was really chuffed that he had seen them again. As no one but Phil knew the order in which the artists would appear that evening, the other lads had no idea that their next musical encounter would be such an assault on both their minds and eardrums.

The stage curtains had been closed after the Californians had finished with their new single, 'Golden Apples', and, as the MC began to attempt to speak, what sounded like someone tuning his guitar noisily suddenly switched to the first heavy chords, accompanied by the drums and bass rhythm, and then the whispered opening lyrics of 'Foxy Lady'.

Solos ensued, featuring the inimitable James Marshall Hendrix on guitar, while his band, the Experience, maintained their steady-tempo rhythm throughout a set that featured 'Hey Joe', 'The Wind Cries Mary', the recent top three hit 'Purple Haze' and the barnstorming finale, Hendrix's amazing version of the Troggs 'Wild Thing'.

The four lads were speechless. Neither Joe nor Martin had been let down by either Hendrix's guitar playing, or his on-stage antics, seemingly playing some numbers with his teeth and others with the guitar behind his back. They were a tad disappointed that he hadn't set his guitar alight, as he had done at the start of the tour, at the Astoria in London in late March. As that had resulted in a hospital visit for Mr Hendrix, maybe he wasn't planning on a trip to New Cross Hospital, in Heath Town, later that evening.

After the coyness of the Californians, this brash and booming audio assault seemed to come from another planet and, just as the audience found their voices to dare to ask for more, Nick Jones was back on stage to introduce the tour's guest artist – 'the artist who had sold more singles than anyone else so far in 1967 – Engelbert Humperdinck'!

Martin and Joe were determined that they wanted to leave, but Phil said he was going to stay for the second half as he very much wanted to see both Cat Stevens and the Walker Brothers. The four of them quickly shuffled out of their seats and looked for a refuge far away from the coiffured balladeer, who none of them had really forgiven for keeping the Beatles 'Penny Lane/Strawberry Fields' double A-side off the number one slot last month.

In the café area, they felt both elated and indignant. The five musical Hendrix gems were still ringing in their ears, but to be denied further guitar brilliance by a crooner – who belonged much more to their parents' generation, and whose records they would never ever think of buying, never mind listening to – was hard to swallow. And not only that, it was well-known that he was a Leicester City supporter.

The thought of their parents reminded them that they would need to change back into their school uniforms, discarded when they had met at Joe's house earlier, before returning home with their carefully rehearsed list of topics that they had supposedly been revising that evening. That would be an easier deception than explaining the reek of cigarette smoke, that gave the Gaumont café a smog which hovered about a foot above their heads. It was agreed that the easiest explanation was that both Joe's parents were chain smokers.

They returned to the auditorium and the second half started just like the first, with the Quotations back on stage, not just to play their new single 'Cool it', to be released on Decca later in the year, but also to act as a backing band for the remainder of the concert. Then Nick Jones introduced Cat Stevens, recently described by the music press as "a fresh-faced teen star", who ambled languidly on to the stage to the accompaniment of shrill animated screams from all the girls in the front stalls.

Joe and Martin grimaced but Phil wasn't at all disappointed by Cat Stevens' performance, easily the best of the evening to his mind. Cat Stevens had already had two top ten hits that year – 'Matthew and Son' and 'I'm gonna get me a gun' – both enthusiastically received, as was his version of the Tremeloes hit 'Here comes my baby', which he had written. John and Mick of the Californians could be spotted, stage right, adding backing vocals.

And if the lads had loathed the reception Cat Stevens got, then the deafening sound that greeted the Walker Brothers was on yet another level, although totally undeserved. Both their style and sound had had its day and their last two singles hadn't even managed to get into the top twenty. It was also evident that they weren't getting on, as a band, never mind as brothers, which of course they weren't.

Even with excellent support, from the Quotations again, they were far from being top-of-the-bill material and so, after a few knowing looks, the four lads headed for the exit and off to Thornley Street to catch the bus back to Joe's, to resume their ruse of grammar school pupils keen to succeed in the O-level exams in just over two months' time.

The next day at school was very much as expected. Some of the sixth form had seen the four lads at the Gaumont but didn't associate with them. Why would they? Most of their form mates were amazed though that the four had been allowed to attend a concert in midweek, especially as some of them had actually spent much of the evening revising or reading the set texts for English literature.

"I'd swap Hendrix's guitar solos for Donne's sonnets or Chaucer's tales any day," mused Martin and, as usual, Adrian agreed with him.

For Phil, it had been a totally new and captivating experience. He had never actually been to a live concert like that before. He had seen some of the local bands in village halls and at youth clubs, but never on a stage as grand as the Gaumont, with tall banks of speakers on either side and never in the company of so many other fans. He had seen many top groups and artists performing in concerts on TV, as they all featured regularly in the *NME* Annual Poll-Winner's concerts which were always recorded live, then shown later on ABC Weekend Television.

Last year, Dusty and Cliff had again won the best British female and male singer, respectively, with Dusty also winning the world category, and, predictably, Elvis pipping Cliff for the world award. The Beatles won best group, together with the best song 'Eleanor Rigby'. The best new group, and also best R&B group, were the Spencer Davis Group, with their singer Stevie Winwood voted best new singer. The least likely surprise was that the Shadows were once again the top instrumental group, for the fourth year in a row.

This year's concert was scheduled for early May and Phil had seen, from the *NME* in February, that the Beach Boys would be performing and that once again the Spencer

Davis Group had won awards. Worth watching, he thought, just to see Stevie Winwood play live and to hear the Beach Boys perform 'Good Vibrations', one of the coolest singles to be released in 1966, and probably in this decade so far, in Phil and Martin's opinion.

Lessons that day were pretty mundane but Phil was looking forward to double physics in the afternoon. Not because he was that good at physics but Taff Williams, his teacher and second in department, was a great fan of space exploration and was keen to make sure his pupils were up to date with developments around the latest NASA missions. More specifically, the on-going Surveyor unmanned series of spacecraft which had been sent out to explore the surface of the moon and become the first-ever terrestrial objects to land anywhere in our solar system.

Phil had become hooked on this topic last May when Surveyor 1 had sent back over 11,000 photographs of the moon's surface. The pictures were mainly of rocks, boulders or dust, with the occasional horizon in view, but, to Phil, it was the enormity of the event – that mankind had actually sent a rocket to the moon which had then successfully landed and was sending back pictures – that had so enthralled him.

Surveyor 2 had been launched just after they had come back from the summer holidays last year but, after an engine failure, the spacecraft had crashed on to the moon, making this third attempt crucial to ensure the Surveyor missions continued. Phil had been surprised, talking to Taff, at the end of one physics lesson, to find there was someone else who found that this was easily the most important event of last year, even more significant than England winning the World Cup at the end of July.

Surveyor 3 was about to be launched in just over a week and should land on the moon on 20th April. Taff explained to Phil that his old university friend, now at NASA in America, had told him that this lunar craft was equipped with a digger-arm for the very first time. Its purpose was to dig up moon soil samples, photograph them and send the pictures back to earth so that scientists could evaluate the properties of the moon's surface.

Taff commented that this was obviously to rule out that the moon wasn't made of cheese. He laughed heartily when Phil replied: "But if it is made of cheese, any idea what type?"

Phil had first discovered science fiction much earlier in his teens, when his brother, Matthew, would pass on his comic, *The Eagle*, for him to read. It wasn't Sergeant Luck of the Foreign Legion or Harris Tweed, Special Agent, who captured Phil's imagination but the adventures of Dan Dare, 'Pilot of the Future', pitting himself and his crew against his arch-enemies the Mekon and Xel.

Dan Dare always seemed to Phil more grown-up than the other popular ITV puppet series, such as Fireball XL5, Supercar or even Thunderbirds. And anyway, Phil's parents had a TV that only received BBC programmes or so they told him when they first moved back to Wolverhampton in August 1960.

It wasn't only space travel that had begun to fascinate Phil - time travel also made a startling impression on his imagination. It was around the beginning of his first term at senior school, that Doctor Who, together with his companions – Phil wished he could be one – began to introduce him to alien species such as the Voord, the Zarbi, the Cybermen and, of course, the dastardly Daleks.

And then the Doctor would travel back through time to meet Vikings, Romans, Greeks or Aztecs, as well as Napoleon, Marco Polo, Nero and even Wyatt Earp. Maybe that was when Saturday evenings really became something special to look forward to.

With books, comics and TV series, Phil could lose himself in their fiction and adventure. The Surveyor missions were real though and Phil wanted them to succeed just as much as he wanted Wolves to gain promotion.

The paths of the Corner Boys, as they became known at school, had first crossed at the beginning of the second term at senior school. There was no rhyme or reason as to why they became good friends. None of them lived close to each other and they had all gone to different junior schools: Phil to Woodfield Avenue, Joe to Fallings Park, Adrian to Warstones and Martin to St Michael's. But they had all passed the 11-plus and each of them had elected to go to Wolverhampton Grammar School.

Actually, Phil was the odd one out because, although he had been born in Wolverhampton, at the Cedars maternity home in Penn Fields, in the summer of 1952, he had only returned three years back, whereas all the other lads had never really ventured further than Wednesfield, Warstones Estate or Finchfield.

Phil's father was an ambitious teacher, keen to be promoted and so, having taught at Wolverhampton Grammar School in 1948 for four years, the family then moved to Brackley, in Northamptonshire, just a month after Phil was born. There Dad continued as a science teacher at Magdalen College School, whilst Mum brought up Matt and Phil, except for a few months around Christmas 1954 when sister Rachel made her appearance in the world.

Just over four years later, Phil began infant school in the Bedfordshire town of Leighton Buzzard, famed firstly as the home of the Barron Knights and secondly as being near to the location of the Great Train Robbery in 1963.

Dad spent another 4-year spell as head of chemistry, at the Cedars Grammar School in the town, before applying for, and getting, the post of deputy head at Wednesfield High School, resulting in the family's return to Wolverhampton, when they bought a house in Penn.

None of the Corner Boys had started in the same form at Wolverhampton Grammar, as first-year pupils went into 1X, 1Y and 1Z, on an ad-hoc basis for the first term, until they were 'streamed' into 1Alpha, 1A and 1B in the spring term. Alpha boys were expected to do O-levels in four years rather than five, going on to take A-level exams two years later. Then, if they were bright enough, to sit for Oxford or Cambridge entrance. Phil, Joe, Adrian and

Martin were all alpha boys and were all expected to be at university by the start of the 1970s.

Their friendship was completely down to the seating arrangement on their first day together in 1Alpha, as they occupied the four desks in the left-hand corner of the classroom, where notes could be passed, and unspoken grins and grimaces exchanged. As they progressed through the school, to 3Alpha and 4Alpha, they stood their corner, rather than their ground, with neither classmates nor uninformed form-masters able to break up the Corner Boys who, in truth, gave little trouble to the latter, and often provided entertainment and information to the former.

Languages had always been Martin's speciality. He was now studying Greek and Latin at O-level and would continue to do so at A-level, before probably going on to Cambridge University. His passion though was pop music, embracing the current teenage obsession of buying single records, or 45s as they were known, although, in Martin's case, he had started his collection well before he had become a teenager.

There wasn't a sport that Joe didn't excel in. Each year, he played for the school cricket and football teams, as wicketkeeper and goalie respectively, as well as badminton, basketball, and fives. If the school had played tennis, hockey or rugby, Joe's name would have appeared on the team sheet. He also seemed more at ease with girls than the other boys which Phil put down to his involvement in mixed doubles tournaments at Heath Town Park tennis courts throughout the summer months.

Adrian was the personification of local-boy-made-good. Raised on a council estate by his mother, as his father had died suddenly when Adrian was just six, he had easily passed his 11-plus and was taking the Grammar school by storm. Not only did he excel in all academic subjects he was also a talented athlete, destined to represent the school at all age groups.

He never bragged about any of this, probably because his three older sisters and his mother wouldn't have let him, but also his manner was to agree in order to get along, conduct which had served him well. He was likely to be head boy in a few years' time and to follow that with a place at Oxford, more than likely the very first pupil from Warstones Junior School to do so.

Phil's forte was figures – always near the top in mathematics – and, during the more boring lessons, he would compile the form's Top Ten, assimilating his classmates' favourite pop singles each week into their very own chart. He was probably destined to work in a shop or a bank or maybe a company accounts office, although, like Martin, a career involving pop music, in some way or another, would be much more to his liking.

Phil couldn't remember when music – mainly today's pop music – had become such an important part of his life. He had had piano lessons, sung in the church choir, and school choirs, and played E-flat horn in the school brass band but, until now, listening to music hadn't held such a fascination. His parents were not avid music listeners, preferring either classical music on the radio or going to light opera concerts by local ensembles who put on the works of Gilbert and Sullivan.

Listening to the radio had always been actively encouraged by Phil's parents. "Radio broadens your imagination, television dulls it" was one of his Dad's favourite sayings, often after he had spent most of the afternoon listening to the cricket on Test Match Special on the BBC's Third Programme, whilst ostensibly doing marking or lesson planning.

From the early days of listening together to 'Listen with Mother' or 'Children's Hour', with the 'Just So Stories', 'Journey into Space' and 'Norman and Henry Bones', to the weekend lunchtime laughter that accompanied 'The Navy Lark', 'Educating Archie' and 'The Clitheroe Kid', the radio seemed very much part and parcel of home life in Brackley, Leighton Buzzard and now Wolverhampton.

Phil had two favourite radio programmes that had become 'must-listen-to' appointments every week. Before Saturday morning school became unavoidable, 'Children's Favourites', with Uncle Mac, would introduce Phil to a wide-ranging mix of music, from classical to pop, or country and western to nursery rhymes.

After it finished, Phil might have enjoyed 'Saturday Skiffle Club' on the Light Programme in the late fifties, which became 'Saturday Club' in the early sixties. However, Mum often had other ideas, usually a list of chores, such as car cleaning, clearing up the leaves in the garden, or shopping at the greengrocers on Penn Road, which meant parting Phil from the valve radio in the kitchen.

But all these chores had to be completed by 12:30 p.m. which was when Jack Jackson would "take you for a ride on his Record Roundabout". Half an hour of records, mainly easy listening tracks, intermingled with surreal comedy clips – a quite bizarre offering on the airwaves at the time and one that Phil loved.

Then, as Phil became a teenager, the radio fare on Sundays began to be less spiritual and more contemporary, especially with the morning's 'Easy Beat' show and late afternoon's 'Pick of the Pops', with the brand-new top-20 chart, with more lunchtime comedy from 'Round the Horne' in-between. This show was often met with disapproval from Dad which meant, to both Phil and Matt, that they should try to listen on their transistor radios, whilst Mum and Dad preferred the Home Service on a Sunday.

The gift of his own transistor radio, at Christmas 1964, had made such a difference to Phil and his listening habits. Not only was he able to listen more privately to stations such as Radio Luxembourg – at that time the only radio station to feature just pop music, although only on the air in the evenings – but at 10 on Monday evenings Phil would be tucked up in bed chuckling, as quietly as possible, to the sheer madness of the characters, skits and sketches from 'I'm sorry I'll read that again', often dozing off as the 'Angus Prune' tune closed the show.

Phil had bought his first-ever record at a church summer fete in Penn in 1961. He had to part with a sixpenny bit for Lonnie Donegan's 'My Old Man's a Dustman', a 10-inch shellac record which played at 78rpm. Not that Phil heard it often as his Dad's radiogram only had speeds of 45 and 33-and-a-third revolutions per minute, so he needed to find a record player with the right speed.

His classmate from junior school, Hugh, had the solution so Phil would pop down to his house in Osborne Road, to listen to this skiffle classic. Not an ideal arrangement but there was a bonus in that Hugh was also a massive Beatles fan and had not only bought all their first singles but also the two EPs, 'Twist and Shout' and 'All my loving'– great listens, all of them. At that time, you were either a fan of the Beatles or the Stones, but never both!

The first 45rpm single Phil bought was a year later: 'Telstar' by the Tornadoes. He loved the instrumental hits of the early sixties, especially guitar bands like the Shadows and the Ventures, but the sound of 'Telstar' combined his interest in space travel and music so much that he was happy to save up his six shillings and three pence to buy this record. He wasn't the only one, as it became a chart-topper in Wolverhampton, across the whole of Britain, as well as in America.

Halfway down Hollybush Lane, Phil was glad he had worn his coat. It might be April, but Wolverhampton always seemed to be much farther north than the Midlands suggested, and this unseasonal cold snap had meant that supporters on the terraces had been well wrapped up that afternoon at Molineux and that the cloakroom at Springdale Methodist would be chock-full this evening.

Walking along Warstones Road, he could see several cars dropping off teenagers, mostly at a distance from the youth club. Since many wouldn't want their friends to see mum or dad giving them a lift there, or collecting them, around 10 p.m., the standard curfew time for most fourteen or fifteen-year-olds, several rendezvous points had been agreed since the youth centre had opened.

As Phil approached the entrance, he smiled on seeing Brian collecting the entrance fees, one of his many duties now he was on the club's committee. They exchanged comments regarding the Wolves win that afternoon. Brian's Dad was a season-ticket holder, so Brian rarely stood in the vastness of the South Bank with the other lads. And when Phil asked who was on stage that evening, he was delighted to hear that it definitely was the Californians.

Phil hung his anorak in the cloakroom and went in search of Martin. To Phil, Saturday evening was all about the music and there was no one better than Martin to talk to about that very subject. He found him drinking tea near the stage, having a chat with the Californians' manager, Roger, so Phil let him be and looked around to see who else was there.

The Wednesfield contingent hadn't arrived yet but if they knew that the Cali's were performing tonight then they would be. Spud's band hadn't really got off the ground. They had played a few school gigs and he had even asked Phil if he wanted to join them on lead vocals, but he said he didn't think he had enough experience or bravado. In truth, he didn't feel confident enough to stand out front and belt out Chris Farlowe's 'Out of Time' or Los Bravos 'Black is Black'. He knew he had a good voice, but strong enough under the spotlight on stage? Maybe not.

Mel, the Cali's roadie, had set up Keith Evans' drumkit, without a seat as Keith preferred to play the skins standing up, and then positioned and tested all the amps and speakers. He would then sort out the microphones, probably the most important part of his job, as the Californians were an outstanding harmony band, usually sharing the vocals on most songs. John O'Hara was the lead singer, but Phil thought Pete Habberley, the bass guitarist, who had a high alto voice, was the one that made the sound just right.

The club was filling up. Regulars had taken up their usual places in the hall: the girls ready to dance near the front, the lads hanging back, towards the rear and at the sides of the hall. Suddenly there was a buzz as Mick Brookes came through the crowd clutching his lead guitar, quickly followed by John, Pete, and Keith. This was one of the few venues where the band had no option but to get to the stage through the throng of their fans, and there were times when they felt that they took their lives in their hands, like at The Woolpack in town where the stage was in the farthest corner from the dressing rooms.

However, this evening the clientele were younger and more in awe of four lads, just a few years older than themselves, who were giving up their evening to entertain them. The band looked relieved to climb the few steps onto the raised stage and guitars were plugged in and microphones tested yet again before Keith counted them in with his drumsticks for their first number. It was 'Sloop John B', a top ten hit for the Beach Boys this time last year, followed by the Cali's own version of the Sam Cooke song, 'Another Saturday night'.

Covers of recent British chart hits followed. Herman's Hermits 'There's a kinda hush'; the Fortunes 'You've got your troubles', then the Tremeloes 'Here comes my baby', after which John asked if anyone had seen Cat Stevens last week at the Gaumont as he had written that last song and had agreed to let the band play it live on stage from now on.

Quite a few hands were raised including Joe, Phil and Martin, with Adrian following suit as usual.

"They are pretty good. Sounding better than last Thursday," said Phil.

"They know their stuff. They know which songs will work for a youth club. They should do. They have been doing live gigs every week since they formed last year, so their manager said. He's got them well organized," replied Martin.

John then introduced the next few songs saying that these American artists had been very influential on the band's style, groups whose origins were in the surf music scene in California. You could see why the band has chosen their name. He went straight into the semi-spoken intro of the Four Seasons 'Let's hang on', with Mick coming in with the sharp lead guitar riff.

All four harmonised with Pete's falsetto voice really standing out, as it did with Jan & Dean's 'Surf City' and 'The little old lady from Pasadena' which, Pete chipped in afterwards, had also been covered by their number one favourites, the Beach Boys.

None of the girls had left the dance floor since the band had started. The songs were very so well-known that groups of girls, and couples, had danced to all of them, some more energetically than others. Phil liked to dance. Often Angie asked him to dance because Spud never danced. He just wasn't made that way, he would say.

"You won't know this one," said John. "It's the B-side of our very first single which was out in the shops last month. We haven't played this much but we like it, as it has that surf sound. Hope you enjoy it. It's called 'Little ship with the red sail'".

Many stopped dancing and listened. It wasn't usual for bands to play their own stuff and very few knew that the Cali's had a record deal. Phil had heard the A-side – they had finished their set at the Gaumont with it – and he'd liked it, although it was different from their normal stuff. This B-side was fab, he thought. Very much their style.

The song finished and there was a very positive reaction from the crowd – big smiles across the stage. Mick thanked everyone, saying: "Please go to Voltic Records or Beatties, or wherever you buy your 45s from, and buy our new single and, you never know, Wolverhampton might just have a top twenty hit this summer. We're going to have a break in a minute but to end this half, here's a new Turtles track 'Happy together'". It was just the right song to send the teenagers off for refreshments while the band took a well-earned breather.

The Californians were back on stage twenty minutes later and Phil missed the start of their first song, the band's version of the Mamas & Papas hit 'California dreaming'. The next few tracks were much slower and again showed that American hits were influencing the band as much as British ones. 'Groovin'' by the Young Rascals was followed by the Lovin' Spoonful's 'Daydream'.

"The next two tracks are about to be massive hits in the States," said John. "Anyone heard of the Association or Harpers Bizarre?" he asked. A lone hand went up. It was Martin, the devourer of all the music knowledge he could lay his hands and eyes on.

"Great," said John with little sincerity as the first chords of 'Cherish' filled the hall. Both that song and the '59th Street Bridge Song' were more ballads than dance tunes so the only teenagers still on the dance floor were couples swaying slowly in each other's arms.

This was obviously the plan, as the songs continued in that vein with the Searchers track 'What have they done to the rain?', followed by the Merseys' hit 'Sorrow'.

"Anyone here called Juliet?" called out Pete, after 'Sorrow' had finished. But without looking to see if anyone responded, they played the Four Pennies guitar intro from the song of the same name.

By now most of the teenage lads had moved to the back of the hall leaving the loving couples entwined on the dance floor. Whilst he liked to dance, Phil wanted more upbeat songs from the band so had fallen into conversation with Joe about the merits of the afternoon's performance at Molineux.

"Right, we're going to finish now with our new single," said John. "As Mick said earlier, it went on sale in March, so it would be really bostin if you can all go out and buy a copy this week. Ta for listening to us play this evening. Not sure when we will be back here, but we love playing local clubs, especially after all the Gaumont dates across the UK, so we hope to see you soon. Here it is – our new single – it's called 'Golden Apples'."

They played the song and there was a ripple of applause. It was very different, a bit Beatlesque, with a sort of sitar sound, played by Mick, but with very little rhythm. Great harmonies as usual but it just didn't seem to stand up as a live track. Keith looked at John and then at Roger, their manager. Phil could see him shake his head and then motioned to carry on. Keith beat out a bass-drum rhythm and Mick caught on with a guitar intro.

"Just time for one more then?" said John and caught the beat seamlessly to sing the Ivy League's 'Funny how love can be'. As soon as that had finished, Pete decided he wasn't going to be left out and began a bass riff. Martin's head was nodding in time. Phil looked puzzled.

"It's a Mamas & Papas song, 'Go where you wanna go'," said Martin. "Great song." It was just the right song to end the evening as the last chorus could go on forever, with everyone singing along. The enthusiastic applause confirmed that Roger had been right to keep them playing.

The band trooped off to the back of the hall and the lights went on. The Wednesfield lot had left already as the last bus into town was at 10:15. Phil looked at his watch. He was meant to have been home by 10 and Dad had said that, if he was late again, then that would be it for Saturday evening youth club visits. Off he went to get his anorak, with a quick cheerio to Joe and Martin. Adrian just nodded.

Running up Hollybank Lane, and turning left onto Penn Road, he knew he could just about make it by around 10:30. That might not be too bad and maybe with some extra effort at home, he could placate Dad. After all, he would be sitting in the choir stalls, as usual, tomorrow evening at church, with all his homework done. Well maybe.

Chapter 2 – Flowers in the rain

It was a quarter to seven in the morning and Phil was downstairs making a pot of tea. It would be a very special day.

"Why on earth are you up at this hour on a Saturday morning, Phillip?" asked his mother, as she came into the kitchen.

"You know what today is, don't you?" said Phil.

'It's Saturday, September 30th," said his mother. "Nothing special about that. You don't have Saturday morning school anymore, so why the early start?"

"Can I put the radiogram on in the front room, Mum?"

"Yes, of course," she replied. "What's on?"

"It's the launch of Radio 1," said Phil.

"Oh, is that all?" came his mother's response.

Phil sunk into the comfy armchair next to the radiogram and waited for it to warm up. He usually listened to his small Perdio transistor radio upstairs, which was great for tuning in to Radio Luxembourg late in the evenings. However, this momentous event warranted the full valve experience, in glorious stereo, rather than the tinny mono sound which came through his radio earpiece. Fine if you were dropping off to sleep but this occasion demanded quality.

The radio had warmed up and Phil tuned it to the frequency 247 metres on the medium wave dial, just in time to hear the words "*And, good morning everyone. Welcome to the exciting new sound of Radio 1*", followed by Tony Blackburn's theme tune, including Arnold barking in the background, before Tony introduced the number 3 song in the Radio 1 Fun 30, 'Flowers in the Rain' by the Move.

Phil was elated. To be able to hear many of the chart hits, plus tracks from new albums, and learn about new bands, was a life-changer. Until now, other than good old 'fabulous' 208 – Radio Luxembourg – all these musical wonders had mainly been the domain of the ten offshore pirate radios stations, such as 'the all-day music station' – Radio Caroline, North or South, 'wonderful' Radio London or 'swinging' Radio England. But they could only be heard in the West Midlands if you had a massive radio mast in your back garden, and there was no way Dad was ever going to agree to that.

Now there would be something worth getting out of bed for every single day. The situation had all come about because the Labour government, in particular, the Postmaster-General, had 'outlawed' the pirate radios stations, claiming that they were not paying royalties to anyone – artists, publishers or record companies – when they played records, and so were not contributing to the nation's economy. Also, more seriously, they were a danger to other shipping, as their broadcasts might interfere with important emergency calls.

Whether these reasons were valid or not didn't bother Phil. He had read about closing down the pirate radio stations in his Dad's *Times* newspaper over the summer and really wasn't worried as to why it was happening. He just couldn't wait to hear this new BBC station, Radio 1. And here it was. Phil wasn't to know that the station was only broadcasting in mono – the sound on Dad's radiogram was so clear, vibrant and exciting that he made two important decisions there and then.

First, over the weekends to come, all homework would be done in the front room, right next to the radiogram and, second, he desperately needed to save up to buy a bigger and better transistor radio. It would be a while until any Christmas gifts might materialise and Phil knew that his weekly pocket money wouldn't be nearly enough. Maybe he might even have to get a part-time job.

He drank his tea and listened to the latest singles from the Bee Gees and the Tremeloes, followed by an album track by Simon and Garfunkel, and hits from Cliff Richard and the Supremes before Tony Blackburn introduced Engelbert.

"No better time to get another cup of tea and see what was for breakfast," thought Phil.

"Well, was it as good as you thought it would be, Phillip?" asked his Mum.

"Yes," answered Phil. "Can I have a boiled egg and toast for breakfast?"

"Go back and listen to the radio, Phillip, and I will do yours and your father's. It'll be a while before Matthew and Rachel will be up and about," said Mum

Back in the front room, the radio was now playing 'Homburg' by Procol Harum, the follow-up to their massive chart-topper earlier that summer 'A Whiter Shade of Pale'. Phil had championed it as a smash hit as soon as he'd heard the song and, although he wasn't often listened to by the other lads, on this occasion he had been proved right. He wasn't as confident about their second single.

"It's obviously too similar," thought Phil.

People were calling this the summer of love but Phil hadn't noticed any love coming his way. Well, not from the direction to which he longingly gazed on many an evening, as he waited for a glimpse of the girl from across the road who was always later home from school than he was, and who wore a uniform he didn't recognise. She always got off the bus just before Muchall Road, then walked halfway up the hill before disappearing into one of the large houses, with a very long drive.

Some years back, Phil, Pete and Hugh used to go into the garden of Muchall Manor, a very old and foreboding house near the top of the hill to get conkers. But that was more of a dare as all the boys thought it must be haunted and no one had ever been seen coming or going from the house. If they heard a dog bark, they ran down the full length of Muchall Road, with or without their conkers. And anyway, they were only 11 or 12 then, so easily scared and with no interest in girls.

Phil heard his father come down the stairs. He stopped in the hall and peered into the front room. "Why on earth are you up at this early hour, Phillip? And on a Saturday?" he enquired.

"That's what Mum said," replied Phil. "Am I the only person in this house excited by the launch of Radio 1?"

"Hmm. Looks like it," said Dad and went to get the newspaper, still stuck in the letterbox.

"Are you involved in any football today? Are the Wolves at home? Will you need a lift anywhere?" Always questions from Dad thought Phil. By the time he had thought of any answers, Dad had gone into the kitchen and unfolded his newspaper.

"Breakfast is ready, Phillip," called his mother and Phil turned the radiogram off and shuffled into the kitchen in his slippers. As he sat at the kitchen table his father asked, "Who's Frank Zappa, Phillip, and why would he call his daughter, Moon?" Phil dropped his toast on to his plate. Dad was interested in pop music!

"He's an American musician, Dad. He's the leader of a band called the Mothers of Invention and he's named his daughter that because he's nuts."

Dad looked none the wiser and Mum just smiled.

Phil had been back at school for just over three weeks. His O-level grades, from the exams in June, hadn't been earth-shattering, unlike Matthew's who had been awarded mainly grade ones or twos, with just a single three out of nine subjects.

Phil's results matched his regular termly school reports which usually read 'quite able but needs to work harder and apply himself'. So, as he had just scraped through five out of the nine subjects taken in the O-level exams, with grade five or six, where six was just a pass, that seemed to him to be about right.

Besides, it had been enough to get him into the sixth form and to begin his A-level studies in chemistry, mathematics for science, and physics. With the latter, he was able to continue his welcome chats with Taff Williams about the space programmes, currently being intensified between America and Russia, as they battled to outdo each other and become the first nation to get a man on the moon.

Taff was always using President John F Kennedy's speech, made over five years ago, in his physics lessons, whenever a tough problem was raised by a student, who might complain that he couldn't do what was asked:

> "We choose to go to the Moon in this decade, and do the other things, not because they are easy, but because they are hard; because that goal will serve to organise and measure the best of our energies and skills, because that challenge is one that we are willing to accept, one we are unwilling to postpone, and one we intend to win."

Taff knew that speech word for word and, after a few terms of his lessons, so did most of his students. To Phil though, quoting his teachers wouldn't help him to convince his parents that he would be studying any harder or applying himself any better now that he was in the sixth form. Throughout the summer holidays, there had been constant prods, from both of them, about Phil's lack of purpose when it came to his education.

It hadn't been so in the early weeks of the summer break, in late July and early August, as the exam results weren't out until mid-August and, by then, they were well into their second week of their annual holiday in Tenby. But, as soon as they returned home, the envelope was lying on the doormat and, whilst to Phil the achievement of gaining nine O-level passes was something to celebrate, his parents were not that impressed with his grades.

"Matthew got mostly grade ones and twos, Phillip, so what went wrong?" they both asked. To Phil, the answer was nothing. He needed five O-levels to get into the sixth form and he'd got nine. His only problem was having an older brother who had passed his 11-plus at nine years of age and then continued to get top grades throughout his time at the Grammar School.

The latter part of August and early September should have been a reasonably idyllic holiday for Phil, but a schedule of household tasks and errands was organised to 'help' him accustom himself to what his parents thought would be a much greater challenge – studying for A-levels.

So, each day was greeted with a wake-up call followed by a list of the jobs he was expected to have completed before having any time to attend youth clubs or football matches. Phil was finally glad to get back to school in

September and by the time the month had ended he reckoned he might be able to broach the subject of going to Venturers again.

"Is it OK for me to meet Martin, Joe and Adrian at Venturers this evening, Dad?" asked Phil.

"If the lawn's been mown and the car cleaned, including the chrome, then OK. But home no later than 10 tonight!" replied Dad.

"No problem," said Phil, suppressing a smile, as he had already spotted that the Wolves away game, at Sheffield Wednesday that afternoon, was going to be the main game on 'Match of the Day', later that evening, and he would want to be back home in time to watch it.

Brian was waiting just inside the entrance at the Springdale church hall, as Phil approached.

"Do you want to know today's score, or do you already know it?" he asked Phil.

"I heard it on the radio, on 'Sports Report'. Sounded a good game. I'm going to make sure I'm home to watch it on the tele later," Phil replied.

"Me too," said Brian. "You coming in? That'll be one and six."

"I've been under curfew for the past month so I've no idea who you've had down here recently. Who is it tonight?" said Phil.

"It's Herbie's People," replied Brian. "They're a great band."

"Weren't they known as Danny Cannon and the Ramrods a few years back? They're from Bilston, aren't they?" asked Phil.

"Yep, on both counts," replied Brian. "They've played the Royal Albert Hall, the Civic and most of the big venues round here and they've been on the radio quite a bit too, so this will be a tad different for them, playing to teenagers like us! They've been around a while so they should be good."

"What sort of music do they play?" asked Phil.

"Martin will be able to tell you," said Brian. "He's in the kitchen making a brew and chatting to Danny, the lead singer." As usual, Phil didn't want to interrupt Martin's chat so he went to hang his coat up. Andy, known as Coops, was in the cloakroom.

"Spud and Angie coming over?" asked Phil.

"No. The band's got a gig," replied Coops.

Phil was disappointed. Not because he had missed out on singing for Spud's band but, without Angie here, if he wanted to have a dance, he might have to summon up the courage to ask someone else.

He could hear the band's roadie testing microphones, guitars and drums, so he wandered through to the main church hall. It was the most modern part of the building and had high windows on two sides which made for intimate surroundings when there was a performance. As always, on youth club evenings, the stage was right up the front – a set of wooden podiums, bolted together to elevate the group just a few feet above their young audience.

There were no stained-glass windows to tell you this was a church hall and, as it was so new, there was also very little in the way of religious information which, in fact, made most club members feel more at ease. The hall was beginning to fill up and regulars were taking up their customary places; once again the girls standing nearer the stage, ready to dance, and the boys on the fringes, mainly to listen, but with one eye on the girls.

There was an expectant buzz in the room. The band tonight had been around since the early sixties and had an unrivalled reputation in the local area. A few years back, as Danny Cannon and the Ramrods, they had finished equal first in the finals of the 'New Sound of '64' competition, held at the now-famous Cavern Club in Liverpool, so understandably the assembled throng had high expectations.

The confident five-piece strolled through the crowd, Alan Lacey taking his seat behind the drum kit, with Mike Taylor, Pete Walton and Len Beddow plugging in their guitars while their main man, Danny Robinson, stepped up to the microphone.

"Really great to be with you on this late summer's evening. Let's get started with a couple of songs you'll know and love."

One guitar chord was all that was needed for the four voices to harmonise instantly for 'I get around' by the Beach Boys, with Mike and Pete's strong falsetto voices making the song just the right opener and getting the girls dancing straight away. Then Alan's drums took the band straight into the McCoys' hit 'Hang on Sloopy' with Danny's lead vocals sounding better than the original. They finished to great applause and Phil could tell this was going to be an excellent evening of music and dancing.

"That's two bostin songs from bands we really like, from a few years back, and now we're going even further back, to the man who was a great inspiration to all of us in the band. This is a Buddy Holly song, and it's called 'Listen to me'." It was a slower tempo but didn't stop the dancing, as the girls swayed, many with eyes that rarely left Danny as he seemed to sing to each of them individually.

Joe was mightily impressed, which wasn't surprising as he thought he was Buddy Holly's number one fan as he had all his albums. Actually, his older sister owned them, but to Joe that was good enough, and for once he inched forward to listen to the band. "They're a cracking band," he said to Martin.

"Well, they have been playing at venues everywhere in this area for over five years," Martin replied. "So, it ain't too much of a surprise that they know their stuff and, when they were Danny and the Ramrods, they won the Big Beat Contest, at the Gaumont, a few years back, beating Steve Brett and the Mavericks who were then the best band in town in the early sixties. Although they're very accomplished, I'd still like to hear some of their own stuff."

As if he was listening, Danny said, "Here's a song which was our first single, released last year in late

November. It's called 'You thrill me to pieces', and was written by our manager, Bill Bates – if you don't like it, he's sitting at the back there so you can lynch him, not us!".

Bill was safe and smiled. He had written hits for Mike Sarne and was friends with Ken Lewis and John Carter, who had penned chart successes for the Ivy League, Brenda Lee, and Peter and Gordon, so he knew what made a good song. The band laughed.

"Bet Danny's used that line before," said Joe and, before there was any response, Len had opened with the guitar riff.

At the finish, Danny said, "Two more songs coming up that were written for us by the great songwriters Carter-Lewis, but we have been too busy doing live appearances to get into the studio so far this year to find time to record them. This one is called 'Thank you for loving me'."

Danny knew how to work his audience, continuing to gaze towards the girls at the front of the hall as he sang the ballad, with the band playing effortlessly behind him. Then, with hardly a break, they went into the opening harmonies of 'Let's go to San Francisco', doing just as good a version as the Flowerpot Men who had topped the charts with it earlier that month.

When the applause had died down, Danny was up at the microphone again. "We'll do some more of our own numbers a bit later, but this next song may be something you have heard this year from a little band from Liverpool." As Len hit the first eight chords on his lead guitar, Phil immediately recognised the Beatles song 'Getting Better'.

Phil had played that Beatles album over and over again, loving some tracks first time round whilst others, like 'Day in a life' and 'Fixing a Hole', were growing on him with each play.

And as far as 'Getting Better' was concerned, it was, and the Herbie's version was also a terrific cover. They followed this with their version of the Kinks 'Dead End Street', a song from a band who were, as far as Phil was concerned, right up there with the Stones and the Beatles.

"I reckon Ray Davies writes better songs than either Jagger-Richards or Lennon-McCartney," said Martin to Joe and Phil, and Adrian nodded in agreement as usual.

"Love that song and the arrangement," said Danny to the crowd, as it finished. "This next one was also written by the Kinks, and the Pretty Things did a great version. It's called 'A House in the Country'," he continued.

"Herbie's People are a great covers band. They deserve a hit of their own," said Phil to Martin and, as if Danny had again been listening, he said, "Right coming up two of our singles. The first is called 'One Little Smile' – we released it last November, but it seems to have escaped and never made the chart."

"Sounds like another Beatles song. Catchy too," Joe said, as the song began.

A couple of minutes later, the song had finished, and Danny announced that they would take a break after one more track. "This single was released earlier this year and is still available if you want to buy it. Again, it was written by Bill and we love it."

The whole of the band moved up to their microphones and the acapella harmonies to the beginning of 'Humming Bird' filled the hall, followed by Len and Mike's clever guitar interplay which worked really well. It was the first song in the set where all the band had performed as one on vocals and was loved by the young crowd.

Joe, Martin, and Phil were already at the refreshments before the last harmony chord had finished. They knew only too well the wait they would have if they left it until the song had finished and they were all ready for a drink, albeit a soft one at the youth club.

"They must be the best band we have had here for ages," said Joe.

"I bought that last single," said Martin, to no one's surprise. "And their live version was not only longer but much better than the recording. The *Melody Maker* said it was overproduced and they were right. With better production and better promotion that could have been a hit. Good song."

Phil glanced at his watch. It was a quarter to nine. The band would be back on stage just after nine, but he must get away by half-nine, to get home by ten, or his parents would have his 'guts for garters' as his Mum would say, although he wasn't sure what that really meant.

When the band returned to the stage, there was much more of the same, more covers starting with a really energetic version of the Yardbirds 'Over Under Sideways

Down' and then a belting version of the Easybeats' 'Friday On My Mind'.

Two belters to get everyone back on the dance floor and both performances as good as the originals with the band really making the songs their own with fantastic playing and singing.

"Back to our own stuff now. We were supposed to have the first shout on this song. Geoff Stevens wrote it and we went to the studios to record it and then another Mann recorded it, if you get my drift," announced Danny.

Those in the know realised he was referring to Manfred Mann who had had a top 5 hit with 'Semi-detached suburban Mr James'. The Herbie's version was just as good and got great applause when it finished before they went straight into the next song

"That was the B side to Humming Bird," said Danny as it finished. "It's called 'Residential area' and is one of the first songs we've written as a band." Len Beddow was on top form on lead guitar and there were some great bass lines from Pete Walton.

"Copies are still in the shop, so please go and buy it. We are really chuffed when it was included on the soundtrack of the film 'Poor Cow'. Enough of us. Are you having a great time? Even if you are having a bad time, it might be good," Danny said smiling before the youngsters' puzzled looks turned into smiles as the band began the Tremeloes latest hit 'Even the Bad Times are Good'.

"Time for me to go," said Phil. "Really want to be home in time for 'Match of the Day'. Wolves are on as the main game," and he said cheerio to Martin, Joe and Adrian and slipped out of the hall, singing the la-las of the chorus all the way down Warstones Road.

As he came in through the kitchen door, Phil could hear the 'Match of the Day' theme playing in the living room at the back of the house. There he found Dad in his favourite armchair with Matthew and Rachel sitting on the sofa.

"Come on, Rachel, time for bed. We'll leave the boys to their football. Straight to bed, Matthew and Phillip, as soon as it has finished," said Dad.

"Mum already gone up?" asked Phil.

"Yes, your mother has to do the flowers at church early tomorrow morning, so keep the volume down on the TV. And no cheering or I will be down to turn it off!" replied Dad.

"OK Dad," said Phil as he went over to the set to turn down the volume a notch, before settling himself into the other armchair. "Night, Dad. Night, Raich."

"Thought you would be back early," said Matt. "Dad knew it as well. He wasn't fooled by you agreeing to be home by ten, just to please him and Mum. He knows you are more passionate about the Wolves than any of us, ever since he took us both to see them soon after we moved back here."

It was true. Dad was really a rugby union man having played at Oxford University in the mid-forties, but he had insisted on taking both boys to Molineux, to stand on the South Bank, on 31st August 1963. The opposition was

Stoke City, freshly promoted to the first division, with a 48-year-old winger named Stanley Matthews. Dad had reckoned this was probably his last season and so it was.

He was pleased that both boys could witness this brilliant player, maybe not at the height of his career, but could say they had seen him play. Wolves came out 2-1 winners and, from that day on, Phil would be a dedicated Wolves devotee.

Soon, the black and white screen showed the players running out onto the pitch at Hillsborough and the distinctive voice of David Coleman began to go through the two sides, Sheffield Wednesday first, as the home side, and then the Wolves team, which included two birthday boys – Alun Evans, just 18, and the brilliant Peter Knowles who, at 22, was being compared with George Best.

"Alun Evans is only a year older than me," said Matthew.

"He's older and better than you, Matt," replied Phil with a smile.

Matt threw a cushion at his brother and they both laughed. Matt was a pretty good player, representing the Grammar school first 11, either on the wing or in midfield, but he was short and slight, so was often left out when they played the more physical sides.

Wednesday looked to start the game with more energy and confidence, not surprising as they were currently third in the league. Then, with nearly five minutes gone, the ball broke to Wolves left-winger, David Wagstaffe, half-way in his own half. He then went on one of his characteristic dribbles, beating defenders with ease and advancing into the Wednesday half. After a quick exchange of passes with Dougan and Knowles, he crossed for Evans to lay it back to Knowles to curl it past Springett for a goal to Wolves. The boys exchanged smiles.

"That was a super move and a brilliant goal," said Matt and Phil just grinned, sitting forward on the edge of his seat. They both knew the result but to be able to enjoy watching the Wolves in the comfort of their own living room was a real bonus this Saturday.

Earlier in the year, Wimbledon had been the very first television programme to be shown in colour and it was predicted that, within the next 12 months, most BBC sports coverage would also be in colour. Whether the boys could convince Dad to change the TV to a colour set would be another matter entirely.

The first half continued with Wednesday continuing to attack but the Wolves defence held firm. Holsgrove and Woodfield looked to have the measure of the Wednesday forward line and Phil Parkes had only been troubled by Jim McCalliog, who was easily the best Sheffield player. Then Wednesday got a corner, with around 20 minutes gone, and Sheffield defender, Vic Mobley, outjumped Woodfield to head in the equaliser. Both boys slumped back in their seats.

"Even when you know they are going to score, you hope it won't happen," said Phil.

Wolves were not being outplayed at all and, in an end-to-end game, both Wagstaffe and Evans created good chances and Bailey had two powerful shots blocked. Then, close to the end of the first half, another great passing move saw Peter Knowles break clear on the left and place a delightful cross to Evans whose shot was blocked on the line by Mobley.

Dougan claimed it was clearly handball, but the referee wasn't interested in the appeal and the first half finished even at 1-1.

Wolves started strongly in the second half and Terry Wharton soon set up Peter Knowles for what looked like his second goal, but it was cleared off the line. Wednesday started to get back into the game and, before long, their centre-forward, John Ritchie, had a great chance.

"Ritchie must score," announced Coleman but Phil Parkes came off his line to make a brilliant save. Wolves had the ball in the net soon after, as Wagstaffe made another searing run from the halfway line and put Evans in on goal to slot it home neatly. However, the linesman's flag had gone up for offside.

"That would have been as good as our first," said Matt. "If only Evans had just timed his run better."

"Bet the Owls score now," said Phil, as Peter Eustace floated a great pass over the Wolves defence and Ritchie ran through to dispatch it past Parkes to put Wednesday 2-1 up. Wednesday kept up the pressure and seemed to be controlling the game.

"David Coleman keeps going on about Sheffield being the superior side but I think Wolves are really playing well, especially being away from home," said Phil, and Matt nodded. Just two minutes to go, and Wolves hadn't given up.

The Hillsborough crowd were encouraging the referee to blow the final whistle when Knowles brought the ball out of defence and spread it wide to the skipper, Mike Bailey. His cross bypassed Dougan and ran straight to Alan Evans who crowned his birthday by hitting the late equaliser. It was the last kick of the match.

"I reckon we deserved that draw," said Phil, as Matt got up to turn the television off.

"Come on, Phil. Off to bed, as Dad said. I've got some A-level revision to do tomorrow and I bet you've got some homework," said Matt.

As the two lads tiptoed to bed, knowing which stairs to avoid so that there weren't any loud creaks, Phil thought what a special Saturday it had been. The start of Radio 1, seeing the excellent band Herbie's People, and a draw for the Wolves away from home.

'Can't top that,' he reflected.

On the first Monday morning in October, Phil was up again with the lark to begin his new paper round. It had taken ages to persuade Mum and Dad that taking on his very first part-time job wouldn't affect his sixth-form studies. Phil wasn't an early riser, never had been, and his paper round would be a real struggle.

He cycled along the pavement on the Penn Road, across Woodfield Avenue, and on to Stewarts Newsagents, which was in the middle of the row of shops between the entrance to the allotments and Coalway Avenue.

Phil understood the basics of the job. He had helped Hugh with his evening round throughout the summer holidays and knew he would be given a bag to put the papers in, emblazoned with the local evening paper, *The Express & Star*, together with a route for the deliveries. Then there would be details of which paper, comic or magazine should be delivered to which addresses, and finally the bundle of all the items to be pushed through letterboxes or left in front porches.

Whether Mr Stewart was being kind to him or not he didn't know, as his round started back down one side of Wynn Road, down along part of Coalway Road and then up Leighton Road, back up the other side of Wynn Road, taking him back to his house, just two along from the junction.

"Blimey, there are over 200 houses just in those two-and-a-bit streets," he pondered, but then remembered that not everyone had a morning paper, and not everyone went to Stewarts for their deliveries, some opting for the Coalway Road Newsagent.

Phil had left home at 6:30 a.m. and had collected all the papers for delivery by 6:45. Could it be done by 8, to get back home for some cereal or toast, before the cycle ride to school in Compton Road? Well, unless he got on with it, he would never know, so the pedal clips were fastened and off he sped, back along the main road, still using the pavement. Phil may well have passed his cycling proficiency test some years back, but there was no way he was going to waste time making two challenging crossings, through very busy traffic, on that main road.

There were fewer broadsheet papers – *The Times, The Telegraph and The Guardian* – than the tabloids – *The Daily Mail, Express and Mirror*, which were easier to fold and slot through the letterboxes. Just a few addresses had the new daily, *The Sun*, which had replaced *The Daily Herald*. Phil had never heard of the *Morning Star* before but there were only a couple of those to deliver.

Occasionally he delivered the *Financial Times*, wondering why it was printed on the same coloured paper as the *Express & Star Pink*, the local weekly Saturday sporting edition.

There was also an assortment of men's monthly magazines. There were occasional sporting ones such as *Playfair Cricket Monthly, Angling Times, Chess Monthly* and *Horse and Hound*, but by far the most popular were about motoring – *Practical Motorist, Classic Car, Motorsport* and *The Motor-Cycle*. None of the 'top -shelf' magazines at the newsagents were delivered – for collection only, Phil had been told.

Most women's magazines were often weekly rather than monthly, *Woman's Own*, and *Woman's Weekly* being the most popular although Phil's mum always had one just called *Woman*. They weren't very imaginative when it came to titles, thought Phil. His mum wouldn't have gone for *The Lady* or one of the glossies, like *Vanity Fair,*

Vogue, or *Woman and Home*, which she would often read whilst under the drier when she was having her hair done.

There were a few children's comics each week. Rachel still had *Bunty* delivered but as she was about to become a teenager in a few months' time, Phil could see this being replaced by something more romantic like *Valentine*, where the lyrics of many chart hits were portrayed in comic strip.

Matt had always had *The Hotspur* in the early sixties and Phil's enjoyment of stories like 'Tough of the Track' from *The Victor* or 'Billy's Boots' or 'Roy of the Rovers' from *The Tiger* had waned since the early years at secondary school. Like Martin, his pocket money now went on something less fanciful and more in line with his new passion – pop music.

Monday wasn't a heavy day for magazines and comics though, so he was home by 7:45 a.m. and pleased to be ahead of plan on his first day.

"How did you get on?" asked Mum.

"Fine," he replied. "There'll be more comics and magazines to deliver later in the week, but Mr Stewart has given me a route right next to home so I should be OK getting to school on time."

Phil sat down to his bowl of cornflakes and a cup of tea, very pleased that his first week's paper deliveries would result in a brilliant start towards the 32 shillings and 6 pence he would need to buy another long-playing record.

Mum looked pleased too, but she didn't know that, by the end of the week, either the paper round or the cycle ride to school would be delayed by the weekly arrival of Phil's favourite reading material – the *New Musical Express* or, as the lads knew it, the *NME*.

All these early starts would be well worth it though as the money he made would go a long way to funding his record collection which, at this moment in time, was particularly solitary. He had used all his birthday money in June to buy his very first long-playing record, the Beatles 'Summer of Love' LP, Sgt. Pepper's Lonely Hearts Club Band.

Phil had already decided on his second purchase. It had to be the eponymously titled debut album from Procol Harum who had topped the charts, from mid-June to mid-July, with their uniquely brilliant single 'A Whiter Shade of Pale'. He had first heard their second single 'Homburg' on Radio Luxembourg, and then again on Radio 1, and to Phil, it was their distinctly different sound that really resonated with him.

With two band members on keyboards – Matthew Fisher on organ and lead singer, Gary Brooker, on piano – they were able to combine blues, psychedelic rock and classical influences into songs which no other bands were proffering at that time. Add a superbly raucous guitar from Robin Trower, on top of an equally solid drum and bass team of B J Wilson and Dave Knights, and their recordings stood out from the everyday songs being released over that summer.

Phil had read pre-release reviews of this album in the music press, and Radio 1 was quick to preview LP tracks in some of its new shows, presented by more enlightened DJs such as David Symonds, Pete Drummond and Dave Cash, included on his weekly 'album review' show.

Many of the press and radio comments suggested that the album was being rushed out to cash in on the group's hit success, which was probably true, but Phil had heard enough for him to be interested in making this his second LP purchase. Most bands had begun to write their own songs but again Procol Harum were a mite unusual in that their lyricist, Keith Reid, was included as a band member but never played an instrument nor appeared on stage with the other five. To Phil, his lyrics were another intriguing reason why he enjoyed their sound.

Like their hits, there were four or five tracks that continued to use classical themes to develop the songs' melodies. 'Salad Days', 'A Christmas Camel' and 'She wandered through the garden fence', all sounding similar to the two single releases, whereas short tracks such as 'Mabel' and 'Good Captain Clack' were obviously novelty album fillers to make up the then-requisite 10 tracks, both sounding like tracks lifted from Bonzo Dog Doo-Dah Band albums.

'Something follow me', 'Cerdes', and 'Kaleidoscope' revealed the blues roots of the band which would have come as no surprise to the fans who had seen the line-up in the early to mid-sixties, as The Paramounts, a more than capable band from Southend, who usually covered R&B and soul tracks. However, it was the first and last tracks on the album that Phil began to want to hear more and more as the weeks went by.

The first – 'Conquistador'– would have been a much better choice as the band's second single, Phil thought, having a great chorus, brilliant organ solo and a driving bass and piano rhythm. Its lyrics were again strange and mournful, but it was a much more upbeat track than either their massive hit or 'Homburg'. Phil loved its excitement, mystery and panache.

The final track – 'Repent Walpurgis'– was very different from the rest of the album. First, it was an instrumental and secondly it was the only track credited as written by the band's organist, Matthew Fisher, although there were some obvious musical prompts. It starts very slowly, in a classical style, then builds with Robin Trower's very hard-hitting emotional guitar playing which, after a calming piano mid-section from Gary Brooker, is repeated in the second half of the track, only with more gusto. Phil loved the contrasting sounds, the changing dynamics and the calming nature of parts of the track before the brutal final crescendo. It was simply a great piece of music.

He was made to wait though as, for weeks on end, neither Beatties' Record Department nor Voltic Records could get hold of a copy of Procol's first album to confirm Phil's expectations. The reason was that the band's record label had decided to release the album in the States in September before making it available in the UK, thinking that, following on the coat-tails of the 'British Invasion', this would result in much-improved sales.

The US version also included 'A Whiter Shade of Pale', as the lead track, but it mattered not to the American public as, although they bought over a million copies, it didn't even make it into the Billboard chart. By the final months of 1967, the 'invasion' was practically at an end and, back in the UK, other than Phil, there weren't many fans waiting to get hold of Procol Harum's first album and it didn't make the album charts here either.

But he wasn't bothered about chart success. If he liked what he heard, and it made him want to hear more, then that was good enough for him. So, with Christmas still a few months away, amassing a further 32 shillings and 6 pence from his paper round would be enough to double the number of albums in his record collection.

Chapter 3 – Hello, Goodbye

When you are in your mid-teens, Christmas can be a somewhat perplexing time. Phil was just eight years old when the family moved back to Wolverhampton in August 1960, taking up residence on Penn Road. Those early sixties Christmas Days still seemed warm and cosy occasions. Christmas Eve was always spent singing at church, as both Matt and Phil were in the choir at St Aidan's, described as a 'mission' church, in Mount Road.

Phil had absolutely no idea what a 'mission' church was or why, as a family, they didn't attend St Phillip's, the local parish church. To him, going to a church with his name on it seemed a much better idea. So, as Dad was a lay preacher at St Aidan's, then St Aidan's it was, and the choir was as good a place to be as any on Christmas Eve. And, after the service, refreshments were laid on, which was a real plus, before home and off to bed and then hours spent trying to get to sleep so that Father Christmas would visit.

Upon waking, one of Dad's rugby socks would somehow have materialised on Phil's bed, full of satsumas, chocolate coins, possibly a sugar mouse and small presents such as dinky toys and balsa wood gliders, as well as those small wind-up toys that usually broke by the beginning of January. Matt also had a sock full of presents but, as the eldest child, many of these were educational, like geometry sets, or games such as Owzthat. Rachel had a sock on her bed but to Phil, in his pre-teens, it was all girls' stuff and of no interest.

There were two things that puzzled Phil on Christmas morning. First, what happened to the fourth sock? Phil was certain that Dad didn't have three legs and rugby socks usually came in pairs. And second, how did Father Christmas get hold of Dad's socks to fill them on Christmas night, and why hadn't he managed to get rid of the liniment smell that always seemed to accompany any sport Dad was involved in?

Phil knew that, on Christmas morning, family traditions would be faithfully maintained, so breakfast would have to be eaten and cleared away before the three children would be ushered into the front room, eyes closed, to be greeted with the sight of three pillowcases full of their main Christmas presents.

In the early sixties, presents from aunts, uncles, grandparents, and godparents were often comic annuals. The *Eagle, Swift* and *Robin* had been replaced by *Biggles, Rupert,* and *Girl's Own,* then superseded by *The Victor, Hotspur,* and *Bunty*. Often Matt would get Meccano sets or Airfix models. There would be Lego or Matchbox toys for Phillip, and string puppets or Mister Potato Head for Rachel.

There might be a board game for them all to play, as well as jigsaws, often educational – maps of the world or such like – and one year Matthew was given a chemistry set with which he managed to stink out his bedroom something rotten. None of them had ever worked out what they should do with a kaleidoscope although they were most entertaining to look through – well at least until the end of Boxing Day.

Chicken was the family choice for both Christmas and Easter, Dad always commenting how dear it was well before it got anywhere near the roasting pan and then articulating how delicious it was, over dinner, adding that it was well worth the expense. The other festive meats – ham, pork pie, scotch eggs and sausage meat – were all collected, with the chicken, from Percy Salts, the butchers, on the corner of Coalway and Penn Road.

That was usually a task for either Phil or Matt on Christmas Eve, with the other having to visit Moores, the greengrocers, to collect Mum's order of all the fruit and veg for the festive period. The standards were potatoes, carrots and apples, but, at Christmas, there would be grapefruit, parsnips, walnuts, and the obligatory sprouts. If Phil's parents were hosting a soiree over the festive season, then there might be a pineapple to go with cheese cubes on cocktail sticks.

It was also one of the few times in the year when extra items were delivered by Colemans, the local grocer whose shop was next door to the hairdressers, just two down from Stewarts. They would supply the chipolata sausages for the 'pigs in blankets' although Mum would make her own stuffing and bread sauce. There would be glace cherries, spices, fruit peel, currants, sultanas and demerara sugar – all destined for the Christmas cake which Mum, along with the Christmas pudding, would dutifully make every year, with help from Rachel, mainly with the stirring.

Phil didn't particularly like figs, mixed nuts, glazed fruits, or the orange and lemon slices, that appeared on the sideboard each year, preferring the contents of the large tin of biscuits that sat beside the cheese crackers. And recent additions such as yule logs and chocolate fingers made Christmas tea another feast to look forward to, especially if Rachel had also helped with the marzipan and icing enveloping the fruit cake beneath.

If she was allowed to stage the Christmas scene on the cake, it would resemble her new-found love of all things cricket, with Father Christmas at the crease, an angel keeping wicket, a robin in the slips, and a snowman at mid-off, with Christmas trees marking the boundary. The Christmas tree always stood in the hall but was always late in arriving as it came from Dad's school and only when it could fit into the back of the Hillman estate after the end of term. Tree decorating was done immediately it arrived.

Streamers, made from expanding crepe paper, were fixed from light fittings to all corners of both living rooms. Christmas cards lined the window ledges and balloons, holly – kept sensibly apart – together with crepe paper balls, snowmen, Santas, and Christmas trees were hung from wherever was reachable.

Besides the festive tableaux on the many greetings' cards, the religious aspect wasn't forgotten with a nativity scene set up in the window of the front living room, becoming a tad shabby having been assembled over and over again for at least the last fifteen years. Rachel was the only one who still asked for an advent calendar, knowing there would be Christmas scenes to greet you when you opened each door, finishing with a pictorial stack of presents on Christmas Eve.

Phil had decided that there were definitely some relatives who had no imagination at all when it came to presents, as they always sent socks, gloves, or a scarf, but then there would always be a large selection box of chocolates, supposedly from Father Christmas! Mum and Dad always bought each other a special present – just the one – and the three youngsters were all encouraged to save enough of their weekly pocket money to buy each other a small present.

As ages reached double figures, so the number of presents fell, as larger presents were requested, such as a bicycle or maybe a new pair of football boots and, for Phil, it would be either a transistor radio or a tape recorder. Aunts and uncles actually stopped sending presents, sending postal orders instead, usually included in a seasonal card. Matt would receive books or book tokens mostly, while Rachel seemed to acquire too many clothes to fit into the wardrobe and chest of drawers in her bedroom.

Whilst board games were still a lot of fun, and selection boxes remained a delectable treat, by the time Christmas 1967 arrived, Phil was only interested in receiving one kind of Christmas present – record tokens. This was a very hopeful wish. The postal order was still very much the relatives' Christmas present of choice, always with a note suggesting that it should be saved so that, when something important came along, like a new coat or maybe driving lessons for Matt, it would be most useful.

However, a record token could only be used to buy one thing – records – whether singles, extended-play 45s – EPs – or, what Phil dearly craved, long-playing albums – LPs. This desire, however, was not universally approved of by Phil's aunts and uncles. The least amount for a record token was six shillings and then you would just need a few pence to buy a single. A thirty-shilling token would be just a few shillings and sixpence short of a brand-new album, easily made up from paper-round earnings.

The highest amount you could get on a token was fifty shillings, but Phil hadn't any relations who would stump up that much at Christmas, nor many who shared his passion for recorded music unless it might be opera or classical symphonies. But there were some enlightened relatives who realised that this was exactly what he wanted.

They had sent some on his birthday, last June, and continued in the same vein this Christmas. Phil calculated that, with two six-shilling tokens, and a ten-shilling one, from generous Uncle Frank, added to the obligatory postal order from a godparent in Ireland he had never met, the total of 32 shillings and 6 pence for that next album could well be reached. But which one to buy?

Since the launch of Radio 1, three months ago, on Sunday afternoons Phil could often be found in the front living room, between 2 and 4 p.m., diligently attending to his weekend homework, or so he told Mum and Dad. Of course, the radio on the radiogram would be tuned to 247 metres medium wave and DJs Pete Drummond, John Peel and Tommy Vance would be presenting a programme called 'Top Gear'.

It was the only show at that time that favoured playing album tracks, rather than chart singles, had contemporary groups or solo artists playing live on air, and was described in the *Radio Times* as playing "the coolest record sounds around". It was also the only programme on BBC radio described as a progressive music show.

Phil was none too sure why this music was progressive or what that meant. He could understand that it was to be listened to, rather than danced to, and that many of the top groups – like the Beatles, Beach Boys, and the Rolling Stones – had all moved away from chart singles to produce albums. Some LPs now had storylines or concepts, others incorporated orchestras or instruments from the Asian sub-continent, like George Harrison playing the sitar on 'Within you, Without you' on Sgt. Pepper's Lonely Hearts Club Band.

It had been in early December that Phil had heard Pete Drummond introduce a song which had him utterly spellbound. It had an orchestral crescendo start followed by simple guitar chords that made the melody both beautiful and sad. The vocal seemed too highly pitched for the singer and it drifted across the stereo speakers for nearly four minutes, ending with a brilliant choral and orchestral sound that Phil loved. He had never heard anything like it before.

With Phil, if he was always waiting to hear a song again on the radio, then he knew that, whoever the group was, they would be worth investigating. In this instance, the band was called the Buffalo Springfield and the song was 'Expecting to Fly'.

On Saturday mornings, in weeks before Christmas, Mum and Dad would take all three offspring into town to do 'Christmas shopping'. Phil would declare that he needed to go off on his own to buy Matt or Rachel a present. Of course, this was just a ruse as whichever present he was supposed to be buying would be much less important than finding his way to the record department in Beatties' basement. There he would target the section marked A to C in the album racks, and painstakingly search for any album by the Buffalo Springfield.

There was no joy until mid-December when amazingly there it was. The cover of 'Buffalo Springfield Again' took the form of a collage with the five band members pictured as if they were behind some cliffs by a lake but looking like giants in front of a massive bluebird. Side 1 track 4 was 'Expecting to Fly'. He carefully took the sleeve up to the counter, knowing that there was no way he could buy it there and then.

"Can I listen to the first two tracks on Side 1, please?" Phil confidently asked the assistant. "Booth number 3," came the indifferent reply and he nonchalantly strolled over to the row of booths. When Phil was tolerating Saturday morning school, his then free Wednesday afternoons were spent, with Adrian and Martin, squeezing into one of these listening booths in local record shops to hear the latest singles by the Beatles, Stones, Kinks, or whatever group Martin had spotted to check out. Phil never bought one, but Martin would, as he had started his treasured singles collection a few years ago.

Phil heard the needle crackle on to the disc; the cool Byrds style intro of track 1 – 'Mr Soul' – was then interrupted by an abrasive guitar followed by a rasping vocal. "Nothing like 'Expecting to Fly'" thought Phil "but a great opening track". The country sound of track 2 followed. 'A Child's Claim to Fame' had a different lead vocal, and again it was nothing like the other two tracks, but he still liked what he heard,

Over the next two weeks, he made every effort to get into Beatties, take the sleeve up to the assistant and ask to hear more tracks. By the time he had made his way to the final track, the assistant was having none of it, until Phil asked if he would be so kind to put the album to one side, and he would be in after Christmas to purchase it. Now all he had to do was convince all or any of his relatives that record tokens were his preferred and required present of choice this festive season.

Early starts on Saturday mornings were now becoming the norm for Phil as doing a paper round had curtailed lie-ins for quite a while, even at weekends. He was usually back in the kitchen by 8:30 a.m. and all the newspapers, magazines and comics had been delivered with a spring in his step today because this Saturday was going to be a fantastic day.

There was plenty to look forward to. Dad was going to drop him off at Venturers that evening. Wolves were at home to the mighty Manchester United that afternoon and, as soon as he had cleared away breakfast and completed his tasks for Mum, he was off on the bus into town, armed with three record tokens and enough extra cash to purchase his third record, the album 'Buffalo Springfield Again'.

By midday, he was home again and ensconced in the front living room, listening closely to all the ten tracks, each one so different from the others. Phil was utterly astonished at the different music styles five musicians could play on one record. If this was progressive music, then he really liked it.

"Come on Phillip," called his mother from the kitchen. "Time to set the table for lunch. You've got a bus to catch if you want to get to Molineux early for the game this afternoon."

"OK, Mum," said Phil. "Just the last track to listen to. I'll be there in five minutes."

Phil was wrapped up warm as he waited in the front room. The number 11 bus stop was just outside their house. They had all got used to the loud vibration of the air brakes and the noise of the doors opening as the bus drew up. The real advantage was that you could see other travellers edge forward, to signal the bus to stop, which was your cue to get from the front room to the end of the bus queue, thus avoiding standing in the cold on a late December afternoon.

When Phil had arrived back in Wolverhampton in the early sixties, for over six years he had delighted in riding in and out of town on their trolleybuses, a public transport system that once had the accolade of being the largest trolleybus system in the world. Sadly, the last trolleybus ride had finished, at the Dudley terminus, in early March that year.

Phil, like many others, missed the very smooth, comfortable ride, reasoning that trolleybuses were much quieter and altogether nicer. The new fleet of diesel buses was much noisier, and bus rides now seemed more uncomfortable. Trolleybuses seemed to glide along the streets. Surely, the same streets hadn't become bumpier in the space of nine months.

Uncomfortable or not, the bus would get Phil into the centre of the town and, alighting on Victoria Street, just outside Beatties, he would meet up with Joe, Adrian, and Brian by the Prince Albert statue in Queen Square. They had arranged to meet at 2:15 giving them around 45 minutes to get into the ground before kick-off.

"They reckon there will be over 50,000 in the ground," said Joe as they walked through St Peter's Square. "We should get into the South Bank, though", he added "and we need to stand well away from the United supporters." Adrian agreed.

"Cheerio," said Brian, as he went off to the Molineux Street stand to sit with his father. They were both season ticket holders. "See you all at Venturers, tonight," he called back. "It's Finders Keepers. Them bostin."

"What?" said Joe.

"The band on tonight, at the youth club," replied Phil. "They're called Finders Keepers and they are one of the best around. Should be a great way to end the year."

"It will be for you if you find someone to dance with, Phil," quipped Joe. Phil just blushed. Adrian grinned and nodded. They were nowhere near the ground but could already see how long the queues were to get in. The South Bank at Molineux was one of the biggest football stands in the country, holding around 30,000 supporters, well over half the capacity of the entire ground. And today, it was going to be jam-packed.

"If we get split up going in, then meet up at the usual place – on the left, by the side stanchions," said Joe. "Adrian's tall enough to see but you and I can stand on the lower struts to give us a better view, Phil," he added.

They were in their places, waiting for kick-off, with just 10 minutes to go. Adrian was studiously reading his programme. Phil's was in his pocket. He would read it on the bus home. He looked across the stand. The United fans were in their usual red colours – they had been known as the Red Devils for some years now – and they were in full voice.

They had hammered Wolves 4-0 at Old Trafford on Boxing Day and their fans were eager to let everyone know just who had been crowned first division champions last season, and there would be no chance of any success for Wolves today. The chants of 'We are the champions' and 'United, da-da-da, United, da-da-da, United' resonated around the ground.

The cheerleaders, in the centre of this vast red throng, were very vocal. The stragglers, round the edges of this section of the crowd, were not so sure as they nervously looked at the many Wolves fans occupying the terraces around them. They had nowt to fear though as most of the more belligerent Wolves fans always stood – chanting and singing – at the opposite end, the North Bank. The South Bank was for those who just came to watch the game, not to start a fight.

Phil had always believed there was safety in numbers there, even though they always stood at the side of the stand, well away from the opposing fans. The United fans were very quickly silenced when Wolves scored within the first 30 seconds of the game!

"They weren't expecting that!" whispered Phil to Joe.

"Neither was I!" exclaimed Joe. "Paddy Buckley wouldn't be playing if Dougan had been fit but he met that cross brilliantly with his head and we're one-nil up."

The South Bank was a mix of smug but muted smiles from most of the Wolves fans, and a discontented murmur from the mass of United fans, situated bang in the middle of the stand. That sort of start didn't happen to their team.

"Amazing considering we've a few first-team regulars missing. No Dave Woodfield, no Terry Warton, no Ernie Hunt, and no Doog. Not really our best side," said Joe. "And Evan Williams is still in goal, keeping Phil Parkes and Fred Davies out of the side."

"And have you seen who's playing at inside right in place of Dave Burnside?" Phil declared. "That's Stewart Ross! He was head boy at school when we first went there. I thought he was like a Greek god, standing at the front of big school at every morning assembly!"

"Well, he's really made it now," said Joe. "I know he's been picked to play most weeks for the reserves. He must have been playing really well to get in the first team. What an incredible game to make your first division debut! Good on 'im." Adrian nodded in agreement.

As the first half continued, it was evident to the lads that this patched-up first team were out to cause a real division 1 upset. After the Boxing Day hammering, you wouldn't have known which side was top of the league and which was languishing in the bottom half. Wolves passing was crisp and accurate, a real credit to the players, and they held onto their lead until the half-time whistle blew.

The lads grinned at each other.

"Another 45 minutes of this and there will be some headlines on the back pages of tomorrow's papers when I deliver them," said Phil.

"45 minutes can be a long time," chipped in Adrian. "Did you see Hawkins limping off? Can't see him coming out for the second half."

"You need to have faith," said Joe, but Adrian was right as the teams emerged and it was announced that Gerry Taylor would replace Graham Hawkins. "I guess Stewart Ross will drop back from midfield into defence now," Joe said out loud.

But, before the Wolves re-jigged defence could sort themselves out, United were on level terms. Straight from the kick-off, the ball found itself at the feet of World Cup winner, Bobby Charlton, and his brilliant shot, from a really narrow-angle, was nestling in the back of William's net, before some of the fans had even taken their seats in the Waterloo Road stand. It had taken the division 1 champions just 15 seconds to equalise.

And, within the next 7 minutes, they had established a 3-1 lead and the game had slipped away from Wolves completely. The second goal came from their left winger, young John Aston, and the third from the 18-year-old Brian Kidd, who had only made his United debut a few games ago.

Both goals were laid on by the brilliant George Best who seemed to have come out in the second half with bags more energy and was now at his crowd-enchanting best, making dazzling runs and beating Wolves defenders with ease.

"I don't know what was in George Best's tea at half-time," quipped Joe. "Peter Knowles could do with some if we are going to get back into the game." The lads nodded. "Mind you, let's hope Knowles doesn't sit on the ball on the half-way line again. If you remember he did it in the middle of a game last season and really wound up the opposition!" continued Joe.

"Wasn't that in the FA Cup against United, when we were two-nil up and they got so incensed they came back and won four-two?" asked Phil.

"Yep, that's right," agreed Joe. "He needs to be right on his game now if we have any hope of even getting a draw out of this."

After 67 minutes, there was a glimmer of hope, as the Wolves captain, Mike Bailey, hit a screamer from 20 yards out, beating United keeper, Alex Stepney, literally all hands up. Stepney was to be United's saviour though, as he denied Dave Wagstaffe a late equaliser with a superb save.

The Red Devils were now in full song, to the right of the lads in the South Bank and, as the final whistle went, all three lads looked at each other with long faces. They say football is a game of two halves, but for Joe, Phil and Adrian they would have welcomed the referee blowing for full time around 55 minutes ago.

As they left the ground, they noticed the weather had changed. They had entered the South Bank two hours earlier with little optimism but with a warmth generated by knowing they were about to watch what everyone reckoned was the best team in the land, not their side but the opposition, who had now proved just why they were top of the league.

The cold of that late December afternoon had disappeared with Wolves early goal which brought beaming smiles to their fans throughout the stadium.

Smiles like that can look like winter sunshine, both of which are usually pretty rare in this part of Staffordshire.

But, by full time, those smiles had returned to standard supporter frowns as the Wolves fans' mood mirrored the weather – dour, overcast, and likely to be frosty to anyone who enquired as to the outcome of the game, later that evening.

Phil caught the bus home from Queen Square and went upstairs to read his match programme. He always enjoyed 'Notes by "Wanderer"' but this time the exhortation to welcome "old friends Manchester United" seemed somewhat hollow now after that result. But he agreed that their "acknowledged high standards" had resulted in an under-strength Wolves side playing very well and putting on a good show, even if they came away with nothing.

The journey home would take around 15 minutes; Phil decided to get off a stop early and wait to pick up a copy of '*The Pink*', the Saturday evening sporting edition of the *Express & Star*.

As he stood up, he saw that, right behind him, for the whole journey, had sat the girl who lived up Muchall Road. She looked at him and smiled. A comely smile. As he walked down the bus aisle to get off, Phil felt he was blushing.

"I need to be at my scout meeting in 20 minutes, Phillip," called his Dad, up the stairs. "If you are not in the car in the next minute, you'll have to walk to Venturers and be late."

"Just coming," replied Phil. "Can't find my shoes."

"They're here, in the hall," said Dad. "Tie your laces in the car. Hurry up!"

In the car, Dad said "You've been very quiet since you got back from the Molineux. You didn't really expect the Wolves to beat Manchester United, did you?"

"Suppose not," was all Phil said.

"Do you want to get out at the Pinfold Lane junction?" asked Dad.

"Yes, that will be fine," replied Phil.

"Pick you up as usual in Hollybush Lane at 10?" Dad asked.

"No that's alright. It's a fine evening. I'll walk home, thanks Dad," said Phil as he got out of the car.

"OK, if that's what you want," replied Dad. "And cheer up! The Wolves won't get relegated just by losing to the league leaders. Don't make too much noise when you come in and no later than 10:15. You've got homework to finish before school on Monday."

It wasn't the warmest of evenings, but the weather didn't seem to matter to Phil as he walked past the shops on Warstones Road. His smile returned as he thought of the evening ahead. Tonight's band, the Finders Keepers, were a top attraction in the Dudley and Wolverhampton pubs, like the Cleveland Arms and the Staffordshire Volunteer, both key venues if you wanted to make it big. By the time he had reached Springdale Methodist Church, the smile had vanished again.

"You've got a face like fourpence," said Brian, in his usual place at the door. "They didn't play that badly, and if Waggy had beaten Stepney, right at the end, we would have got a draw. Not bad against a top side like Man U."

"Suppose not," replied Phil and handed over his 1 shilling and 6 pence.

"It'll be 1 and 9 in the new year," said Brian. "The committee's cashing in on the club's popularity. Mind you, if we keep getting top bands like tonight, then it will be well worth it. Still cheaper than the pubs and clubs in town."

"Martin here?" enquired Phil.

"Yep, usual place. In the kitchen making a brew," replied Brian.

Phil hung his anorak in the cloakroom and collected his ticket from Janice whose job it was to make sure coats, scarves and hats were safe. Not that that mattered to Phil so much, but many of the members had bikers' leathers and helmets, and a Crombie coat was a valued adornment to those who still considered themselves as mods.

"Missed a good performance at Moli this after," said Phil to Martin. "Even though we didn't win, they put on a good show."

"Not my cuppa tea," replied Martin. "Talking of which, you want one? Two sugars? It might sweeten you up. You look as if you have real cob on this evening! Who's given you the hump today?"

"Oh, no one," replied Phil and quickly changed the subject. "They're supposed to be really good, Finders

Keepers. Haven't they been out in Germany this year? What sort of music do they play? Haven't seen any of their records? You got any?"

"Blimey, you're all questions – yes they've recorded a couple of singles. Their first single, called 'Light', was produced by Scott Walker. You remember, we saw the Walker Brothers at the Gaumont in April. Well, that's what their manager, Roger Allen, says but then he always likes to boost the publicity for his bands. And they've got a brand new one out this month, but I haven't heard it. I expect they will play it tonight."

"How do you know all this?" said Phil.

"I spend as much time in the record department in Beatties or in Voltic Records as you do at Molineux. Your passion is the Wolves, mine is music – pop music that is," replied Martin.

'I like what John Peel calls progressive music on 'Top Gear' on Radio 1," said Phil.

"You won't hear much of that tonight," said Martin. "This lot are mainstream pop, but pretty good as far as I've heard," he said as the evening's first guitar chord rang out.

Ian Lees, who for some unknown reason was known as Sludge, was the only bandmember on the raised stage at the far end of the church hall. He had been the band's roadie until, when they arrived in Germany, they had been told that the promoter had expected a five-piece so Sludge took to the stage from then on, sharing the vocals with Roy Kent, whose also had a nickname – Dripper. It seemed to

Phil that in order to be in Finders Keepers you had to have a nickname that related to water!

Sludge still carried out his duties as roadie and was ensuring that all the guitars, amps, drums and mics were in working order and securely taped to the stage. Finders Keepers were known for fooling around on stage and the last thing they wanted to do was to trip over a rogue cable or collide with a wrongly placed piece of equipment.

Satisfied, he disappeared to the back of the hall. The club members were dotted around the hall, some seated, some chatting. Others near the stage – nearly all blokes – were having a quick gawk at the band's gear and, close to the front of the stage, assortments of handbags, piled together, with no apparent owners. These small assemblages designated the dancing places of girls who, once the band were on stage, would dance together but with their eyes fixed on whichever band member was, in their view, the best looking.

Phil was only too aware, from uneasy personal encounters, that asking any of them to dance would be met with an icy stare and no conversation whatsoever. Most club members seemed a tad impatient that evening. They all felt that this should be a special event. The last Saturday of 1967 and one of the best local bands to entertain them.

They were not disappointed. From their very first appearance, it was evident that the group members of Finders Keepers not only knew the right mix of songs to play but the banter with the crowd was also at just the right level to keep them smiling throughout the evening.

David Williams on drums and Phil Overfield on bass guitar provided a solid rhythm for the early openers – the Hollies' summer hit 'Carrie-Anne', and the nonsense top three hit, 'Zabadak', for Dave Dee, Dozy, Beaky, Mick and Tich. Sludge and Dripper shared the main vocals with lead guitarist, Alan Clee, adding great harmonies.

"Those are as good cover versions as you'll hear anywhere," said Phil to Martin.

"Not really progressive or psychedelic though, is it?" replied Martin. "But they know how to make a song their own and have fun with it."

"I saw Dave Dee and his lot do that song on 'Top of the Pops'," said Phil. "But not with as many smiles as Dripper and Sludge had. They really enjoyed doing that."

"Any of yow young ladies know what those words mean?" asked Dripper to the throng of girls in front of him. They all shook their heads. "Pity," he said. "I hoped that some of you could explain the meaning of that song to us, cos we ain't got a clue." Everyone laughed.

"These next two songs have been written by some of our Brummagem mates. Yow'll know the next one, if yow went to see the film," and they went straight into the vocals of Traffic's 'Here we go round the mulberry bush', followed by the Move's 'Flowers in the rain'.

"Great songs those," chipped in Sludge. "Not all the best songs come from Liverpool and London, you know. Even America has some great songwriters. The next song was written by an American guy called John Stewart, who also wrote our first single which we released in 1966".

"And it's never been seen since!" added Dripper with more laughs from the band. All the crowd knew the words to the Monkees' 'Daydream Believer' but very few had a clue about the Finders Keepers' single 'Light'.

"Bet you've got a copy of that," said Joe to Martin.

"The B-side's rubbish though," said Martin. "It's a country and western song called 'Come on now'. That type of music doesn't suit the band at all."

"We're going to have a break soon. Alan needs to oil his guitar. Sounds a bit creaky to me," announced Dripper. Alan grinned. He'd been the butt of Dripper's jokes for a while. "But we have some great songs lined up for the second half, including our brand new single. These next songs have both been chart-toppers this summer for the Turtles and the Foundations."

Alan hit the opening chords and the full band went straight into the harmonies of 'She'd rather be with me'. As the band did their rendition of 'Baby now that I've found you', the lads made their way to the refreshments.

"Not bad for a regular pop act," said Joe. Adrian nodded.

"Not found anyone to dance with, Phil?" joked Joe. "Plenty of talent on the dance floor – none taking your fancy or not good enough for yow?"

"Neither. Just don't feel like dancing," said Phil.

"Blimey, if Finders Keepers can't cheer you up, no one will. They're having fun on stage. Love the banter between them. They really love performing," said Martin.

"Can you make sure I am off home by 10, Martin? I've forgotten my watch and will really be in for it if I am late home from here again," asked Phil.

"Sure, no probs but only if your first New Year's resolution is to put on a happy face on Saturday evenings here or Brian and I will get you banned," answered Martin.

Phil's face was a picture. He looked at Martin who smiled and said, "Only joking, mate. But any chance you can cheer up for the rest of the evening. You've already made the milk in my tay go sour. If that's what you're like when Wolves lose, then maybe you should stop going to Molineux."

With a quick poke in Phil's ribs, Martin led the lads back into the hall just before the band took to the stage again.

Dripper looked at his audience. He was a showman and entertainer and, with this audience, he was in his absolute element. He paused and then said, "Hit it, Dave". Five drumbeats followed by a bass intro and Dripper sang 'Give me a ticket for an aeroplane' the opening line of 'The Letter'. 'Walk away Renee' by the Four Tops, 'World' by the Bee Gees and the Dave Clark Five's 'Everybody Knows' followed – all ballads. Phil struggled to raise a smile with these starry-eyed tunes. Martin grinned as he looked at him.

"OK, that's enough smooching," said Sludge, as most of the dancing was now couples embraced in each other's arms. "Great songs, but you've lost the party mood, Dripper. You've made it into a Friday kind of Monday."

"Good title for a song that," answered Dripper having moved to the keyboards where he was playing a repetitive four-note refrain.

Harmonies followed from Alan and Sludge, and the rhythm was upbeat again with the band's new single. It had the crowd up and dancing again, and with Dave Williams's drumming and Phil Overfield's bass giving it a tremendous rhythm, smiles were back, including Phil's. The song came to an end, to an enormous cheer. A song that probably no one there had heard before had made a fantastic impression.

"Wow," exclaimed Dripper. "Yow liked it?! That's our brand new single. It's called 'Friday kind of Monday' and it's on the Fontana label. If yow've got any record tokens left after Christmas, yow can buy a copy next week and give us a hit record in early 1968. And, if yow want to know what's on the B side, this is what it sounds like."

Dripper looked at the rest of the band and began playing 'On the Beach' on the keyboards, which was much more of a progressive sound but got the same reception from the youngsters who were loving the band.

"Glad you like that," said Sludge. "That's the first track that we recorded what we actually wrote. So whichever side you like, let's have our record in the charts in January."

"Here's a song that's already a hit," continued Dripper. "In fact, it's been number one for a few weeks but then aren't the Beatles always number one at Christmas."

And as he sang 'You say yes, I say no, you say stop, and I say go, go, go', Phil realised that 'Hello, Goodbye' meant it was time for him to think about going home.

"I'm off," he said.

"We've noticed," replied Martin with a wide grin, and Phil actually smiled, handed in his ticket to Janice, put on his anorak, took his gloves from his pocket, together with his Wolves bobble hat, and set off up Hollybush Lane.

"Shame I didn't dance tonight," he thought. But then there wasn't anyone there with such a comely smile that he had witnessed earlier that day. "Maybe next time," he said to himself as he arrived home, bang on time.

Chapter 4 – Bend me, Shape me

The spring term began at school on Monday 1st January 1968. Scotland had treated New Year's Day as a holiday for decades, but in Wolverhampton workers were expected on the shop floor, clerks to be seated in their offices, and school bells rung, bright and early, on the first day of this new year.

Although there was no Stewart Ross as head boy in big school assembly on that Monday morning, his name was on everyone's lips as pupils at the grammar school were excited by the news that 'one of their own' had made his debut for the Wolves first team against Manchester United on Saturday. And he had played really, really well.

Phil Morgan, regular reporter for Wolves matches at the *Express & Star*, wrote:

> "Wolves even went so far as to 'blood' a first division newcomer but ex-grammar schoolboy Stewart Ross did not let them down. He was in the thick of it and several times, by quick thinking and determination, helped in the first-half frustration of United. Wolves can call on him any time they like without a qualm. He gave as much as the rest, all of whom rose to the occasion splendidly – unfortunately for so little reward."

The pride of many scholars, across all years at the school, was plainly evident as results from the under-13 football team through to the first 11 improved week on week. This was in contrast to that of Wolves, who lost in succession to Everton, Leicester City and West Ham United. By the end of January, they were just above the relegation places in division 1, as well as tumbling out of the FA Cup to lowly Rotherham United. Phil went to each and every one of these home defeats and, on every bus trip home, he would always read his programme whilst now making sure he knew precisely who was in the seat behind him.

Joe usually sat behind Phil at school. They were in their second term in lower sixth science, and Phil was beginning to struggle with two out of the three subjects he had chosen for A-level studies. He had always been a very capable mathematician so the maths for science lessons were no problem to him.

Disappointingly for Phil, his physics lessons were no longer overseen by Taff Williams, as had been the case for O-level studies. Now, some of the other students were taking great delight in winding up their new teacher who, whilst obviously very expert in his subject, was struggling to keep control of twenty or so less-than-respectful teenage lads.

Often practical work would be interrupted by what was, in Phil's mind, unhelpful and attention-seeking antics, which did nothing to help students who, like Phil, were already labouring with many of the physics topics newly encountered at this level.

Likewise, in chemistry, Phil was struggling, although this was not really his fault. He had never been a bookish pupil so having a teacher who appeared at the start of a lesson, instructed his students to read certain pages from whatever chapter of the primer was next, before disappearing for the majority of that double period, was never going to help Phil.

It was strongly rumoured that many of the science staff enjoyed their hands of bridge so much so that some teachers, particularly those who taught chemistry, would continue their recreations even when classes had started after break or lunch! Given the option of reading the recommended text or delving into his duffle bag to find the copy of his latest *Melody Maker* or *NME*, was a no brainer to Phil. The latter always won.

At lunch, on that first day of term, Taff Williams was on duty, seated on a bench by the music hut. He was wrapped up in his overcoat and college scarf. Phil thought that Taff only had two coats – his overcoat and the lab coat he wore when teaching. His characteristic bow tie was, Taff insisted, standard uniform for scientists and was a much safer option than ordinary ties when demonstrating practical concepts. His accord to uniform in teaching could be seen by the elbow patches on his jacket, worn down from seemingly endless staff meetings, or so he said.

Although Phil's Dad said that teaching tended to make you lose your hair somewhat prematurely, Taff was into his late 30s and this hadn't been the case with him although there was often a need for a comb. Unlike many of the other teachers, however, he made time for his students especially those who would enter into conversation about his favourite topic – space exploration and the current race to get to the moon.

"Can I sit here as well?" asked Phil.

"Of course, Minor," replied Taff. "How's Oxford?"

Taff had nicknames for many of his students and Matt's was 'Oxford' – after the car – and the fact that he was destined to go to university there.

"He's fine. Just waiting for the results of his entrance exams," said Phil. "He's hoping to get into New College, where Dad went, to study chemistry."

"Oxford should get in okay. Your father taught here, didn't he?" enquired Taff.

"Yes, from 1948. It was his first teaching post. He's a headmaster now," replied Phil proudly.

"Good for him," said Taff.

"No football here, lads!" bellowed Taff, as a few lads started a game on the green grassy strip between Derry Hall and the fives courts. "If you want a kick-about then either go onto the junior school playground or down to the valley fields, although that's likely to be full of mud maids this time of year!"

The boys looked at Taff with total bewilderment, but he just smiled. "So, who's going to win the space race this year, Minor?"

"Must be the Americans as they have made two successful landings on the moon during last term and the Soviets haven't done much in the past year," was Phil's view.

"Ah, never trust a quiet Russian," came Taff's reply. "They may have been quiet, but I bet they have been very busy."

In early 1968, the space race between the Americans and the Russians was about to come to a head, as both nations continued to work towards successfully landing men on the moon, and then returning them safely to earth. It had been nearly seven years since Taff's hero, President John F. Kennedy, urged America to send astronauts to the moon.

In 1966, whilst most of this country had both eyes on World Cup football, the race looked neck and neck, with the USA's unmanned robotic spacecraft Surveyor 1 landing on the moon just four months after the Soviet craft Luna 9 had done the same. Both nations seemed to make progress later that year and again into 1967, with the Soviets concentrating on orbiting the moon, whereas the Americans had succeeded in making four soft landings on the surface.

The Americans launched Surveyor 7 on January 7th, 1968. Phil and Mr Williams continued a daily dialogue on the progress of its journey until it successfully touched down three days later. Taff's contacts kept him informed as to the number of photographs sent back from the moon, although they were both disappointed to learn that this would be the last of the Surveyor programme of space ventures.

Their despondency grew when the Soviet mission centre announced that the latest launch in their Luna programme would take place on February 7th. However, the craft suffered a launch failure and it would be another two months before the Soviet programme was back on track, with yet another Russian spacecraft orbiting the moon.

By this time, the powers at NASA had decided to put all their efforts back into the Apollo programme which, a year earlier, had made a terrible start with all the crew perishing in a launch fire on Apollo 1. Further launches were postponed until November 1967, when the programme resumed, and by early 1968, the Americans believed they then had a spacecraft that would be capable of transporting their three-man crew to the moon and back. Such a prospect excited Phil who hoped he would be in Taff William's physics set for his second year in the sixth form.

Little of this though would help Phil to gain a good top grade in the A-level physics exam. Knowing the location of the Tycho Crater on the moon and the fact that it wasn't on the moon's equator like the other four Surveyor moon landings had been, was unlikely to come up in any exam. Once again Phil was coming up short when it came to applying himself to learn about the thermal properties of materials or even the kinetic theory of gases.

His studies continued to be somewhat wayward throughout the spring term, although his parents would have been none the wiser as he seemed to be at ease with his schoolwork. Every Sunday afternoon, he would take up residence in the front living room to work on his weekend's school assignments. As he had promised himself late last September, any perusing of organic chemistry textbooks or solving questions on differential equations or understanding vector analysis would be accompanied by dedicated attention to 'Top Gear', now solely presided over by John Peel.

These two hours, together with *Melody Maker* and the *NME*, introduced Phil to an array of music, ranging from superior, but often less-popular, three-minute pop singles to album tracks by new artists from both sides of the Atlantic. His main problem was that this glut of new sounds just begged more questions than his chemistry homework.

Why was psychedelic music so in fashion? What was rhythm and blues music, or R&B as the DJs called it? Was soul and blues music only from the deep south of America? It was true that soul labels, such as Stax and Sun Records were both based in Memphis, Tennessee, but Tamla Motown hailed from the north, in Detroit, and the Atlantic studios were in New York.

Since the beginning of the year, soul music had seen a surge in popularity following the tragic death of Otis Redding in a plane crash last December. Phil had heard some of Otis's songs, played at local dances at Compton and Tettenhall youth clubs, and wasn't overly impressed with the more up-tempo tracks such as 'Mr Pitiful' and 'Respect'.

Otis's ballads, like 'Try a little tenderness', passed him by completely at the end of each youth club dance as, by that time in the evening, he was invariably getting his coat from the cloakroom ready to cycle home. To Phil, the best soul tracks were those that you could easily dance to which came pretty well exclusively from Tamla Motown. Many of these had been chart hits, for the Four Tops, the Supremes and Phil's favourite, the Temptations, and all had that distinctive 'Motown Sound'. He would often say that if you can't dance to Motown, then you just can't dance.

However, for someone approaching his 16th birthday, this sudden musical miscellany was all very mystifying. All Phil knew was that he really enjoyed listening to radio programmes that embraced different styles of music, and to some presenters, like John Peel, who never seemed to have any particular musical preferences but just gave the impression that they were really happy to be able to bring the listener such a varied and entertaining selection of tracks, whether singles or from Phil's choice of record purchase, albums.

However, whilst he continued to put a shilling or two aside each week from his paper round, it would still be a few months before his next birthday, which meant at this time of the year his finances were very much in line with the national picture, certainly not on the way up. Nonetheless, he still had no concept as to why the pound had been devalued, as the Labour Government had announced last November, and why any pound that found its way into Phil's pocket would be worth any less than it was before.

Doing a paper round ensured that he came across bold front-page headlines which at that time exalted readers to 'Back Britain' in order to boost the nation's economy. Unsurprisingly that campaign ran out of steam when it was revealed that the T-shirts promoting it were actually manufactured in Portugal! Phil had also heard the campaign theme song, 'I'm Backing Britain' by the entertainer, Bruce Forsyth, on Radio 1, and thought it was pretty naff and thankfully short.

The *Express & Star* wasn't that positive about local prospects either reporting on the closure of the Baggeridge Colliery, in nearby Sedgeley, bringing to an end nearly 300 years of coal mining in the Black Country and adding to growing unemployment in an area where work had been plentiful for over a decade. Whether local or national, the struggling economic picture seemed of little consequence to Phil who just knew he didn't have enough pounds or shillings in his pocket to augment his record collection.

Things changed for the better towards the middle of February when 'Top Gear' began to play tracks from a brand-new type of record release, known as a sampler album. The record in question was 'The Rock Machine Turns You On' and with each track he heard, he knew he wanted to hear more. And the real bonus was that this 15-track collection was only a penny under 15 shillings, less than half the cost of a full-priced album!

There were tracks from established singer-songwriters such as Bob Dylan and Leonard Cohen. The latter had released his first album just a few months ago but it had spawned plenty of good cover versions from established artists and led to more success in Europe than in his native Canada. Phil wasn't a fan of either singer but liked their songs.

Some artists were new to Phil such as Tim Rose and Roy Harper, neither of whom he had heard anything by before and whilst both tracks might well have been lyrical masterpieces, to him they didn't have enough melody.

Familiar artists, such as The Byrds and Simon & Garfunkel, pleased him more, together with the jazz-rock sound of Blood, Sweat and Tears, and two foot-tapping tracks, 'Statesboro Blues' from the singer Taj Mahal, and 'Killing floor' from a barnstorming blues-rock band called The Electric Flag.

Other outlandishly named psychedelic bands, like Elmer Gantry's Velvet Opera, The Peanut Butter Conspiracy, Spirit and Moby Grape, all had attention-grabbing tracks and whilst most tracks were by American artists – not surprising as they all recorded for CBS, based in New York – the stand-out for Phil was Side 1 track 5, 'Time of the Season' by the Zombies. And they were from St Albans in deepest Hertfordshire!

So, on the morning of the first Saturday in March, Phil ventured forth to Beatties' Record Department to purchase the fourth LP in his somewhat paltry, but already eclectic, record collection. Buying 'The Rock Machine Turns You

On' would use up most of his savings, but he had enough to make the purchase, with the help of 6 shillings borrowed from Matt, on the condition that Matt could listen to it, as part-owner, when he wanted to, especially the Dylan and Cohen tracks.

Later that day, Phil boarded the Number 11 bus into town. He had borrowed the money from Matt so that he would still have enough for what was yet another chock-full Saturday. The mighty Liverpool were the visitors to Molineux that afternoon and then, later in the evening, he needed money to get into Venturers, as the band appearing were the 'N Betweens, another local band with an outstanding reputation for entertaining and performing. Neither of these events was to be missed at any cost.

Brian and Adrian were already standing close to the famous statue of Prince Albert in Queens Square. To most locals, it was known as the 'man on the `oss', rather than any mention of Queen Victoria's consort. Most would also be amazed as to how much her majesty had taken such a shine to Lady Wulfruna's town, unaware that, just over a century before, a group of Wolverhampton widows had written to ask if the queen would visit them as they were concerned about her overlong period of mourning. Having been touched by their concern, she made Wolverhampton her first visit upon returning to public duties.

None of this meant much to these lads, who had forsaken history studies for science, languages or classics a few years back when choosing their academic options.

However, they had all been informed that the stately statue had a major fault – that all the horse's hooves were flat on the ground, a posture that would have resulted in the princely steed falling over. Not very regal really!

Joe was late. It was well past 2:30 p.m. as he ran up Lichfield Street, having stepped off the Wednesfield bus at Horsley Fields Depot. It was a good thing that he was fit as a butcher's dog, as Shorty Robertson, the PE master at school, would have said in his broad Scottish burr, so he could leg it through town to meet the other lads by the statue.

"Yow'm late," said Brian. "I'm going to have to get down to the Molineux Street Stand sharpish to get in with me Dad or he'll go in without me. See you this evening at Venturers, Joe."

"Ok. Tara a bit. See you later, Bri," replied Joe.

"Sorry lads, but me Dad kept on finding summat for me to do right up to lunch, and then the bus was late," explained Joe. "Still, we should get into the South Bank easily today. Can't see there being a big crowd after the run of results we've had with no wins so far this year – only one point in five games and that point is just keeping us above the relegation places!"

"But it's Liverpool today, Joe," replied Phil. "They might win the league this year and they're full of British internationals like St John, Callaghan and Lawler, with Yeats and Smith in defence and Roger Hunt up front."

"We'll see," Joe said. "Shall we stand in the usual spot or do you fancy our chances in the middle of the stand with the `Pool supporters?"

"Why not. They aren't any trouble usually, the `Pool fans. They love to talk about the footie. I've stood on the Kop with my cousin, Steve, and they were really friendly then," said Phil confidently.

The three lads – with Joe having been proved right as there were no queues to contend with – cautiously took their places behind a barrier about ten yards to the left of where the away fans were, singing the Liverpool anthem 'You'll never walk alone', made famous by the group Gerry and his Pacemakers, five years back.

As the teams came out at 10 to 3, Phil leant across to Joe. "Why are there so many cameramen on the pitch?" he asked.

"It's Derek Parkin's first game at right-back," Joe replied. "Wolves paid £80,000 from Huddersfield for him. Hope he's as good as the other famous Terriers full-back, Ray Wilson, who went to Everton for big money and then helped us to win the World Cup in '66."

When it came to finding answers for all things about pop music, bands and the charts, Phil always deferred to Martin. But with football, Joe was like a walking soccer encyclopaedia, keeping up with who had had been transferred where, who was scoring most goals, who was looking to win the title, or which team might be relegated.

"Mind you, the bosses need to spend some of the money they've made from selling half the team since we got promoted last summer," Joe declared.

"Yeh. Big Ron Flowers and Ernie Hunt went at the start of the season. Really surprised that we let Wharton go to Bolton. I wouldn't have paid £65,000 for him," chipped in Adrian, surprisingly.

"Yow'll never have £65,000," laughed Joe. "Then they have sold Paddy Buckley, Graham Hawkins and Fred Davies since the New Year – all regular first-team players. And replaced them with who? Mike Kenning from Norwich and now Parkin. Six out and two in doesn't make sense to me. No wonder we can't win a game this year."

"I heard they are about to sign a fella called Frank Munro from Aberdeen," said Phil.

Joe wasn't budging. "Munro won't get in the side. He's a centre half and we have Woodfield and Holsgrove playing well enough right now. It's up front we need new players. It's all about scoring goals and at the moment there's too much resting on the Doog's shoulders."

The game kicked off with a flurry of attacks from Wolves but they just couldn't score which meant that Joe knew he was absolutely spot-on. Liverpool were relying on their wingers, Thompson and Callaghan – who had both been ignored by England's manager Sir Alf Ramsey as regular internationals, but who were very skilful players – to take the game to Wolves. Scottish international, Ian St John, seemed to be everywhere.

Both keepers made comfortable saves in the first 30 minutes but with just over 10 minutes to go before half-time, Wolves deservedly took the lead. Wagstaffe had been on the end of some agricultural tackles from the Liverpool defence so far this half, but, following another long clearance from Wolves keeper, Phil Parkes, the ball went out to Waggy on the left wing where he evaded Tommy Smith's desperate lunge and set Peter Knowles off down the wing. Knowles just got the cross in, before it went over the byline, and there was Derek Dougan, towering over the `Pool defence to head home at the far post and put Wolves one up.

"We deserved that," declared Joe. "We have been the better side all half and that was a brilliant cross from Knowles. He's been playing better and better. Controlling the midfield."

"And Liverpool have had to resort to clogging tactics, mainly on Waggy and Alan Evans," chipped in Adrian. His comment was drowned out by the crowd on the North Bank, singing the Doog anthem – 'I'll walk a million miles for one of your smiles, Oh Doooogan'.

As the first half drew to a close, Wolves should have made it two-nil, as once again Wagstaffe was clattered by Liverpool's Lawler. From the resulting free kick, Peter Knowles floated a delightful cross into the `Pool penalty area. Doogan rose majestically, made full contact and headed goalward, only for Tommy Lawrence, Liverpool's keeper, to make a fingertip save and push the ball out for a corner.

"That was superb from Knowles again," said Phil and both Joe and Adrian nodded, totally engrossed in the game. Liverpool continued to create chances but Wolves defenders, Woodfield and Holsgrove, were keeping both Hunt, and Liverpool's new signing, Tony Hateley, in check. The half-time whistle blew and the lads grinned at each other.

A Liverpool fan nearby looked across at the three of them, then smiled and said "Hey lads. Why are you lot down the bottom of the league? You're playing some good footie."

"We always play better against the top sides," replied Joe. "We're home to Sunderland next week and I bet we won't play half as well as this against them."

As the sides came out for the second half it was evident that the Liverpool tactics had taken their toll. Wagstaffe's right foot was heavily bandaged and Evans was walking very hesitantly. Still, Wolves made another strong start with Peter Knowles having two cracking shots saved by the `Pool keeper, Lawrence. Then, midway through the half, Evans couldn't play on any longer with his back injury and was replaced by John Farrington.

"We just need to hang on," said Joe. "This would be a superb win and raise the team's confidence. It would be a bostin result for the Wolves. Get us back to winning ways."

"Now that would be something new," replied Phil as they all bit their fingernails.

The crowd had gone quiet. Liverpool were still pressing for an equaliser and with just 10 minutes left, a strong shot from Callaghan, easily Liverpool's best player on the day, was saved by Parkes. A couple of minutes later, Callaghan again tormented the Wolves defence finishing with a snapshot which Phil Parkes was in place to comfortably save.

Then the referee gave Liverpool a free kick for a late tackle by Parkin on winger Thompson. Tommy Smith floated the ball into the Wolves penalty area only for Liverpool's centre half, Yeats, to head the ball goalward but wide. A lack of communication between Parkes and Holsgrove saw the defender put it out for a corner when he could have safely let it go out for a goal kick.

"Why did he do that?" asked Joe anxiously. "There was no one near him! What a pillock!"

"Playing safe, I suppose," replied Phil, but he knew it could be costly.

Callaghan took the corner and his cross was met decisively by Yeats who this time was on target, but it hit his own teammate, Hateley, on the goal line. Before any of the Wolves defenders could react, Roger Hunt dashed in to tap the ball into the net. There were shouts for offside, handball, or anything that might chalk off the equaliser, but the referee was pointing to the centre circle and the game was all square at one each.

The last few minutes were played out and at the end of the match, the lads were understandably crestfallen. The nearby Liverpool fan came over.

"Didn't think we would come away with a point," he said. "Well played, lads," he continued as if the three of them had actually been on the pitch.

"We'll be playing you again in division 1 next year, if you can play like that and if you can hang on to some of your players. Your defenders were great, and Knowles is your real star. Better than that Manc lad, Best. Cheers lads."

As the lads left the South Bank, Joe was obviously narked.

"All we needed to do was to hold on for seven minutes to get two points rather than one," he said. "Call themselves title contenders. All they did was kick lumps out of our lot and then miss their chances. We ended up playing most of the second half with ten men after the injuries inflicted by them in the first 45 minutes. Waggy could hardly run in the last half hour. We were the better side throughout. We wuz robbed."

"Well look on the bright side," said Adrian. "That's doubled our points tally for this year."

Both Phil and Joe glowered at him and the three lads trudged silently back up North Street and into Queen Square to catch their buses home.

Seven-thirty that evening saw Phil approaching the entrance of the Springdale Methodist Church in Warstones Road. Another Saturday's evening's entertainment in store and today it was the turn of, arguably at that time, the most respected band in the area, the 'N Betweens.

The four-piece had been one of the mainstays of the local music scene for quite a few years now but recently, having found a more settled line-up, had moulded their repertoire around the soul and R&B sound which made them sound more earthy and heavier than other local bands.

Like other local bands, they did a lot of cover versions but theirs were much more obscure tracks rather than the regular chart hits, or Monkees' or Beatles' songs. Martin had described the band to Phil some weeks ago at school, saying they were probably the most accomplished local outfit doing the rounds, but he wasn't surprised they hadn't had a chart hit. It wasn't their style.

It was a bumper crowd in the youth centre and not the regular gender balance. A lot more blokes than usual and plenty of new faces.

"Word got around that the 'N Betweens were playing tonight," said Brian as Phil went in. "We could have charged two bob and made a packet. Do you like their type of music?"

"Never seen them before," replied Phil. "Martin says they are the best band around. Let you know later."

Phil saw Martin near the back of the hall and jostled his way through to have a chat. Just as he reached him, the band's drummer, Don Powell, ambled towards the stage, checked his kit was secure and sat down on his drum stool. Then Jim Lea, bass in hand, followed and plugged his guitar into his Ampeg B15 amplifier and began a few test bass lines.

Happy with it, he looked across at Don, which was the cue for the pocket-sized Dave Hill to take a run to the stage, with his guitar slung across his back. Finally, Noddy Holder, with his rhythm guitar, appeared on stage as if he was just one of the crowd.

All guitars plugged in, and with just a few practice chords from Dave, the band were straight into their first song. 'I sit here every day, looking at the sky' sang Noddy as they played the Small Faces track 'My Mind's Eye' and then, without any need for any introduction, the rhythm of Noddy's guitar led into the Yardbirds' 'Shapes of things', both tracks that were definitely hits, but had been given the distinctive 'N Betweens treatment – guitar work just as good, rasping vocals and never a beat missed by Don and Jim.

"Ow do," barked Noddy. "How yow awl doing? Them two were great songs from two of our faves – Small Face and the Yardbirds. Great blokes. Crackin' songs. This one'll surprise yow! Any Dave Dee Dozy Beaky fans in tonight? Well, hold tight."

It was the same song as the 1966 hit but the 'N Betweens version was a lot rougher and Dave's guitar solo was an eye-opener – he could really make a noise. At the song's abrupt ending the place went wild, caught up in the energy that just a band with just three guitars and drums could bring.

"Bet the Beatles felt like that when they were playing the Cavern," whispered Phil to Martin.

"It didn't take them long to get this crowd going," replied Martin. "I reckon that by now they know just the way to do things down pat. They have been around since the Steve Brett and the Mavericks days. And they have done stints in Germany, just like the Beatles, so I reckon they know their stuff."

The band looked dead chuffed. "Thanks," chipped in Dave. "We recorded that back in 1966 but it was never released although this next one was. It's a Young Rascals' track and was a hit in the States for them, but not over here and it wasn't for us neither!"

The riffs on the intro of 'You better run' preceded the arrival of Noddy's vocal, stressing the 'whatcha' in the repeated line 'Whatcha tryin' to do to my heart'.

"Doesn't sound American to me," said Phil. "But maybe that's what the band intends. Sounds more like the Animals or Them". The band then went straight into the B side of that single, 'Evil Witchman', both tracks being well received by the crowd.

"We wrote that B side", said Dave "together with an American producer who said we were the 'next big thing'. Well, he's back in America and we are back in the Black Country enjoying ourselves on a Saturday evening. Maybe being the 'next big thing' can wait a few years. Noddy, Jim and Don all laughed. "Now, two of our versions of songs by bands that should be – in our minds – the 'next big thing'. This is a song called 'Painter Man'."

"I've got this single," said Martin to no one's surprise. "It was nearly a hit here – got a lot of play on the pirates.

It's by a band called the Creation. They're really great, like the Who." When the 'N Betweens went straight into their next song – 'My Friend Jack' – it was Martin who again piped up. "Got this one too. Love it. It's by the Smoke".

At the finish, the crowd showed again how much they were already enjoying the band. It might not have been the greatest song ever written but they were a great live band and could make an average song sound lively and bright.

"Who's recently bought an album called 'Disraeli Gears?'" called out Jim. A few hands shot into the air. "It's like being back at school," laughed Noddy.

"Well", continued Jim, "this track is entitled 'She Walks Like a Bearded Rainbow' but on the sleeve it's abbreviated to SWLABR....and it's bostin."

Dave Hill was in his element on lead guitar, attempting to emulate the deific Clapton and Noddy's vocals were again passionate and loud. The band then went straight into another Cream song – 'Outside Woman Blues' – again given the 'N Betweens treatment.

"Is that R&B then?" Phil asked Martin.

"Well, I suppose so," replied Martin. "I think it's an old blues number given a rock treatment, so I guess that's what rhythm and blues is. Pretty well most of the songs they have played tonight are R&B, except the Dave Dee cover. Good, though, init!"

"Right, you lot," growled Noddy. "We need a break, so here's two numbers we recorded with that American producer. The first one's called 'Need' and the other is a cover of the great Otis Redding's song 'Security'."

At the end of the second song, the cheering was probably the loudest Phil had ever heard and, by this time, he and Martin had met up with Brian, Adrian and Joe at the refreshments counter.

"What do you think?" asked Phil and before anyone could reply, Adrian was heaping praise on the band.

"Absolutely fantastic," he said "Best band I've ever seen….anywhere! Brilliant! All of them!"

"Say what you think, Ade," joked Joe. "Don't go round the Wrekin about it!"

"I love this style of music. I just do," responded Adrian. "I may even have a dance in the second half."

Joe looked at Martin. Martin looked at Phil and then they all burst out laughing.

"This I have to see," said Joe. "Me too," said Martin. Phil said nothing.

They stopped laughing when they heard the sound of someone on the drums.

"Come on, the band are about to re-start," said Martin still grinning. Adrian had already gone back into the hall and made his way towards the front.

"There seem to be more people than before," said Joe and Brian chipped in that they had a steady stream of club members coming in all evening.

"Word got around, then," said Phil.

"Yep. Told the committee we should have charged two bob. Nobody listens to me," responded Brian.

"Pardon," said Joe and Phil in chorus, still smiling.

By then, the 'N Betweens were all back on stage and a roll of the drums by Don, followed by the guitar intro from Dave lead to Noddy beginning the Small Faces 'All or Nothing'. When the song ended, the crowd went wild again and Noddy held up his hands.

"Hush now, yow lot. Always start with a Small Faces song – gets us in the mood. You won't know this one though but it's from the Pretty Things and it's called 'Midnight to Six Man'."

When it had ended, Dave chipped in: "We love The Pretty Things. They let us record one of their songs on an EP we made a couple of years back. Never got released in England. Shame, it wasn't bad at all. Here's the Pretties song 'You don't believe me'."

The band followed that with their version of the Sorrows hit 'Take a heart' with Don Powell really enjoying himself on drums and Noddy's vocal snarling and coarse. Great applause again.

"That was on the lost EP, as well," said Noddy. "This next one's in the charts this week – but this is how we would have done it."

'Bend me, shape me' was, as Noddy said, performed in their own rough and ready fashion. "Time we did some blues songs and you can marvel at Dave's guitar playing," joked Jim as the band stood back, leaving Noddy stage front to sing into the mic 'I gotta woman, mean as she could be', before the band joined in on background vocals and, true to form, Dave gave it all on the guitar solo.

John Mayall's song 'You don't love me' was next up, and again Dave and Noddy battled vocals against guitar, with Don and Jim keeping the 12-bar rhythm right on the beat.

"That last one was off the first album from the king of British blues, John Mayall, and before that, it was 'Mean woman blues' that our Brummie mate, Spencer Davis, recorded," said Dave.

"Superb playing," mouthed Martin to Joe. "Bet that's got Adrian moving. Where is he, by the way?"

As Noddy introduced the next track, saying that everyone would know that this was by the Rolling Stones, the lads scanned the room. "There he is over in the corner," whispered Martin. "And he's dancing!"

"With a girl?" enquired Joe, grinning.

"Yeh, but I can only see the back of her," said Martin.

Phil looked across as to where the other lads were staring and, sure enough, Adrian was dancing, slowly to the beat of the Arthur Alexander classic 'You better move on'. To Phil, there was something familiar about the girl Adrian was dancing with but, as Martin had said, Phil could also only see her back.

Her height was the same. Her hair looked the same. No, it couldn't be the girl from up Muchall Road, could it? And if it was, then why was Adrian dancing with her? The song came to an end and Adrian and the girl chatted, whilst Noddy introduced the next song as their latest recording.

"We recorded this next one at Abbey Road – yeh, the Beatles studio – with their engineer, Norman Smith and it's called 'Delighted to see you'."

Phil heard none of this as he hadn't taken his eyes off the girl Adrian had been dancing with. The track was much poppier, more like a chart hit than the R&B they had been playing, so Adrian shrugged his shoulders, turned to watch the band and the girl walked away from him, but still with her back to Phil.

Phil moved in her direction.

"Where yow off to?" asked Joe.

"Need to get home soon," replied Phil casually. "Thought I'd get me coat to get away pronto."

"Bet they do a couple more songs," said Martin. "They won't finish on that. It's too slow and not their style."

Phil wasn't listening, and moved towards the cloakroom, as Dave Hill played the intro to 'Baby please don't go' by Them. Phil was humming along quietly as he tried to position himself to where he thought the girl was moving to. He saw her back and tapped her on the shoulder. She turned and smiled. It wasn't the same smile.

"Sorry. Thought you were my sister," Phil blurted out and then quickly carried on out of the hall. He gave his ticket to Janice, put on his anorak, and, without looking back, he was striding off home sharpish, just as he'd said. As he left, he heard the 'N Betweens begin their last song, the Animals' hit 'Baby, can I take you home' and Phil was in no doubt that he was blushing now.

Chapter 5 – Time of the Season

Saturday seemed to become the one day of the week that changed as you got older. Evenings and afternoons became more your own time, as youth clubs and football matches were occasions to really look forward to. Conversely, Saturday mornings often seemed to be regimented by others.

Following the family's return to Wolverhampton in 1960, these mornings became full of chores – shoe cleaning, going to the local shops to get vegetables, car cleaning or just the ever-present tidying your room. Starting at the grammar school, in September 1963, meant that all this changed for Phil, as attendance at Saturday morning school was compulsory. The only breaks to this new regime were regular and frequent trips to Birmingham, catching the number 126 bus from the town centre and travelling the whole route along the Birmingham New Road to visit an orthodontist on Hagley Road.

These outings were to align Phil's teeth, which not only meant he had the dubious delight of having to wear a brace in those early years at secondary school, but also he had to endure the soulless trips down the A4123, witnessing the dour landscape along this major Black Country thoroughfare. The winter smog, worsened by the unceasing smoke-belching chimneys, often gave the surroundings an industrial gloom through which the sky never really stood a chance.

To find sunshine or blue skies, you had to venture out of the county, to Shropshire or Worcestershire maybe, because you were unlikely to find it on the way to Birmingham. The new-fangled dual carriageway was bordered by council estates, usually at least three storeys high, interrupted by either manufacturing works or seemingly endless lines of single shops, with cheerless flats above them. Rumour had it that the schools which served these estates often ran special day trips to the countryside, just to glimpse blue sky and sunshine.

The morning of Saturday, April 27th was different. The family was off to the south coast for the last week of a late Easter holiday, to stay with Grandma, Dad's mother, and to enjoy the wonders of the seaside, at a place called Hayling Island, with all its motley delights.

These consisted mainly of the funfair, pitch-and-putt golf, and endless games of cricket on the sand, all centred around a beach hut where tea was regularly made on the Primus stove, sandwiches eagerly devoured with potato crisps, after shaking the salt on them from the little blue sachets, and where you could get warm again after a bracing dip in the sea.

Phil missed the excitement of getting on to Hayling Island in past holidays when he was much younger. It was often his job to pay the threepence toll on Langstone Bridge, when they travelled by car, although sometimes they would take the class A1 steam train, 'The Hayling Billy', from Havant to West Town on the island. This was not a long trip but a very emotive one, stopping to take on more holidaymakers at Langstone Harbour and North Hayling before the stroll up the tree-lined Staunton Avenue to the beach.

As this family had taken the journey south from the Midlands many times before, over the past eight years, the family car, a Hillman Minx Estate, could now be put on autopilot, finding its way along the A449 and A491 to Stourbridge, then on to Lickey End, before skirting Redditch. Dad always stuck with the A44, passing through Woodstock, then stopping at Oxford for lunch, and a chance for him to have a brief wander down Memory Lane, also known as New College, evoking memories of his carefree university days.

With the family fed and watered, the journey would then resume down the A34, taking an age to get through the numerous roundabouts at Newbury, and then on to Winchester where the car knew to take a left-hand turn towards the historic Hampshire village of Wickham. Then all three teenagers would play the game 'Who's the first to see the sea?' as the winner would be excused from washing up later that day or maybe even longer.

The sea usually came into view as they drove over the brow of Portsdown Hill, with Portsmouth and Southsea spreading before them. The road then wound along the hilltop and on through Dad's hometown of Havant to Grandma's bungalow in Emsworth.

Throughout the first half of this journey Phil was as quiet as the proverbial church mouse as, between 10 o'clock and midday on Saturdays, Kenny Everett was on Radio 1. Kenny Everett had become something of a legend on the pirate radio stations, with his whacky and quirky shows, initially partnering Dave Cash on Radio London. As he had been unable to hear those shows, Phil had never heard him until Radio 1 started up the previous year. From then on, Kenny soon became one of his favourites, for the most part as he now had a weekend show.

On last week's show, Kenny had announced he would be playing every single track of the brand-new LP from the Zombies, called 'Odessey and Oracle'. This was the album from which the track 'Time of the season' had appeared on the sampler album Phil had purchased a few weeks previously so there was no way that he would miss more of the same.

It was then pretty well unheard of to play a whole LP from start to finish on any Radio 1 programme. That might be the case on the Third Programme, or Radio 3 as it was now known, but on the UK's only 'pop music' station such accolades were usually reserved for the Beatles, or possibly the Rolling Stones. The Zombies were not thought to be in the same league, but Kenny had already called it "the album of the century" and often had members of the band in the studio, helping him with his zany programme jingles.

And it wasn't the first time Kenny had been involved in broadcasting a full album. Nearly a year before, he had held court on a show called 'Where it's at', then on the BBC Light Programme, with John, Paul, George and Ringo, interviewing them and playing all the tracks from 'Sgt. Pepper's Lonely Hearts Club Band'.

So, Phil had made sure he was totally prepared for the journey. A new battery had been fitted in his transistor radio, he had a spare in his pocket, and the plastic earpiece had been cleaned. The sound was a clear as a bell – well, as a tin bell with a piece of string – but good enough for him to enjoy Kenny and his wonderfully imaginative style of broadcasting, taking Phil into his own auditory world.

All of a sudden, Matt elbowed him in his side.

"What was that for?" complained Phil.

"Mum's talking to you," smirked Matt.

"You're very quiet, Phillip?" said Mum. "Are you feeling all right? Last time you were this quiet, you were carsick. Not feeling queasy today, are you?"

"No. I'm fine – thanks. I just want to listen to Kenny Everett on Radio 1. He's got every track from the new album by the Zombies," replied Phil.

"Of course," said Mum looking at Dad who just kept on driving with an expression on his face that mirrored Mum's comment. Matt smiled, and Rachel giggled.

Kenny came to the end of the opening track, the highly melodic 'Care of cell 44', and announced that the track had been the second single taken from the album last November, demanding to know why it hadn't been a smash hit. He went on to say that the single's B side was the next track on the album and played 'A Rose for Emily'. It simply featured Rod Argent's solo piano, together with Colin Blunstone's wistful vocal. Phil thought it was wonderful.

The third track – 'Maybe after he's gone' – was just as exquisite but more the entire band's work, written by rhythm guitarist, Chris White, and full of the Zombies' trademark harmonies. Chris wrote the next two tracks, the melancholic 'Beechwood Park', followed by the haunting and harmonic 'Brief candles'.

Rod Argent penned the final track on side one – the atmospheric 'Hung up on a dream' – which featured an instrument called a mellotron which Rod had found at the studios at Abbey Road, in London, where the band had been recording the album. It was also the sole track to highlight lead guitarist, Paul Atkinson – unusual as most tracks were dominated by Rod's keyboard playing.

Phil was overjoyed. All the songs were magnificent and the Zombies sound, with their harmonies and melodies, came from the best band he reckoned he had ever heard. He knew this had to be the next LP for his record collection, but where was he going to find the money to buy it? He still had a couple of postal orders from Easter, from his generous godparents, but with a few bob saved from his paper round that only came to 15 shillings in total. He would need at least another pound to get the record.

As Warwickshire became Oxfordshire, and the signposts showed that they were well past Stratford-upon-

Avon, Phil set his mind as to how he could raise the money for the album. First things first: he would have to get into Havant, the nearest town to Grandma's home, and visit the Sound of Music record shop, near the park, to see if they had or could get a copy. That couldn't be done until Monday, as all the shops would be closed tomorrow, which meant he had at least another 24 hours to come up with a plan to get that vital pound.

Kenny Everett was still praising the album on the radio as he introduced 'Changes', track one on side two, again full of choral phrases, and a beautiful intro and outro which sounded like a flute. On first hearing, Phil thought the next track should be their next single.

'I want her, she wants me' had been covered by the Mindbenders a couple of years back and sounded like an early 'Beatlesque' number. It was the band at its poppiest and Phil loved it.

Just as he thought there wouldn't be anything to top that, piano chords from Rod were joined by Hugh Grundy's drums and Colin sang 'This will be our year', with a trumpet appearing from nowhere in the chorus line. The smile across Phil's face was as broad as could be until he heard the very eerie sounds that started 'Butcher's Tale', followed by what sounded like the church organ at St Aidan's. It was a very strange song which was not at all to his liking. It wasn't Colin on lead vocal and didn't have the summer sound the other tracks had. Very strange.

The penultimate track renewed Phil's wavering faith. 'Friends of mine' was full of melody, and the harmonies behind Colin's lead vocal delivery were sublime. Surely this would be another hit for the band. At the end, Kenny announced it had been the first single to be released from this glorious album, back in October but once again, beyond belief, it had failed to get anywhere near the singles chart.

"And finally, this last track has just been released, so, come on folks, get out there and make it number one for the wonderful Zombies – third time lucky," urged Kenny, as the percussive intro to 'Time of the Season' began to play. After a further mesmerising three and a half minutes, his show came to an end.

As promised, Kenny had played every single track from the album, claiming that in his humble opinion it would remain "the album of the century" forever, and asking every listener to go out and buy a copy. Phil needed no encouragement, just the means to make the purchase.

Rachel was the one who spotted the sea first as they came towards the end of their journey south so Phil and Matt knew they would be on kitchen duty at Grandma's for the weekend at least. That set Phil's mind to thinking about how he might earn some money during their stay. Phil's Grandfather, Will, had passed away five years back, having taken an ill-advised morning dip in the local harbour, too soon after a heavy cold and then developing pneumonia. So, without a man about the house, there would be plenty of jobs that needed doing.

Phil knew that trips to Hayling Island beach would not happen every day, so if he offered to do some of these chores, then both Dad and Grandma might be forthcoming with enough extra pocket money. He knew that Matt had brought some reading with him to do before he started his summer job at a laboratory next week. Dad had also promised Matt some driving practice before his test in June, and it was improbable that they would ask Rachel to do such household tasks, so the field was clear for Phil to earn some extra cash.

The estate car bounced up the unadopted road where Grandma lived and turned into the short drive. Dad was somewhat surprised by Phil who greeted Grandma warmly with a big hug before offering to help unpack the car. Mum looked on bemused and Matt nudged Rachel.

"He's up to something," he said. Rachel smiled. "Probably to do with what he was listening to on the trip down here," she replied.

On Sunday morning, while they had breakfast in the front room, plans were made for the week ahead. Mum wanted to do some shopping in Portsmouth. Dad wanted to visit his sisters in Bedhampton and, as they had rented the beach hut for the whole week, getting across to Hayling Island would definitely be on the agenda.

"Can we go across on the Puffing Billy?" asked Rachel.

"Afraid not," replied Dad. "The line was closed by Ernest Marples five years ago. Don't you remember?"

"And I think you mean the Hayling Billy, Raich," added Matt. "I think the Puffing Billy railway is down under, in Australia."

"Can I go into Havant on Monday morning?" asked Phil, oblivious of the railway conversation.

"Expect so," replied Dad. "What for?"

"I want to go to Market Parade," said Phil "Isn't the Sound of Music record shop there? I just need to pop in to see if they have a record I want."

"And if they have, where's the money coming from to buy it?" asked Mum.

"I need to talk to Dad and Grandma about that," replied Phil as Matt and Rachel exchanged knowing smiles.

Negotiations went well on Sunday, with a list of jobs being drawn up, with amounts to be settled when complete. And Phil was pleased when Dad said he could drop by Market Parade on the way to see his sister, Elizabeth, on Monday morning. Although this meant Phil would have to accompany his father on the family visit, it would be well worth it and, anyway, Aunty Elizabeth was his favourite aunt.

Monday went even better than Phil had hoped, as the man in the Sound of Music promised they would have a copy of the Zombies LP 'Odessey and Oracle' by Thursday lunchtime when their regular weekly delivery of new records was due in, and he would definitely put a copy aside for Phil.

By Thursday morning, the lawns at Grandma's bungalow looked pristine; the front step had been polished;

all the grime from the journey down had been washed from Dad's car; the vegetable plot had been dug over; and the windows at the front of the house had been cleaned. Phil had been on sole washing up duty for four days solid. Matt took pity on him on Wednesday, after dinner, and offered to help.

"Doing bob-a-job over all those years must have been good training for this week, Phil," he quipped. "Mind you, you must really want this new record. Is it really worth all this?"

"It's fab. No, it's more than that," replied Phil. "Anyway, I reckon I've really helped Grandma a lot. She says she's missed Will over the past five years and it's been a bit of a struggle living on her own. Although some of our cousins only live a few miles away, they are mainly at college or working, so she doesn't get much help from them anymore."

Thursday morning saw most of the family pile into the Hillman. Matt was staying behind to concentrate on his reading and, other than Phil, everyone was off to Southsea to visit the department stores. Phil would get out in Havant, armed with enough postal orders and cash to buy "that LP", as the family had called it since Sunday breakfast.

He cashed the postal orders at the Post Office in West Street and made his way to the park where he waited until midday, watching an entertaining local cricket match and trying to spot whether his Uncle Fred was playing. As St. Faith's church struck midday, he walked across to the Sound of Music record shop. The owner was busy, so Phil started to flick through the LPs in their racks and study the singles and album charts on the wall.

After nearly two months since entering the charts, Louis Armstrong's 'Wonderful world' had finally made it to number one, which didn't thrill Phil a great deal, although it had dislodged Cliff's Eurovision winner 'Congratulations' from the top slot. Bob Dylan's 'John Wesley Harding' was still the biggest album seller, which would really please Matt although Phil thought the track on the Rock Machine sampler, 'I'll be your baby tonight', was a bit slushy and not as distinctive as Dylan's early stuff.

'Hello," said the record store owner. "You're the young lad who wants the new Zombies record, aren't you? Let's have a gander to see if it's in yet."

For an eternity, or so it seemed to Phil, he slowly went through the pile of LPs behind the counter. The owner could see Phil's frustration and continued the monotonic and repetitive commentary.

"No, no, not that one, no, no, this one – no," he intoned and then turned to Phil. "Doesn't look as if they've included it this week." He saw the hopelessness on Phil's face and then smiled. "Only joking, I looked for it as soon as it came in this morning and put it aside for you. They sent two copies, so I have been playing one, but this is yours – untouched by any living stylus. It's a really excellent album, isn't it. I'll order a few new copies for next week. Should be a good seller."

Phil's face had quickly shifted from gloom to rapture as he saw the gaudy hotchpotch cover of 'Odessey and

Oracle'. Like many contemporary LP covers, the artwork was stunning. Phil read the notes on the back, which revealed that the cover was done by Terry Quirk, a friend of the band. There was also a quote from William Shakespeare which made no sense to Phil but then neither had anything from the Bard that he had read before. Phil suddenly became aware that the shop owner was waiting.

"You going to pay for it then?" he enquired.

"Of course," responded Phil, somewhat embarrassed and produced his one pound, twelve shillings and sixpence. The album, in its protective plastic sleeve, was then placed carefully in a brown paper bag.

"Enjoy," said the record shop owner.

"I will," was all Phil could reply.

Once out of the shop, Phil looked at the album again. What did the record shop owner say? 'Untouched by any living stylus!'

It was only then that Phil remembered that Grandma didn't have a record player. She listened to the radio, the Home Service, as she still called it, and the Third Programme. Then Phil remembered his visit to Aunty Elizabeth's on Monday. His cousin Celia had a record player!

He returned to Grandma's bungalow over four hours later.

"Where have you been?" stammered his mother. "We've been wondering where on earth you had got to?"

"After I bought THAT record, as you all keep calling it, I realised I couldn't listen to it here cos Grandma hasn't got a record player, so I went to Aunty Elizabeth's and played it on Celia's Dansette."

"What's a Dansette?" asked Mum.

"It's a record player, Mum. All teenagers have them," informed Matt. "At least Phil's safe and I bet Aunty Elizabeth looked after him," he continued.

"Yep, her cakes are as tasty as ever and I had a great chat with Uncle Fred. He was home for lunch. Celia wasn't there but they let me play my new record twice in her room. I would have let you know but they aren't on the phone yet in their council house. And I didn't have any change for the phone box. Sorry," apologised Phil, trying to look sorry although he'd had such a brilliant day.

"How did you get home?" his Mum asked.

"Walked," said Phil.

"That's over five miles," said Mum "You'll sleep well tonight! Get ready for tea. Still, your turn to set the table. It'll be ready in ten minutes."

Phil slept really well that night, dropping off with the melodies and harmonies of the Zombies "album of the century" going around and around in his head. He wasn't sure which was his favourite track, but he knew that he couldn't wait to be sitting in the front room back home playing both sides of the record again, on Dad's radiogram.

The trip home, on the first Saturday in May, seemed to take an eternity – in fact, it was actually quicker than the journey had been a week ago. It should have been longer, Matt had quipped, as going back to the Midlands, from the south coast, was surely going uphill! Rachel looked puzzled but Phil had heard it once or twice before and just groaned.

The battery in his transistor radio still had enough juice so he was back in his own auditory world again, sitting in the back of the car with a contented smile, soundlessly listening to Radio 1 throughout most of the journey, first to Kenny Everett, and then to the Scottish drawl of Stuart Henry.

Although the start of the summer term would be bright and early next Monday morning, for everyone except Matt who would have an even earlier start for work, they all seemed to have enjoyed the week's break on the south coast and the mood in the car matched the weather – bright, cloudless and sunny.

Their return midway stop was at Woodstock, with lunch at The Feathers Hotel, and, by the time the signposts read Stratford-upon-Avon and Henley-in-Arden, their Penn Road home wasn't far away. Phil guessed they would be back by teatime and, whilst he'd have missed the season's penultimate home game against Chelsea, he reckoned he had time for a bath, get changed and ready for an evening's enjoyment at Venturers.

His efforts, helping Grandma, had resulted in more than the pound in extra pocket money which meant he still had enough for the club's entrance fee. Dad had been so pleased with his efforts that he had agreed, not only to get back in time for Phil to go to the youth club but also to take him there and pick him up later.

"See you back here at 10 o'clock," said Dad as he dropped Phil off at the usual prearranged spot. "No later!"

Approaching the Springdale Methodist Church, Phil could see that the throng of teenagers waiting to get in had not only spilt out on to the pavement but also went around the corner into Rutland Avenue. He spotted Joe and Adrian in the queue.

"You're back then," said Joe.

"Obviously," replied Phil. "What's this all about?"

"Coz of the band tonight," informed Joe. "They need to set up before the doors open."

"Which band?" asked Phil

"They're from London, so Martin says," chipped in Adrian.

"But who are they?" continued Phil, beginning to get a tad riled.

"Named after some posh hotel in the smoke, I think," said Joe. "Never heard of them, me. You better join the queue, Phil. Looks like the doors are opening."

The queue slowly and politely shuffled in and as Phil got ready to pay his entrance fee, he was met with Brian's beaming mush.

"Evening, Phil," he said. "Glad you could be back for this. It's two bob tonight on account of the band. We're lucky to book them."

"I've only got half a crown," replied Phil "Not much left for a drink."

"I'll stand you a cuppa later," said Brian. "Seen the result from the Moli, today? Assumed you weren't there. Cameras were, so it should be on 'Match of the Day' later."

"Good," replied Phil. "I'll get home for that, as Dad's giving me a lift. So, WHO is this BIG attraction at the club?"

"Top blues band from London. Already released two albums. Should be a brahma of an evening," informed Brian.

"But what are they called? The band's name?" said Phil sounding exasperated.

"No need to get shirty," Brian responded. "Haven't you heard of Savoy Brown?"

"No," said Phil as he paid his two shillings and went in.

The hall was packed. There was a constant murmur of promise and anticipation. No one had much idea about what to expect. How many were in the band? What style of music would they play? Was it this new progressive music? Some people called it prog rock! Some had been told they were a blues band but were they like the Pretty Things or The Animals, or did they stay true to the old-style American blues?

From the set up on stage, Phil could make out three guitars – two six-string electric and a four-string bass – and there was a keyboard to the left-hand side. There were three microphones and an extensive drum kit. The lights dimmed and six figures came through the crowd of teenagers in hushed reverence. Venturers had never had a band from London before and certainly not one with two albums already to their name.

The band was led onto the stage by Kim Simmonds, blonde and flamboyantly attired in blue velvet trousers, a paisley shirt, with a dark fringed buckskin jacket. The rhythm section – Bob Brunning on bass and Hughie Flint on drums – wore more workaday attire – jeans, t-shirts and denim jackets, as did rhythm guitarist, Dave Peverett, though his jacket was leather. Bob Hall sat down at the keyboards. He could have been in any pin-up group of the decade, with his boy-next-door good looks and shoulder-length dark hair.

They all had long hair, longer than many in their audience, including some of the girls. And then, there was the lead singer, Chris Youlden, who looked as if he had just finished his shift at an undertaker. Dressed in dark velvet trousers and jacket, collarless grandad shirt and a black top hat perched on his dark curly hair, he looked sinister and the band looked as if they meant business.

With all the instruments plugged in, Kim Simmonds counted two, three, and they were straight into the Jimmy Rogers classic 'Walking by myself', with Simmonds' sparkling guitar combining with Youlden's gravelly bass singing. A great guitar solo from Simmonds had both Joe and Martin open-mouthed in admiration, but when Youlden sang 'You know I love you' he didn't seem quite so menacing. The rhythm section carried the pace throughout the song, and Bob Hall's boogie-woogie piano playing set the tone for the type of music the crowd was in for that evening – good solid quality blues music.

"That's a great blues song from Chicago, back in the fifties," said Youlden. "One of our favourites and a great way to start the set. A pleasure to be here in the Midlands. We don't often play so far north. Most of our gigs are usually around London. Hope you enjoy our music – this is one we wrote ourselves."

The band played the basic 12-bar song 'Stay with me, baby', with great driving guitar work from Simmonds and Peverett, and Hall complimenting the blues vocals with piano counter melody. He then played a great solo towards the end, reminiscent of the old rock 'n' roll pianists, Jerry Lee Lewis or Little Richard.

"Boy, do they know how to play," muttered Adrian to Martin. "The guitar playing is the best we've seen since Hendrix at the Gaumont. I think that keyboard player is brill."

"That's a track from our second album called 'Getting to the point' which we finished recording at the Decca Studios in March and we hope will be in the shops next month," continued Youlden. "The next song is from the band's first album. There's been a few personnel changes since then, but this is Bob's – that's him, over there on keyboards – arrangement of the trad blues classic 'Shake 'em on down'."

Brunning's bass set the tempo with Flint's train-beat drumming keeping a solid rhythm aligned with Hall's repetitive keyboard refrain. The track went on for over seven minutes, with both Simmonds and Hall contributing solos, and Youlden getting the crowd clapping and hollering until his final recurring lyric slowed and the imaginary train, came to a halt. Brilliant stuff and the crowd went wild. They were loving this band just three songs into their set.

"Phew," said Chris Youlden. "That was just fine! Thanks."

He spoke as he sang, in a low intonation which threatened to fall off the end of the piano keyboard. The band continued with tracks from their debut album 'Shake down' – B.B. King's 'Rock me baby' followed by John Lee Hooker's 'It's my own fault' – sumptuous blues standards, performed perfectly and passionately. Not only did the band know their blues music but it was obvious that they loved playing it.

Youlden took a swig of water – or it might have been something stronger – to oil those well-tuned tonsils, and Kim Simmonds took to the microphone and in his Welsh brogue said, "We'll give Chris's vocal chords a rest for a while with a couple of blues instrumentals I wrote – with the band's help of course. Here's the title track from our new album."

'Getting to the point' heavily featured Simmonds on guitar. Joe, Martin and Adrian, were all mesmerised by the slick brilliance of his playing. 'Lonesome' Dave Peverett joined in towards the end, then they duetted on the weirdly titled song 'The Incredible Gnome Meets Jaxman'. As the song came to an end, Youlden strolled back on stage, leading the applause.

"Expect you are used to having a break about now. Well, that's not what we do. Once we are in the groove, we keep on playing – right to the end. The next track is our version of Willie Dixon's 'You need love'."

Hughie Flint's driving train rhythm set the band off on an impressive rework of the song, with each band member offering up solos throughout the 10-minute performance.

The youth club crowd always loved to dance but this week all eyes were on the band, checking out the performance and musical expertise many had never witnessed before. This wasn't a local band playing the latest chart hits or covering their favourite surf or rock 'n' roll or R&B classics. These were thoroughly professional blues musicians, loving their craft and enjoying their performance. As Brian had said, the club was lucky to have booked them.

At the end of each song, the applause grew louder and louder. Youlden was a natural cheerleader and whilst he had the appearance of a malevolent circus ringmaster, the audience hung on his every word.

"Here's two songs which are good advice for you lads," he growled, looking around the hall with a somewhat decadent grin. "I should know, I wrote both of them!"

'Taste and try, before you buy' was followed by 'Big city lights', both tracks stripped down and featuring Youlden's wistful vocals above the excellent musical support on guitars and keyboards from Simmonds and

Hall. He had really taken the musical tempo down to a smooth blues sound.

"This next track just features me and Bob, the master of the boogie-woogie piano. Our manager is thinking of releasing this as a single, with 'Walking by myself' on the other side. Bob and I wrote it and it's called 'Vicksburg Blues'," said Youlden.

Hall played the piano intro before Youlden started to sing. They followed this with the laidback Bobby 'Blue' Bland song 'I smell trouble', again at a quarter pace of the early songs.

Kim Simmonds moved up to the microphone again. "Time to give Chris a rest again – he's getting on you know," he said with a smirk.

"He puts everything into his singing," Phil said to Martin.

"Really great stuff, though," replied Martin.

"Not enough melody for me," said Phil. "But they are brilliant musicians."

The band then played a further two instrumentals – Freddie King's 'High rise' featuring Simmonds unwavering exceptional guitar playing, followed by 'The dormouse rides the rails' which had much more of a pop-song feel to it than most of the blues numbers performed so far that evening.

Youlden had lumbered back on stage. "That was written by Martin Stone who left the band last year. Something about getting more action, I think." There was a wry smile from Simmonds. "Not quite sure about the title but riding the rails fits with our next song, which I hope will be our new single," continued Youlden. "It's called 'Train to Nowhere'."

The low-key guitar intro was complemented by the bass guitar riff, playing together with the bass drum. Then Youlden sang 'You can catch it if you want to ride'. It was the most haunting song of the evening – a spellbinding sound, with the guitars rhythmic interplaying as the song literally built up steam as the train went 'to nowhere'. The song certainly didn't, as the band made their instruments sound like a musical train ride you weren't quite sure you wanted to be on.

Totally brilliant, mused Phil, thinking how quickly the evening had sped by – completely engrossing music. He looked at his watch.

"Blimey, it's nearly 10. Dad's picking me up at 10. I've got to go," spluttered Phil to Martin. "See you at school on Monday."

As Phil and Dad came through the front door, the 'Match of the Day' theme could be heard in the back room.

"Good timing, Dad. Thanks for the lifts. Is Matt in the back room? Where's Mum and Rachel?" asked Phil.

"Rachel's already in bed I expect, and your mother, too. They're pleased to be sleeping in their own beds after a week crammed into two bedrooms at Grandma's," replied Dad.

"Well, at least last week they were sleeping in beds. Matt and I had to sleep in a tent on the lawn and he bagged your camp bed," complained Phil.

"So, are you wanting to stay up for the football or enjoy the comforts of your own bed?" enquired Dad, smiling, knowing only too well that Phil's bed would stay empty for at least another hour.

Matt was already sitting on the sofa watching the TV.

"Are we on as the main game?" asked Phil. "Brian said the cameras were there."

"Not unless you've started supporting either Leeds or Liverpool. They're on first as they are just a couple of points behind joint leaders City and United. At this point in the season, the BBC would have had cameras at most grounds, with only three points covering the top four clubs fighting for the title. Then there could be any one of six clubs, including us, who could go down with Fulham," stated Matt.

"If Wolves win both remaining games, then it's division 1 football again next season. Fingers and legs crossed then," said Phil. "Playing Chelsea and Spurs on the last two Saturdays is tough though. They are both near the top," he continued as he settled down to watch the games.

Jones put Leeds ahead after just 15 minutes but two late goals from Lawler gave Liverpool the win and ended Leeds championship hopes for that year. With Manchester United hammering Newcastle 6-0 at home and City winning 3-1 at Spurs, the first division title would be decided by the two Manchester clubs on the very last Saturday of the season.

The programme then focussed on the relegation battle. With Sheffield United winning, and Coventry gaining a point at West Ham, a Wolves win would practically make them safe as their goal difference was better than either of those sides as well as Stoke City, who were just a point below them but had a game in hand.

Finally, the brothers edged forward in their seats as their game started.

"You avoided hearing the result then?" asked Matt.

"Only just. Brian was about to tell me. I got a bit lairy with him before he could," replied Phil, as the match commentator announced that Wolves had won a corner after 13 minutes. Mike Kenning crossed it from the right wing and there was Frank Wignall to execute a right-footed volley past Peter Bonetti in the Chelsea goal to put Wolves 1-0 up.

"I didn't think much of Wignall when he arrived from Notts Forest in March. Thought £50,000 was a bit over the top, but that's his sixth goal in 12 games, so somebody at Molineux must have known what they're doing," said Matt.

"He's also given the Doog a bit of freedom and if he keeps on scoring and we stay up, then that transfer fee will be money well spent," said Phil.

Fourteen minutes later, Kenning was again the provider from a free kick, with Wignall scoring his second goal with a fine header. His third goal came just after half-time when skipper Mike Bailey's long throw was headed on by Dougan to the feet of Wignall, whose shot, on the turn, had Bonetti beaten all ends up. Chelsea had little to offer in the second half and Wolves ran out comfortable winners by three goals to nil with hat-trick hero, Frank Wignall, presented with the match ball after the game.

"Just a point against Spurs next Saturday should clinch safety," yawned Phil. "I'm off to bed. You watching the rest of the programme, Matt?"

"Yep. I take it Dad locked up when you came in. I'll close down in here in a while. Good band at the club this evening?" asked Matt.

"I reckon so. They were easily the most professional outfit we've ever had there. Showed why some of our local bands haven't made it but their music was a bit too bluesy for my liking. Joe and Martin thought that the lead guitar player was as good as Hendrix. They did a great track called 'Train to nowhere' but that's when I had to leave to get my lift with Dad. Wouldn't have been your cuppa tea, Matt," said Phil.

"You'd be surprised. Just 'cos I play the flute and the clarinet, doesn't mean I only like classical music," replied Matt. "Guess there will be a lot of different types of music at Oxford."

"When do you find out if you have got in? asked Phil.

"Next week, I'm told," replied Matt.

"You seem very calm about it. It's a big step, leaving home and all that," said Phil.

"Not much I can do about it," said Matt. "They know my results. I've done the interviews and I know that because Dad went to New College, that might help, but it's in the hands of the gods now."

"You need a Frank Wignall hat-trick!" yawned Phil.

"And you need to go to bed. It'll be your turn in a couple of years," said Matt.

"You're right. I am still wacked-out from the long walk from Havant to Emsworth last week. Not sure I will be joining you in Oxford though. I'm not a genius like you, Bruv. Between you and me I'm finding it a struggle in six science," replied Phil.

"Thought you should have gone into six maths, really. Easily your best subject," said Matt. "Pity they don't do A-levels in listening to pop music, buying LPs and supporting the Wolves. You would get top grades in all three."

"Now that would be worth going to school for," said Phil.

Chapter 6 – Last Time Around

If 1967 had been the summer of love, then 1968 became the summer of protest. There were student riots in London, Warsaw, Rome, Madrid, Paris and Prague, and America experienced anti-Vietnam war and civil rights demonstrations throughout.

In April and June, two of the most powerful voices for social change had been silenced in America, with the assassinations of Martin Luther King and Robert Kennedy. In England, again in April, Enoch Powell's 'Rivers of Blood' provocative speech, described by the daily papers as 'evil and racialist', had undoubtedly raised racial tensions both locally and across the country. Powell was the MP for Wolverhampton South West, the area in which Phil lived. To say that Phil's parents disliked their parliamentary representative was, to put it mildly, an understatement.

Their liberal views were very much at odds with their MP and both had ardently supported the local Liberal party since their return to Wolverhampton, even though they were very aware that the seat was always a two-way fight between the Labour and Conservative parties. However, they stuck to their political principles whilst always encouraging their three offspring to make their own minds up, the prevailing custom of liberal-minded parents.

A year ago, the Beatles were singing 'All you need is love' and the Stones responded with 'We love you'. But then the new albums in 1968, from these two most successful British sixties' bands, included tracks entitled 'Street Fighting Man' and 'Revolution'.

Protest songs, many with anti-war lyrics, were now being played on some radio shows, having become more mainstream, rather than just side-lined to folk clubs and protest marches. None were chart hits, but singles like 'Sky Pilot', from Eric Burdon and the Animals, would be played by DJs in Britain, like John Peel, even though it was over seven minutes long.

Phil Ochs had long been in the vanguard of protest singers and his 1968 single 'The War is Over' was banned by many stateside radio stations as was 'Unknown Soldier' from the Doors although, despite this, it still became a Billboard Top 40 hit. Even the Monkees were getting in on the act, recording a Davy Jones song entitled 'War games. They were hopeful that this would appear as an album track on their fifth album 'The Birds, the Bees and the Monkees', but their management had other ideas and the recording stayed in the RCA Victor vaults for over four decades.

And how did Phil's parents react to this period of intense social change, musical protest and political unrest? They went on holiday, of course – first, in late April, with their customary trip down to the south coast, and again, in late July, to a hotel in North Devon, in a remote place called Hartland Quay.

By then Phil's father was deputy head at Wednesfield High School and his mother was now teaching mathematics, part-time at the Municipal Grammar School. It was not surprising that as soon as the schools broke up at the end of the summer term, holidays would be the first thing on their minds. So, on Saturday, July 27th, the family car was once again jam-packed with cases, picnic baskets, windbreaks and raffia sand mats, ready for the off.

This trip would be different. With only four in the car, there would be more room all round. Matt wasn't going on holiday with the family, having taken on a summer job in a local science laboratory earlier that summer, leaving the grammar school having secured his place to study chemistry at Oxford in October.

He would be at New College where Dad had studied the same subject in the late war years. Phil wasn't sure who was more pleased: Matt for getting into Oxford or Dad for the opportunity to revisit old haunts.

This summer holiday, though, was to be a new adventure. In the past three summers, they had gone to The Park Hotel in Tenby, where they had met families from across Britain, many with teenagers, who made friends with Matt, Phil and Rachel, and others with younger families. The hotel owners were very keen to secure repeat business and always put themselves out to make sure all their guests were well entertained from day one.

They ran weekly swimming galas in their outside pool and a range of games on the beach, at the bottom of the north cliff on which the hotel stood. If the weather was dreadful, trips were arranged to the local cinema. Matt and Phil saw the Beatles film 'Help' there but came away none the wiser as they couldn't hear the dialogue or any lyrics of the songs because of all the girls screaming.

Rachel and her friend, Alex, from Edinburgh, went to see the 'Sound of Music' film three times and Matt even had a holiday romance, with a girl called Sheila, who lived near North London. Phil had a girl 'friend' – Maureen from Darlington – but he wouldn't say that a quick kiss, when you were 14, round the back of the swimming pool maintenance room, made it a romance. He and Maureen became pen-pals which surprised Phil's parents as he was easily the worst at doing his thank-you letters after birthdays and Christmas.

When the weather over Carmarthen Bay was at its best, typically warm rather than hot, you could learn to snorkel or go water-skiing. Lads versus dads' football or cricket matches seemed endless on the beach and the ice-cream van would drive along, just when tea was being served by the hotel staff to the grown-ups. Over the years, friendships were made, and addresses exchanged so that when Christmas cards were sent, dates were co-ordinated to book the same fortnight. Families returned home happy, rested and some ready to hit the world of education once again.

This year, though, three of the families had said they wouldn't be able to go at the same time and as other summer holidays, particularly abroad, were becoming more accessible and reasonably priced, they were looking for a change especially with older teenagers. Phil's parents decided to go to somewhere they had never visited before, booking a double, and two single rooms at The Hartland Quay Hotel.

"The trip should be straightforward," said Dad. "Down the A449, skirt Worcester and once you are on the A38 we don't need to come off it, except to have some lunch around Bristol, and then on to the A361 for the last leg of the journey. All aboard!"

He was right. Getting to Bristol was such a breeze that they had plenty of time for lunch in a hotel just off the A38, near a place called Keynsham.

"Spelt K-E-Y-N-S-H-A-M," said Phil grandly.

"Yes, we can see how it's spelt from the road signs, Phillip," said Mum.

"It's from a Radio Luxembourg advert, Mum. It advertises Horace Batchelor's 'Famous Infra-Draw Method'. That's a system that increases your chances of winning large sums on the football pools. We ought to try it. Win a fortune." replied Phil.

"Phillip", said his mother sternly, "you know very well what your father and I think about gambling. Let's hear no more about it."

Phil looked suitably admonished and Rachel quietly beamed at his reprimand.

Lunch over and back on to the A38, the journey, and the holiday, began to take a turn for the worse. Roads down to

Devon and Cornwall, at that time of year, especially on a Saturday, and at the start of the school summer holidays, were very busy and it wasn't long before they were stuck in an extremely lengthy traffic jam.

"Any alternative routes?" asked Mum from the back seat. Phil had been allowed to sit in the front to listen to the radio.

"Not that I know of," replied Dad. "It seemed such an easy route, I didn't bother to look." Mum's eyes moved heavenwards, and she began to look for the map which was usually under Dad's seat. Dad suggested a game of I-spy. Groans all round.

"Better than playing pub cricket, though," he said. "Can't say I've seen many pubs on this road." Eventually, the traffic began to move again and what should have been an eight-hour journey, with an hour for lunch, was now looking more like ten hours.

"I was hoping to get settled in our rooms and have a good look round before dinner," said Mum. "But the rate we're going the other guests will be seated in the dining room and we will have to be served after them."

"Good thing we had an excellent lunch," said Dad, trying to lighten the mood.

When they finally arrived at the hotel, it wasn't the time the journey had taken or the accommodation that dampened Phil's spirits. The hotel stood alone on a rocky headland with just a few cottages opposite. The outside swimming pool was somewhat detached – perched on the rocks a good hundred yards from the hotel. The bay, to the right of the hotel, could be reached by a slipway and you could see the remains of an ancient quay jutting out from the promontory.

But worse for Phil were the other guests – not that there was anything wrong with them. It was just a couple of minor details. Firstly, there weren't many of them. The hotel had 12 rooms and, with their family taking up three, that meant there wouldn't be anywhere near the expansive and sociable company that they had been used to in Tenby.

In fact, there were three other families – one with three young children, one with a boy aged around 12, and the other with two girls aged 11 and 13. The remaining guests were couples, mostly retired. There was no one around Phil's age. This was not going to be a summer holiday to remember.

Mum was right. They did arrive after the dinner gong had been sounded and their entrance was greeted with gazes from all the other guests, with parents quickly telling their children not to stare. The dinner was fine, and they all agreed their rooms were very comfortable. But Dad could see Phil's disappointment written all over his face.

After dinner, Dad said "I fancy one of my Hamlet cigars. Still got a few left over from Father's Day. Better smoke it outside though. Want to join me, Phil?"

"I'm not taking up smoking, Dad", joked Phil, "but I'll come with you."

They strolled down to look at the bay. It was an ideal cove for young children – plenty of safe sandy stretches with lots of rock pools for hours spent finding crabs and other seaside delights. But to a lad in his mid-teens, it suggested complete boredom for the coming fortnight.

"Sorry, Phil. I think your mother and I have got the holiday wrong this year," Dad admitted. "We thought a change of scenery would be just the right thing. There are other youngsters for Rachel here, but I never thought there would be no one at all for you to make friends with. Your mother needed somewhere quieter than Tenby after her operation this year. Can you see that? And can you try to enjoy it for her sake, Phillip?"

"I'll do my best, Dad," responded Phil. "I even wish Matt was here."

"Really?" asked Dad.

"No, not really – he would hate it, too. But I promise I will try to make the next fortnight good for mother," affirmed Phil.

And he did, looking for opportunities that wouldn't have arisen when the Park Hotel put on their hectic list of activities. For the main part, he listened a great deal more to his transistor radio. Some days, when the family were on the beach in the bay, Phil had one ear to the sounds of the sea and the other taking in many of the weekday radio programmes he had never heard because he was usually at school.

And it didn't take him long to realise that, for most of the time, he wasn't missing much! Most of the morning was taken up with the 'Jimmy Young Show' where there was little emphasis on the 'young'. Politics, recipes and listeners' topical observations were interspersed with music from crooners – as Mr Young had been in his time. Often the programme included the latest chart hits but played by the BBC Radio Orchestra, with guest vocalists such as Danny Street or Andy Silver.

Phil couldn't understand why they didn't play the original singles. He would need to tap Martin's brain when they got back. He would know. The afternoons were better on Radio 1, with Dave Cash followed by Stuart Henry and, in their wisdom, the BBC had given Phil's favourite, Kenny Everett, an extra slot, from 6:45 to 7:30 every weekday evening.

He rarely got to hear much of that though, with the hotel dinner gong sounding at seven, but he made a note to have 'Foreverett' tuned in on 247 metres medium wave on the radiogram in the front room at home next term after tea. It would then look as if he just had the wireless on whilst he was reading his inorganic chemistry textbooks or working out those tricky vector analysis problems.

The evenings were the worst time as the radio shows were either re-runs of old comedy favourites, such as 'Hancock's Half Hour' or 'The Navy Lark', followed by specialist music shows – folk, country, big band or jazz. For Phil though, there weren't any programmes featuring the latest American bands or album tracks from some of the better British groups that he liked such as the Kinks, Small Faces or Procol Harum.

In the middle of the holiday, Phil was able to spend most of the weekend enjoying Keith Skues and Emperor Rosko on Saturday, then Stuart Henry and John Peel on

Sunday, all playing a great mix of live recordings from bands, some established and some new. They also featured many of the better chart hits, such as 'This Wheel's on Fire' by Julie Driscoll, Brian Auger and the Trinity, as well as the Crazy World of Arthur Brown's 'Fire' and a new band to Phil, Canned Heat, whose single 'On the road again' seemed to be on every show.

It was this that made the holiday bearable although there were other diversions that surprised Phil's parents. Occasionally he would break into a smile and even look like he was actually enjoying himself. One of the families – the one with a boy aged 12 – spent a great deal of time at the various golf courses in North Devon and, taking pity on Phil's lonesome deportment, offered to take him along with them to the Royal North Devon Golf Club.

Phil had never held a proper golf club before, not counting the pitch-and-putt courses at either Hayling Island or Bantock Park, off Bradmore Road in Wolverhampton. However, he soon realised he had a pretty good swing and, by the end of the day, and a not-that-many-over-par round of golf, the kind family reckoned that Phil was a natural, having excellent eye-to-ball co-ordination and that he really should consider taking up the sport.

When the western gales prevailed and the clouds raced over the nearby headland, trips to Hartland Abbey; to the nearest main seaside resort, Ilfracombe; or to the nearest main town, Barnstaple, broke the tedium. On sunnier days, a trip to the beautiful waterfall at Spekes Mill Mouth seemed to lift mother's spirits and Phil even endured the ferry to Lundy Island rather than stay at Hartland Quay. Sometimes, a brief bout of seasickness is preferable to a long day of boredom and Jimmy Young.

The day the family returned to Wolverhampton was the start of the new football season with the Wolves away to newly promoted Ipswich Town, nicknamed the Tractor Boys. This seemed somewhat appropriate to Phil as their trip home was delayed by a gathering of agricultural machinery on the North Devon roads, keeping the estate car at annoyingly low speeds in the first hour of their trip.

The A38 didn't disappoint either with its sluggishness and Phil, back in the front passenger seat, was called on by Dad to lift the mood by starting a game of '20 questions'. That didn't last long as Phil would choose either footballers or pop stars, resulting in neither his parents nor Rachel having a clue as to who the person was. You would have thought that, in this decade, everyone would have heard of either Jimmy Greaves or Bobby Moore, or maybe John Lennon or Bob Dylan, but not in Phil's family.

Eventually, the car turned into the drive around seven in the evening, having taken, including an excellent lunch near Cheddar Gorge, nearly nine hours to get home with quite a few comfort stops on the way. Then cases were unloaded, clothes piled up ready for washing the following week, and some of the rooms aired having been closed up for a fortnight.

Matt was pleased to see them and had managed to survive without any evidence of piles of fish and chip papers or crates of empty beer bottles. Phil knew that

Matt's friends, Guy and David, would have spent a fair bit of time there while they were away, but Mum and Dad were not only pleased to be home but pleased that their trust in Matt had not been misplaced.

Mum had said that leaving him to fend for himself for a fortnight would be good practice before going up to Oxford at the end of September. Dad knew Matt would be allocated rooms at New College, and that all the rooms on each stairwell had a scout to tend to their welfare, so he wasn't so concerned but, as usual, he agreed with mother.

In the following week, several events helped to lift Phil's mood from his holiday gloom. In early July, before the term had finished, he had begun to enjoy another new science fiction programme, 'The Time Tunnel', in which two American scientists become 'lost in the swirling maze of past and future ages'.

Having watched the pilot episode, in which the temporal travellers found themselves back on the Titanic, Phil was captivated and looked forward to settling down in front of the TV at 6:15 every Tuesday evening. With no homework pressures or parental exhortations regarding revision, he was able to really enjoy this new series and follow the weekly exploits of these time trekkers, Tony and Doug.

In the next episode, they found themselves on the very first manned expedition to Mars, ten years in the future, and while the third episode took them back again into the past, to the early 20th century, appearing deep underground at the time of the appearance of Halley's Comet and endeavouring to rescue a group of trapped miners while the rest of the town thought that the world was coming to an end.

Although Phil had a strong interest in space travel, time travel fascinated him just as much and he would have liked to be either one of Doctor Who's companions or Tony or Doug running down the 'Time Tunnel'. Recently he had considered reading H. G. Wells' book, 'The Time Machine'. He thought about it, but he didn't.

Phil wasn't a great reader. A few years back, every fortnight, he had accompanied his parents to the local library, housed in a converted Nissen hut on the Warstones Road. On each occasion, he would select three books, get them stamped out and two weeks later, those same three books would be stamped back in, unopened and unread. Mum and Dad gave up taking him with them within a year.

Compared with listening to music, particularly on the radio, reading wasn't even a poor second to Phil. Matt read avidly and Rachel always seemed to lose herself in those series of books about girls at boarding schools – 'Malory Towers', 'St. Clare's' or such like. Comics and annuals could keep Phil quiet in his pre-teens but by now even requisite textbooks were an on-going struggle of application and concentration.

Phil had missed episodes four and five whilst they were in Devon, so he had no idea how Tony and Doug got on, either at Pearl Harbour or which side they had ended up on in the American Civil War. He had also missed two weeks of doing his paper round which, more specifically in that instance, adding nothing to his savings for his next record purchase.

Paper rounds continued week in, week out, the only difference being that in the holidays you didn't have to dash around so that you weren't late to school in the mornings. The evening rounds, delivering the *Express & Star*, plus any overlooked magazines, comics or periodicals, could be done any time after five.

On Tuesdays, Phil was now first in line to collect his late deliveries so that he could be back home in good time to catch up with the series, episode five being set near Krakatoa, just as the volcano was about to erupt. To Phil, it had become the most gripping thing on TV all week!

On the Monday morning, a week after his return, Mr Stewart called him into the back room at the newsagents.

"Rob's on holiday for three weeks. Can you do his round as well?" he asked. "I know you can do your round in your sleep – in fact, I sometimes think you do – so a quick whizz back here, pick up Rob's bag and then deliver his. They'll be a mite late, but you shouldn't get much grief as it's summer. It's not that much out of your way really."

Rob's round started at the bottom of Mount Road, all the way up, both sides, then down Muchall Road and back delivering to the few large residences along the top side of Penn Road and back to The Mount Tavern. It wasn't a short round, with many of the houses being detached and most having newspapers, magazines and comics to be delivered. There was another newsagent, at the shops in

Birchwood Road, but Phil suspected that most homes in Mount Road would go to Stewarts.

There were two notable bonuses to this extra exertion, which would undoubtedly take up more of Phil's holiday time, both in the mornings with the dailies then delivering the evening paper to probably half or so of those addresses. Firstly, for those few weeks, this meant earning more than twice as much which would result in increasing Phil's LP collection, making up for his lost holiday earnings.

The second, which made Phil's heart race slightly, was that there was a faint possibility – actually he hoped a probability – that he would have to deliver papers to the home of the girl who lived halfway up Muchall Road. Earning more money was one thing but finding out more about her was far too good an opportunity to ignore.

Phil rushed down Wynn Road that morning, zoomed along Coalway Road and back up Leighton Road in record time, and then back along the Penn Road to Stewarts to start his second round, dropping by home, to let Mum know he would be in for a late breakfast.

Rob's bag was quite a bit heavier than his own and his list of deliveries a lot longer. They'll be even more when magazines and comics come out later in the week, thought Phil, as he left his bike at the gates of St Aidan's Church and started on the lower section of Mount Road.

As he got halfway up the road, he delivered to the Simberts and caught up with Graham who enquired about when the season would start for the youth club team at St Aidan's. They had been friends in the choir for many years and had recently decided to put a team into the town's youth club league, with a side mainly made up of choristers, together with a few mates from school.

"I have to go to the first team secretary's meeting next week," said Phil. "They will hand out the fixture list then, so I would have thought it would be towards the end of August. We've got the Mount Road Rec as our home pitch. Mr Barnwell has fixed that for us, and he said he will coach us. You still up for it?"

"You bet," replied Graham. "And Rob, Wynn and John are in. Be a bit different from our kickabouts behind the church though."

"Gotta get on," said Phil. "Double paper round for a few weeks until Rob gets back from his hols. You'll be seeing a lot of me."

"Oh good!" said Graham, mockingly, as he went back to cleaning his mum's car and Phil crossed the road to deliver Mr Barnwell's papers. As he finished the Mount Road addresses, he turned into Muchall Road and wondered whether he might just bump into the girl who alighted so gracefully from the bus every weekday evening, unaware of his admiring gaze.

Phil was halfway down the road when he approached the drive down which she always disappeared on her way home. There were no deliveries for this address. His heart sank but then he thought: "As I don't usually do this round, no one would know if I mistakenly delivered a paper to this house".

As he walked down the long drive a dour deep voice boomed out.

"No papers for the next three weeks. They've cancelled them. They're abroad on holiday. Didn't the newsagent tell you or aye you just daft?" Phil looked across the lawned terrace, in front of the bay window of the house, to see a man he assumed to be the gardener, hands on hips and looking somewhat sternly at him.

"Sorry, this is my first day doing Rob's round," stuttered Phil turning on his heels and making his retreat. "Thought this was number 33. Won't happen again," he replied, as he continued down Muchall Road, with a lighter bag but a heavier heart.

That afternoon, Phil was again on the racing bike he himself had built. This time, he was going down to Chestnut Way in Finchfield, to Martin's house. Phil and Martin always had one afternoon a month when they would compare notes on the latest songs they had heard, what singles Martin was looking to buy or had bought, and which albums Phil was saving up for.

Martin opened the door at number 10. "Come on up. I've got some bad news, some good news and some even better news," he said as the two lads went up to his room to study the latest music papers.

"Bad news first?" asked Martin.

"Why not?" replied Phil. "My day didn't start well with an extra paper round so whatever it is has got to be a change for the better!"

"Who is your favourite band?" asked Martin.

"I like a lot of bands. Maybe Procol Harum or the Beatles. No, the Zombies – got to be them," reflected Phil.

"OK. Which American band do you like best then?" asked Martin more purposefully.

"Not the Monkees. Maybe the Beach Boys. Love 'God Only Knows'. Or the Byrds with 'Mister Tambourine Man'. Quite like Jefferson Airplane, the Doors and Spirit. So many," reckoned Phil.

"And whose album did you listen to every single track in Beatties' record booths before you bought it?" said Martin, even more exasperated that Phil obviously wasn't thinking straight.

"Oh, Buffalo Springfield!" said Phil. "What about them?"

"They've broken up – gone off to do solo projects," announced Martin. "It's in the *Melody Maker*. Seems Stephen Stills and Neil Young never got on, were always arguing on stage and the others got fed up of their bickering."

"Thanks, mate," sighed Phil. "And I thought today was going to get better – eventually!"

"Well, it could. Here's the good news. The Springfield have a new album out, sort of a swansong – released at the end of July, so you should be able to get Beatties to order it for you and, with all the money you're getting from your extra paper round, no probs. You should have enough, even if you spent all your savings on holiday," said Martin.

"You are joking. It was the worst holiday ever. Two weeks of listening to Jimmy Young and no other kids my age there. I saved all my pocket money. Nothing to spend it on. No coffee bars and no jukeboxes. Nowhere to shop and nothing to do. Played golf though and they said I was pretty good. Might take it up rather than footer," said Phil. "Anyhow, you got any new singles?"

"Have a listen to this," Martin said. "Got it last week."

He played 'Rain and Tears' by Aphrodite's Child and then played some recent singles from Love, the Doors, Family and the Moody Blues, as well as a few old favourites such as 'Sunshine Girl' by the Parade and 'Rainbow Chaser' by Nirvana, probably Martin's favourite band.

"Those two guys are geniuses or is that geniae?" he pondered.

"You should know," said Phil. "You're in six classics, not me! What's the name of the new Springfield album then?"

"'Last Time Around', I think. Very apt," said Martin. "Peely and Stuart Henry have played a track each – sounded good. Think I've got the single 'Uno Mundo' around somewhere."

As Martin delved through his considerable collection of singles, Phil said "Right, I'll go into town early on Saturday, before the game, and order it from Beatties – something to look forward to this month. So, what was the even-better news then?"

'Oh that," said Martin. "You'll never guess who we've booked to play at Venturers this Saturday?"

"No, you're right, I probably won't. Not the Beatles, as they've given up playing live. The Stones or the Who? Love to see the Kinks there!" Phil said smugly, knowing Martin was bursting to tell him.

"Only the Band of Joy with Robert Plant," announced Martin. "They are one of the best, if not THE best, of all the local bands around. Better than The Calis, the Monts or the N' Betweens."

"Sounds like Saturday will be an extraordinary day then. Double paper round, new album to order, Wolves at home to QPR, then a great band at the club – can't wait," said Phil, as he put his coat on to get home in time for tea.

"Oh, by the way, I meant to ask you," continued Phil. "Why does Radio 1 have a lot of the chart hits played by their orchestra with guest singers?"

"Ah, that's to do with what is called 'needle time'," explained Martin. Phil looked none the wiser.

"The Musician's Union will only allow the Beeb to play a certain amount of recorded music every day – I think it's just five hours. So, they use bands playing live cover versions or, as you say, the BBC Radio Orchestra. Daft if you ask me as neither Radio Luxembourg nor the pirate stations had the same problem," continued Martin.

"I knew you would know," said Phil as he got on his bike. "See you Saturday then at the club. Thank your mum for the cuppa. I forgot! Tara."

By Saturday afternoon, just after 2 o'clock, Phil had ordered 'Last Time Around' from the Beatties' Record Department, paying his deposit of two shillings and sixpence so he would get the very first copy that came in. Deliveries were usually Wednesday so he would be back after that to check if it had arrived.

Standing by the 'man on the 'oss' in Queens Square, Phil was glad he had asked Dad for a lift into town earlier. For over a year now, the buses had become less than reliable due to what had become known as the 'Turban Dispute'. It had started last June when a Sikh bus driver was banned by the Wolverhampton Transport Department because he turned up to work with a beard and wearing his turban. Their stance was that the turban violated the dress code and being unshaven was unprofessional.

What was just a local issue had now become a national debate, fired up no doubt by the recent rhetoric of Enoch Powell, and one particular Sikh leader who had said he would set fire to himself next April if the situation had not been resolved. Phil thought it was something about nothing and tended to agree with most of the comments from local passengers reported in the *Express & Star*.

To him, and many others, it was a matter of ensuring that the buses ran on time, rather than how the driver was dressed. Paying your fare wasn't for a fashion show or a religious service but simply the matter of getting to your journey's end at the right time.

He wondered how the others would get here today, as this dispute often led to some bus stoppages and today was one of those days when there had been a walkout by the other Sikh drivers. He then spotted Brian and Adrian walking up from Beatties at the end of the square and turned to look to see if he could spot Joe coming in the opposite direction.

"No sign of Joe yet?" asked Brian.

"Not yet. Your Dad bring you in today?" replied Phil.

"Yeh. We picked up Adrian on the way, but I couldn't get him to go across town to get Joe," said Brian.

"He'll be here soon," chipped in Adrian. "Joe won't miss a game. We might even win this one. They've only got one point from the first two games. Mind you, we ain't got any!"

He was right. Wolves had started the season poorly, losing 1-0 to Ipswich Town, promoted as champions of the second division, in the opening game, then losing again 3-2 to Manchester City, winners of the division 1 title in May. These were sides used to winning – Wolves were not. The only excuse was that both games were away.

It was nearly 2:30 when Joe made an appearance.

"Come on, Joe. We'll only just make kick-off," snapped Phil, but Joe had no breath left to reply, having run into town to get to the game today.

They got in with plenty of time as there were only just over 30,000 fans at Molineux and very few seemed to have come up from London's West End to watch today's opponents, also promoted last May, Queens Park Rangers.

Phil was beaming. The new match programme was called *Molinews*. He usually saved it for the bus ride home but, with Dad picking him up and the novelty of a larger and brighter publication, he was already deep into it, reading through the features, as was Adrian. As the teams were announced, pens would be taken from pockets and changes noted to the line-ups.

Wolves were at full strength with both Dougan and Wignall up front and Holsgrove and Woodfield at the centre of the defence. Knowles and Wagstaffe would provide the skill, Bailey and Kenning the industry in midfield. The Rs had four changes and no really well-known players to speak of. This clearly should be an easy win.

Seven minutes gone and Wolves were one up. Frank Wignall's left foot hit a half-chance past QPR's keeper, Mike Kelly, lifting the spirits all around Molineux. Wignall had scored a brace at Maine Road in midweek although that hadn't been enough to bring back even a point.

"A hatful today, I reckon," said Joe. "About time the Doog got off the mark this season. The defence looks solid enough."

Joe spoke too soon, David Woodfield being easily beaten by Alan Wilks for the visitors, who then laid it on a plate for their right-winger, Ian Morgan, to equalise and it stayed like that until half time – one each. The second half started in the same way, with Wolves taking the lead after seven minutes, this time from skipper Mike Bailey who ran unchallenged all the way from the halfway line, before sliding it past a helpless Kelly.

QPR were dogged opponents throughout and it took until the 84th minute for victory to be guaranteed, as Joe's wish came true and Derek Dougan scored the third, to give Wolves a comfortable but not impressive 3-1 win.

"They'll have to play better than that on Wednesday," said Joe. "It's Arsenal here and they are much more experienced than QPR. You going, Phil?"

"Not sure yet," Phil replied. "It depends if I can afford it. I might be doing two paper rounds at the moment, but I won't see the cash for that until next weekend and I'm hoping that the LP I want will be in midweek. Would like to, but Dad's not keen on giving me money on tick, as Mum calls it. He's always saying, 'neither a borrower nor a lender be'. It's a quote from Shakespeare, I think."

The lads didn't know whether to be impressed or not but none of them really had the time as they hurried away from the ground – Phil, Brian and Adrian off to get lifts home and Joe starting the long trek back to Wednesfield.

"See you at Venturers, Joe?" shouted Phil.

"Hope so. Band of Joy should be bostin," he said, trotting off up Waterloo Road.

Joe got a lift with Spud, Andy and Angie to the club that evening, getting there just as Phil was walking down Warstones Road.

As they approached the entrance, they could sense that all was not how it should be, most noticeably that Brian was not sitting at the door ready to collect entrance money. They all walked in and looked around. All the regulars were in attendance, but everyone was in deep conversation and none of it seemed elated. Phil saw Martin in the kitchen.

"What's going on?" asked Phil.

"He's not arrived," stammered Martin.

"Who? Brian?" replied Phil. "Surely someone else on the committee could do Brian's job on the door. Not so well perhaps, but it's only taking money and making a note of how many come in."

"No, no. Brian's here. He's on the phone trying to get a stand-in," said Martin.

"A stand-in for who?" asked Phil.

"Robert Plant, you moron!" exclaimed Martin. "He cancelled this afternoon. Gone off to London to meet someone important, he said. Something about being asked to join the Yardbirds, I'm told. You know, 'For your love'. 'Heart full of soul'. All those hits."

"Or 'Over Under Sideways Down'," said Phil, but Martin wasn't amused.

"We've got a packed club tonight but no act," he sighed. "Need a cuppa – always helps. Wonder how Brian's getting on?" Just then Brian walked into the kitchen looking smug.

"Well? Any joy?" asked Martin.

"What about Barmy Barry?" said Brian. "Roger says can be here by 8:30."

"He's great but we can't afford him, can we?" continued Martin. "We've let everyone come in for nowt tonight cos we didn't have an act."

"Roger says he owes us, as we've had a lot of the bands from his agency on here recently, so he will reduce the fee and sort it with Barry. We just got to put this down to experience and make the best of it, Mart," said Brian.

"Yeh, you're right. Suppose you want me to make the announcement. Thanks a bunch!' said Martin as he strolled into the hall to let everyone know what was happening.

Barmy Barry was a legend as a DJ in the Black Country area, outrageously living up to his name but also knowing his stuff when it came to what to play, when to play it and how to introduce it, before getting the crowd on to the dance floor. He didn't do radio presenting. He didn't need to, getting plenty of evening DJ work right across the Midlands.

He had his hair dyed in four different colours and looked as he performed – barmy by name and bonkers on stage. He would arrive and act as a roadie, no one taking much notice of him setting up the record decks with a bobble hat on, looking more like Benny from 'Crossroads' than Barry the disc jockey.

He then disappeared into the makeshift dressing room at the back of the club and re-appeared as his stage persona, ready to give everyone maximum entertainment for the rest of the evening.

Barmy Barry played great records for over two hours without any break, including fantastic soul tracks from the Stax, Atlantic and Tamla Motown labels, and introducing many to the wonders of northern soul music. He would mix well-known hits such as the Four Tops 'I can't help myself' or the Temptations' 'Get Ready' with unknowns, like a Gloria Jones song called 'Tainted Love'.

And Barry wasn't afraid to play current chart hits if he knew they were good to dance to, such as Sly & the Family Stone's 'Dance to the music' or 'Mony, Mony' by Tommy James & the Shondells. That was the key to his talent – creating an atmosphere to dance, to smile and just enjoy the evening.

Chart successes, such as 'Baby come back' by the Equals and 'Jumping Jack Flash' from the Stones, would bookend lesser-known tracks such as Gene Chandler's 'Duke of Earl' or Frank Wilson's 'Do I love you' or the Tams with 'Be young, be foolish, be happy'. He knew his audience and he knew how to give them a good time.

He had also sussed that many had come to hear Robert Plant and the Band of Joy, so he included more blues and soul tracks in the middle section of his act. Wilson Pickett's 'In the midnight hour' together with Sam & Dave's 'Soul Man' had the room swaying, and whether you wanted Aretha or Otis singing 'Respect', it didn't seem to matter which one Barry played.

By 10 o'clock there wasn't anyone who hadn't stepped on to the dance floor. Anyone who seemed reluctant was singled out by Barry and pulled into the dancing throng. It was a crazy, brilliant night. Barry knew that it was time to drop the tempo and to introduce ballads on his turntables, like Fleetwood Mac's 'Need your love so bad' or the Temptations' 'You're my everything'. Couples embraced and the dancing slowed. Phil knew it was time to begin his walk home.

"You pulled that one out. Everyone's had a great time," said Phil to Brian as he was leaving. "Bet there isn't anyone who misses Mr Plant now. Great evening. See you next week."

It was a warm balmy August evening as Phil strolled up Hollybush Lane. It's been a bit of a barmy month all round Phil thought to himself, enjoying his own play on words, and made a mental note to listen to more soul music, as well as the tracks he liked on his favourite radio shows.

"Everett may love the harmonies and Peely may champion the unknown bands but when it came to a wonderful evening's dancing there was nothing better, as Arthur Conley would say, than 'sweet soul music'," he thought.

As he turned into Penn Road, he realised the songs Barry had played in his set were still running around in his head and, as he wended his way home, he was still keeping to Barry's barmy beat.

Chapter 7 - The Urban Spaceman

Turning sixteen in the summer of 1968 seemed to bring about an autumnal change in parental attitude towards Phil. Maybe it was because he was now the oldest child at home, with Matthew up at Oxford which, whilst it had brought with it some extra tasks around the home, had also resulted in a somewhat loosening of the filial reins.

So, when he asked whether he could go to a pop music concert at the Civic Hall during half term, there was a surprising absence of argument from Mum and Dad. The usual evening curfew time was extended to 11 and Mum actually expressed the hope that he enjoyed himself.

The concert featured a Birmingham band who had been establishing a growing reputation both locally and nationally. They regularly played to enthusiastic audiences at The Ship & Rainbow, out on the Dudley Road, and had also done quite a few gigs at The Woolpack in the town centre. Earlier in the year, they had played at Mothers, the brand-new progressive music venue in Erdington.

Both John Peel and Kenny Everett championed their music on Radio 1, especially their latest single 'The Skeleton and the Roundabout', a great story song with a quirky melody. Martin was already an ardent fan and Phil was keen to find out what all this fuss was about. They met up with Adrian in Queens Square on a late October evening to stroll down North Street towards the vast Civic Hall foyer.

There were plenty of tickets left for the circle but the lads decided to stand in the stalls area where they could witness the band's performance close up. As always with groups, the 8 o'clock start time meant very little, so when the support act, a local band called Evolution, shuffled on there was just a murmur of excitement.

Evolution had only formed a few months back and they played like it – a bit disjointed with most of their songs having a solid blues edge which Adrian really liked. There were a few cover versions from singles by new progressive music bands, such as Family, Pretty Things, Traffic and Jethro Tull, but they never quite caught the audience's attention.

"I really like them," said Adrian. "Worth coming just to hear them."

"You'll like the main act better," said Martin and, when Evolution had finished, the lads went over to the bar for some refreshment.

They could have had a beer but Martin and Adrian weren't into drinking much and the memory of Phil's experience with cider and cigars, at Jerry's birthday party when they were 14, had stayed with him for a long time and so it was soft drinks all round.

Handing him his drink, Phil asked Adrian "Where's Martin gone?"

"He's up at the other end of the bar, chatting to some fella with really long fuzzy hair," replied Adrian.

"Any idea who he is?" asked Phil.

"Nope," replied Adrian. "Probably attached to one of the bands. You know how Martin is. Always trying to find out some bit of obscure info on these bands."

Martin swaggered back with a grin from ear to ear. "I got his autograph on this beer mat," he said.

"Whose autograph?" enquired Phil.

"That's Jeff Lynne, lead singer of the Idle Race," answered Martin.

"Who?" said Adrian.

"The band we've come to see tonight, you moron," exclaimed Martin. "They're going to be really big. He's a musical genius, I reckon."

"Is that 'really big' like the singles by the band Love that you managed to sneak on to the jukebox at Venturers?" enquired Phil mockingly.

"Not my fault I have brilliant taste," replied Martin nonchalantly as the lights in the main hall began to dim and the lads went to stand near the stage.

The Idle Race sauntered casually on. Roger Spencer sat down at his drum kit, Geoff Masters picked up his Hofner bass, and Dave Pritchard his rhythm guitar, leaving Jeff Lynne to move towards a small keyboard, his guitar slung across his back, to count the band in. Two, three, four and then straight into the intro of their recent single, Jeff extolling everyone to 'Climb aboard my roundabout'.

It went down a storm, with many in the audience joining in the chorus la-la-las. Afterwards, Jeff stepped forward to his microphone and thanked the audience for their applause. "That's our latest single. Still available in all good record stores," he continued.

"Already got it!" said Martin. Neither Phil nor Adrian were surprised.

"And it's on our first album which was released this month," said Jeff Lynne. "As is this track, called 'Morning Sunshine'." The band played a few more tracks from the album – 'Follow me, follow', 'Lucky man', 'On with the show' and 'Pie in the sky'.

"Dave wrote that last one," explained Jeff. "And this next one was written by my mate Roy. You might have heard some of his stuff."

They played their version of the Move's 'Here we go round the lemon tree' before playing cover versions of Moby Grape's 'Hey grandma', the Lemon Pipers' song 'Blueberry blue' and a stupendous version of Tyrannosaurus Rex's 'Deborah' which went on for over six minutes, really showing off Jeff's great guitar work, sometimes sounding like Hendrix, other times more like the rawness of the Kinks.

"They're nowhere near as heavy as that on record," said Martin. "That cover of the Lemon Pipers' song is really great though. It could have been written by the band themselves."

The band returned to more melodic and laidback tracks from their album. 'The Birthday' and 'The Lady who said she could fly' both showcased all four members sharing vocal harmonies which were right up Phil's street. His favourite bands – the Zombies, Beatles, and the Byrds – all depended on strong melodies and good vocal harmonies, so the Idle Race was another to join his faves list.

"What's the album called?" he asked Martin and, as if he had heard Phil's question, Jeff revealed the album was called 'Birthday Party' and it was out on the Liberty label.

"Here's a couple of novelty tracks," he continued and the band played 'I like my toys' and 'Sitting in my tree' before finishing their set with their very first single, the rockier 'Imposters of life's magazine'.

At the end of the song, the band's dedicated fans went wild in the Civic, with hollers, whoops and applause, much more deafening than the lads were used to at Venturers. As the band waved and trooped off the stage, the audience began to stomp for an encore. Unsurprisingly, back they came and played the aptly titled 'End of the road' to finish a great concert.

"Told you they were bostin," said Martin. "Thought they sounded really good even at the Civic. I'd been told that bands often don't like playing here 'cos the acoustics are really bad. The Idle Race are going to be massive and Jeff Lynne will be up there with Lennon and McCartney as a songwriter. That autograph on the beer mat will be worth a fortune in years to come. You agree, Phil?"

"Yep. Liked their softer songs more," said Phil. "I think that's me sorted for Christmas. When I get some more record tokens, it's definitely 'Birthday Party' by the Idle Race as the next LP in my collection. Nowhere near as many as your singles though, Martin. What about you, Ade?"

"Thought they were pretty good, but I liked the support band better," he replied and, as they left the concert, Phil and Martin looked quizzically at each other and shook their heads, making their way back to Queen's Square to catch their buses home.

The 1968 Michaelmas term hadn't gone well for Phil. It had all started going downhill towards the end of the summer holidays when Mum had announced that she was actually joining the teaching staff at his school, the grammar school. She would be teaching part-time, as she had since returning to teaching when she joined the staff at the Municipal Grammar School, to teach mathematics and physics, a few years back.

Having teachers as parents had its downsides. It wasn't the values and expectations they both had, when it came to doing homework or how well you did in class or exams. It was the fact that, when it came to school matters, you couldn't get away with anything. Joe agreed since his parents were also teachers.

Adrian had only his mum, and, as her only son, if he wanted to, he could convince her there was no school and she would always believe him. Mind you, Adrian never did. Neither Phil nor Joe could ever even try to get away with that one.

It hadn't always been a problem. At junior and infants' schools, no one bothered about what your parents did. Your father could be a doctor, telephone repairman, train driver or a teacher. Mums were just mums then. It simply didn't matter. At senior school, it seemed to matter all of a sudden and it wasn't always the pupils who gave Phil grief.

In his second year at the grammar school, his history teacher had told him that, by the summer, he would be top of the class in that subject, not because Phil was a brilliant history scholar but because this teacher was a friend of Phil's father. That didn't sit right with Phil so, from that moment on, he did just enough history homework to get by. He rarely answered questions in class and he didn't come top at the end of the year.

Phil's parents were always of the opinion that it didn't matter if you weren't top of the class, as long as you did your best. Some of Phil's classmates assumed that having teachers at home would be an advantage. But it was often quite the opposite. Phil's parents would argue that it would be for his own benefit if he sorted things out for himself.

There might be just a mere suggestion as to which chapter, or in what textbook, you might find your answers but, as far as Mum and Dad were concerned, teachers taught and pupils learnt. As teachers, they were of one mind and, no matter what stage of education you were at, they would know exactly where you should be, or so they thought.

In Phil's case though, his parents were well wide of the mark. Whilst his ability in mathematics was very evident, he was struggling in both chemistry and physics. In the former, the lengthy teachers' bridge sessions seemed to have become even longer, leaving an embarrassment of time for those less academic students to be distracted away from those key topics, which would undoubtedly appear in the A-level exam papers next year.

However, there were occasional advantages to his mother joining the teaching staff, such as getting a welcome lift to school on cold autumn days, although that meant that if he wanted a lift home he might have to stay late until she was ready to leave. But he usually took the bus, with the promise that his studies would commence as soon as he got home.

This was a dodge, of course, as the number 1 bus, into town, would drop Phil off in Queen's Square and, instead of just crossing the road to get the number 11 home to Penn, he could easily make a short musical detour.

Voltic Records was no more as the Queens Arcade had been hastily demolished earlier in the year to make way for a modern shopping centre named after the Mander family, who had been heavily involved in Wolverhampton's industrial expansion over the past two centuries. Their part in the town's history was undoubted and they probably deserved their civic acclaim, but Phil really missed the ambience and relaxed expertise of the music specialism that was a byword in Voltic Records.

So, for Phil, there was little option than to disappear down into the basement of Beatties department store where their music and records section was situated. The trick was then to get home before Mum and attempt to look as studious as possible when she got in. It worked – most times.

By the time the school choristers, including Phil and Joe, were practising new descants for the impending school carol service, Phil was well behind with his A-level studies and there were also other matters that irked him, which he believed had clearly arisen from Mum's presence at his school.

Both Joe and Adrian had been made prefects during that term, but not Phil. Either of them would be head boy in their Oxbridge year, come next September, but not Phil. He was fairly sure that the staff who chose the prefects hadn't actually overlooked him but if he had been chosen it might have been seen as favouritism.

Taff Williams wouldn't have held such an opinion, being more concerned about Phil's academic progress, or lack of it, than his school status when he asked him to stay behind after a double physics lesson in the last week of the term.

"How's your brother getting on in Oxford, Minor?" he enquired.

"Fine, sir" replied Phil. "Though I don't tend to hear much from him. He phones on a Sunday afternoon usually but speaks to my parents rather than me."

"Expect you miss him," said Taff.

"At times," responded Phil. "My sister Rachel doesn't talk much about the Wolves. She's more into cricket and hockey. And she says the space race is a waste of time!"

"I hear she's making quite a name for herself at the girls' high school, especially in sport," said Taff. "Already at county level in hockey and tennis and likely to play cricket for the ladies' county team as well. Miss Heyhoe speaks very highly of her indeed."

"Yes, sir. She's pretty good – for a girl," said Phil with a grin.

"Glad to see you still like a joke, Minor. Your physics homework is no laughing matter though, is it?" said Taff.

"I struggle to find it fascinating, sir. Topics like wave mechanics, magnetic-field densities or properties of materials just don't excite me," replied Phil. "Now, if it was astrophysics or topics such as space travel or possibly time travel then I might be a tad more enthusiastic!"

"Those subjects aren't studied at this level, Minor. You will undoubtedly come across them in degree courses. But now you have to learn the basics, at this point, to move on and then get to university to study those more interesting matters," explained Taff.

"I'll have to up my game next term, sir," said Phil.

"Yes, you will, if you want to be an Oxbridge candidate next year," Taff replied, quite sternly for him.

Then he changed the subject. "However, I expect you're really looking forward to the launch of Apollo 8 this weekend," he said. "It's going to be an extraordinary event, mankind going to the moon for the very first time."

"I expect you wish it was a Welshman in the space module rather than an American," joked Phil.

"Now there's a thought," countered Taff. "I expect everyone at NASA is just hoping that this mission is a success. I, for one, am really looking forward to the pictures that should come back from space. They should be spectacular. Have a good Christmas, Minor. See you in January."

Whilst he was speaking, he had put on his raincoat, fixed his bicycle clips onto his trouser legs and was moving towards the classroom door, leaving Phil feeling that he had been definitely summarily dismissed.

Saturday, December 21st was going to be a very, very hectic day. Phil was still doing his daily paper rounds, not only to fund his small but well-played LP collection, but also as he needed to save up for driving lessons when he turned seventeen next year.

When he got home, he enjoyed an excellent cooked breakfast before going back to the Mount Road shops to get the weekend veg for Mum, from Moores, the greengrocer. Then there were the regular weekend chores to do. Matt was home from Oxford but was excused chores which, to Phil and Rachel, seemed somewhat unfair just because he had been away at university. By 1 o'clock, lunch was on the table and Phil asked Dad whether he could listen to the BBC lunchtime news on Radio Four.

"It's on 276 on the medium wave," advised Phil.

"I think I can find the Home Service on the wireless," said Dad. "I've been listening to it for over 30 years – man and boy. Why do you want that on? You are usually plugged into that new Radio 1."

"There should be a news report on the launch of Apollo 8 in Florida. It should've taken off earlier this morning," explained Phil.

"What's Apollo 8?" asked Mum. "A new brand of ice lolly?"

Rachel stifled a giggle. "It's the latest in America's bid to win the space race and to be the first to land men on the moon," explained Phil thoughtfully.

"Oh, well then, we had all better listen," said Mum. The BBC news reporter revealed that, at just before 8 a.m., Apollo 8 had successfully taken off from the John F Kennedy Space Centre in Florida, USA.

The space centre had been built on land adjacent to the military base, Cape Canaveral Air Force Station, and had been named after the American president just a week after his assassination in 1962. Phil remembered exactly where he was when the news had come through of the shooting – choir practice had just finished at St Aiden's Church.

It seemed more than fitting that Apollo 8 should be the first mission to launch from the base named after the man who, earlier in the sixties, had promised that *"this nation should commit itself to achieving the goal, before this decade is out, of landing a man on the Moon and returning him safely to the Earth".*

Whilst none of the three-man crew on Apollo 8 – Boorman, Lovell and Anders – actually set foot on the Moon, it was a triumph in every other aspect. The successful launch was followed by the Saturn 5 rocket leaving the Earth's orbit and travelling for nearly three days over 200,000 miles before reaching the Moon.

The spacecraft then completed 10 orbits of the Moon in the next two days, whilst sending the very-first-ever Christmas message from mankind in space. The crew also became the first people in history to witness 'earthrise', observing the Earth coming into view over the surface of the Moon.

None of this wonderment was lost on Phil who was fascinated by the BBC TV news coverage of these historic events, although it was somewhat limited as they happened over the Christmas period, or the reports he eagerly read in Dad's *Times* newspaper.

Over that Christmas period, his paper round took twice as long as he scanned both broadsheets and tabloids for facts and pictures of the Apollo 8 space mission. Whilst newspapers were often infrequent over the festive season, Mr Stewart remained puzzled as to why Phil asked for any unsold copies, concluding that Phil needed some extra wrapping paper, with a difference, at that time of the year.

The spacecraft then returned safely to Earth on Friday, December 27th and was recovered after splashing down in the Pacific Ocean. Phil was more than amused that the Command Module Pilot, Jim Lovell, had confirmed, on Christmas morning, in their daily radio transmission, that, as they left the Moon's orbit, they had 'proof of the existence of Santa Claus'.

Later that afternoon, Wolves were home to Sheffield Wednesday. Phil would be there and, for the very first time, he wouldn't be watching a division 1 game from their usual spot in the South Bank. Brian had gone abroad for the Christmas holidays with his family, spending their time doing something called skiing, and had offered Phil and Adrian his, and his father's, seats in the Molineux Street Stand for this game.

Neither of them could believe their luck. Joe had said that there was no way he would be seen in the 'posh' seats – his Dad would kill him. It was rumoured that Joe's dad was a member of the Communist Party, but Phil thought this was a bit of an overstatement, though he was definitely a Labour Party member and trade union representative at his school.

However, there would be important business to be done in town before Phil met up with Joe and Adrian. He caught the bus after lunch, giving him time to visit the basement in Beatties and spend some time looking through the racks of LP covers, but only after he had placed his order for a copy of the Idle Race's album 'Birthday Party'.

"It won't be in before Christmas," said the sales assistant.

"That's OK," replied Phil. "I won't have enough money to buy it until after Christmas."

"We're shut most days next week. Open on Monday but early closing on Christmas Eve and then back in here on Saturday for just one day," continued the assistant. "Unlikely to be any deliveries either so your best bet is the first Thursday in January."

"Thanks. That suits me," said Phil.

By now the sales staff in the record department had got used to Phil, and Martin, often occupying the listening booths to check out album tracks and singles. They knew there would be a purchase, somewhere down the line, with both lads sure to cough up for an order once they had made their choice.

Phil looked at his watch and saw he was late to meet up with the other lads so it was up the grand staircase and out into Victoria Street to dash to their usual meeting spot.

"Hurry up," barked Joe, as Phil appeared. "It's all right for you and Adrian using Brian and his Dad's season tickets but I have to get into the South Bank."

"There won't be a big crowd today," said Adrian. "What with last-minute Christmas shopping and the fact that Wednesday aren't one of the top sides, you should be fine, Joe."

"We'll see. They'm a tad fickle, Wednesday," prompted Joe. "Wouldn't like to second guess this one."

Joe wasn't wrong and in fact this whole season had been pretty unpredictable with most sides winning as many as they had lost, other than the top four of Liverpool, Leeds, Arsenal and Everton. Halfway through the season and there were only six points separating West Ham in fifth down to Sunderland in fifteenth.

Today's visitors, Sheffield Wednesday, were just two points above Wolves and hadn't won away from home since early November, whereas Wolves had recorded three straight home wins, scoring nine without conceding any, so the lads had every confidence that they were about to witness another lampin'.

The lads split up by the Molineux Hotel, at the top of the South Bank stand, Joe to stand in the queue, whilst Phil and Adrian went around to Molineux Street to take up their seats for the match. This wasn't actually a brand-new experience for them as they sometimes went into either of the seated stands, on the Waterloo Road or Molineux Street, when they came to see reserve games. Then the seats were as cheap as standing in either the North or South Banks. They never used the family enclosure – full of kids!

As always, both lads had bought programmes and, as the teams were announced, Adrian noted the changes to the line-ups. Gerry Taylor wasn't fit so Les Wilson would take his place and Dave Wagstaffe was back in the side, which pleased them both as Waggy, in their opinion, was the best crosser of the ball in the league and should be playing for England, if Sir Alf would ever consider playing wingers.

Injuries still meant that David Woodfield was missing in defence together with big Phil Parkes in goal, but winger John Farrington had just had a run out in the reserves and should be back to match fitness soon. It was hoped that manager Bill McGarry would have a fully fit squad for the

Boxing Day fixture, at home to the Sky Blues, Coventry City.

So, Phil and Adrian settled back in their seats, hopeful that this would extend the Wolves latest unbeaten home run to four games. How wrong could they have been? The first half an hour was laborious, with neither side seemingly bothered as to what the result might be. Unsurprisingly, Wolves were confident as they had beaten Wednesday 2-0 at Hillsborough back in October, but that over-confidence turned to complacency as they became second best in passing, tackling and goal attempts.

The sedate crowd in the 'posh seats' began to murmur with unease as Wednesday took a grip on the game, in particular Jim McCalliog who, not for the first time against the Wolves, was expertly controlling the midfield. Bailey and Knowles seemed listless and to no-one's surprise Wednesday scored just over 30 minutes into the game.

Wolves' keeper, Alan Boswell, seemed hesitant and stayed on his line rather than coming out to cut off the cross from Wednesday full-back Wilf Smith. The Wolves defence thought the keeper had it. The keeper thought the defence would clear it. The result was that the cross found the head of the Wednesday centre forward, John Ritchie, who calmly scored.

To make matters worse, Wolves were two down four minutes later as McCalliog drew the Wolves defence, went to the byline and crossed for Wednesday winger Irvine, standing totally unmarked, to neatly flick the ball past a beaten Boswell. As the half-time whistle went, the murmurs turned to boos as the home team left the field. The lads sat back in their seats.

"Think we should have stayed in the South Bank," said Phil.

"Not much atmosphere here, is there," replied Adrian. "At least in the South Bank there's a lot of noise whether it's from the away fans or wisecracks from the home supporters. Can't say I would want to do this every game. Nice to try it but back standing for me on Boxing Day. Brian won't worry he missed this one. It's been very poor from Wolves."

"Yes. McGarry will need to work his magic over half-time," said Phil. After they had read through their programmes, both teams came out for the second half with few cheers from the home fans. Unfortunately, anything that the manager might have said went out of the window as Wednesday scored their third goal, just two minutes after the restart.

Again, McCalliog was involved as his corner flew right over Boswell who seemed rooted to the ground, leaving Ritchie with the easiest of finishes to give him his second headed goal of the game. After that, it was all over and, despite missing a couple of chances, Wolves didn't seem to have any answers to the tight defensive marking that had kept both Derek Dougan and Frank Wignall very quiet most of the afternoon.

Many supporters started to leave with 10 minutes to go, but both Phil and Adrian saw it through until the final whistle, as they knew Joe would do the same in the South

Bank and they had arranged to meet him by the 'man on the `oss' before going home. When they met, Joe's face was like thunder.

"What was Boswell doing? Did he think he was blinkin' Father Christmas, giving away three goals like that?" snapped Joe. "Call himself a goalie. He couldn't catch a cold and once they knew he was useless at crosses they just rained them in. Surprised we didn't lose by more. Hope big Phil is fit soon. Boy, we could have done with him between the sticks today."

"The Doog would have been better – at least he knows how to jump," joined in Adrian.

"You both down at Venturers this evening, fellas?" he continued.

"Can't say I fancy it today after that display. It's made me real crookid," said Joe.

"Not for me either. It's the second evening of carol singing for my church choir," said Phil. "Club will have to do without me – family orders!"

"Probably won't go either then," said Adrian. "I'm off to get the number 46. See you both after Christmas."

"Hope Father Christmas is as generous to you as the Wolves were today," jested Joe as he left too, leaving Phil crossing over to wait for his bus home to Penn.

He felt somewhat empty after such a lifeless and disappointing display that afternoon but he knew that the carol singing that evening would, as ever, cheer him up and that, if the sumptuous food on offer was as good as it normally was, then the day would end on a high.

The annual St Aiden's church choir carol singing, in the week running up to Christmas, had become both a tradition and a celebration. Since Phil's parents had decided that the mission church was more to their liking than the parish church, both Phil and Matt had been ever-present in the choir.

It had always been an all-boys choir, mainly because the then choirmaster expressed the opinion that young girls' voices were too shrill and thus a male-voice choir would always be better. Not everyone agreed with this but, by the mid-sixties, an assorted collection of Penn lads was not only one of the stand-out choirs in the town but had also cemented youthful friendships that then also involved their parents in many of the choir's activities.

Throughout the year, if anyone – parents, siblings, friends, etc – needed to know where any members of the choir were, all you had to do was to go round the back of the mission church where, from September to May, a large expense of grass would host everlasting football games nearly every weekday of the school holidays. After hours of play, score lines of 29 against 26 were not unusual, and half-time was usually a break for lunch. Fully refreshed, the game would then restart and was normally friendly unless Phil and Matt were on opposite sides.

In the summer months, cricket would take precedence, with a Polish lad called Slim always chosen first when the sides were picked. His surname was Slyminski, which none of the lads could pronounce. None of them knew his first name. He was just known as Slim and he could spin bowl better than anyone else, often sending down a leg-break or a googly to beat even Graham, who was probably the best batsman.

Slim called these unbeatable deliveries his 'cheesy ones' and, if he was on your side, you usually won. The only person who seemed to be able to get the better of him was Rachel, who occasionally turned up, much to the annoyance of most of the lads, not because she was a girl but because she was actually much better at cricket than most of them.

Throughout the year, there were many events that would involve the lads from the choir. The grass needed regular mowing and their roster helped to keep the greensward available not only for their sporting assignations but also the Easter fete, the summer fete, the outside harvest festival, and never forgetting the early November celebration that was bonfire night.

Work on this last event began in early October with planks, broken furniture, cardboard, branches, boxes of leaves, and anything that was combustible being stacked at the top of the church field, far away from the building itself, just in case anyone unconnected with the church fancied an unwanted early blaze.

The most important item to be found was at least one discarded chair, to sit poor old Guy Fawkes on before he went up in flames on the night. He would be made out of discarded clothes, pillowcases, newspapers and straw, stitched together to form a figure, added to which was a painted mask. Sometimes more than one guy was constructed and so two seats or a battered sofa would be needed for both revolutionary conspirators.

It was always a splendid night, with over 20 adults present to deliver a lengthy firework display involving sparkling silver fountains, glittering golden rain and shimmering cascades. There would be volcanos, Egyptian pyramids as well as Mount Vesuvius erupting alongside snowstorms, traffic lights and rising suns.

Later in the evening would come the lads' favourites, the much noisier jack-in-the-boxes, mine of serpents, air bombs and the enduring Roman candles, whilst several dads tried to blacken the chestnut trees at the side of the field with Catherine wheels, whirligigs and airplanes.

Rockets would whoosh into the sky temporarily adding a few more stars to the night and some lads would light a jumping jack to frighten the younger children, as that firework always seemed to have a mind of its own and certainly no sense of direction.

With the large number of fireworks that materialised on the night, there was never any need to collect a 'penny for the guy'. Despite efforts by many choirboys to 'play with fire', there was constant adult observance on the state of the bonfire, even down to making sure it was safe at the end of the evening and fully out, come dawn the next morning.

To say the adults enjoyed the evening more than their offspring may have been a slight exaggeration although not misplaced. There was also an abundance of good warming food ranging from soup, sausage rolls, baked potatoes, pasties and sausages, to iced buns and cakes, including a ginger cake, called parkin, with squash or flasks of tea or coffee to wash it all down.

Nobody went away feeling cold or hungry that evening or without experiencing plenty of oohs and aahs from the pyrotechnic display, amateur perhaps in its conception but always with safety uppermost and entertainment guaranteed.

The togetherness of this congregation was most apparent just before Christmas when the choir would set out in the streets adjacent to the mission church to raise money for charity by carol singing. None of the parents sang or accompanied them but the resting places on each night were at the homes of many of the choristers.

They met at the front of the mission church in Mount Road at 7 p.m. that Saturday. Most of the choir were there – very few would miss this evening of singing and eating, mainly because of the latter. By now, Phil was singing bass parts for many of the carols but he knew all the other voices, from soprano to alto to tenor because, over the past seven years, as his voice had broken, he had moved from the front to the rear of the choirstalls.

Matt and Ian had both re-joined the choir, on their return from university, adding to the other bass voices of Phil and John Shakespeare, with Slim, Graham, Rob and Wynn singing tenor. This quintet had been with Phil from his first days in the choir and they all knew who could handle which solo best or make the most of a difficult tenor descant. New lads, mostly trebles and altos, were still a bit green about the gills and nervous about singing in public but the older lads, especially Matt and Ian, were there to look after them, *in loco parentis*, as Phil's mum would say, especially when it came to going into any pubs in the area.

Walking up Westbourne Road, they stopped under the second streetlight and Steven, the new choirmaster, instructed them to turn to page seven and begin by singing 'Whilst shepherds watched their flocks by night'. Matt and Ian, the two oldest, went door to door to collect for this year's charity, which was Shelter, a fairly new organisation campaigning to end homelessness.

This being the seventh year in a row the choir had done this, most locals were very welcoming and so the collecting tins soon filled with loose change. A further carol, 'Hark the herald angels sing', gave more value for their donation before they moved on to the junction with Goldthorn Avenue. On the corner, as 'We three kings' and 'Once in royal David's city' boomed out into the cold night, curtains twitched, and lights came on in porches.

Then, over to The Battle of Britain pub in Birchwood Road, where many callow choirboys marvelled at their first time in the public bar. They sang the heartier well-known carols 'Good King Wenceslas' and 'God rest ye merry gentlemen' before moving into the snug to sing 'Away in a manger' and 'O little town of Bethlehem' for the ladies. Matt, Ian and Steven were offered half of mild, by the landlord by which time the collecting tins were much heavier.

Back out into the street and the cold, and the short stroll into Westminster Avenue for the first festive feast of the evening, and what a starter this would be at the home of the celebrated Mrs Shakespeare's apple pies.

Well, certainly legendary amongst the St Aiden's choristers and definitely by Phil. And, as is well known, all choristers are expected to sing for their supper, so the avenue's residents were regaled with 'In the bleak midwinter' and 'It came upon a midnight clear'.

Mrs Shakespeare hadn't let them down. Gallons of pop, sandwiches, crisps and the crowning glory, her apple pies. There were mince pies too, but Phil didn't like them, so he had two of the apple variety instead. They absolutely melted in the mouth and their taste was divine, full of lovely fruit.

As he looked for a third, Steven said it was time to move on, so the Shakespeare's kitchen returned to its usual Saturday evening peace, having satisfied well over a dozen hungry mouths. The contented choral crocodile was then led back to Birchwood Road where they huddled under another streetlight to give renditions of 'O come all ye faithful' and 'The First Noel'.

Empty collecting tins had been given to Matt and Ian, the full ones left for Bill Shakespeare to look after, and as they called on houses the donations matched the standard of the choir's efforts. Turning back down Mount Road they again gave extra gusto to 'The holly and the ivy' and 'We saw three ships', before crossing over to sing 'O come, O come Emmanuel' and 'Joy to the world' outside the Simbert's house.

There they were invited in for warm soup and savouries such as pork pie, scotch eggs, sausage rolls and vol-au-vents. Most of the young choristers avoided the latter being unsure of what was in the filling, but Phil and Matt marvelled at how delicious Mrs Simbert's pastry was, compared with their mum's.

Again, fully refreshed and with all the required amenities used at their second stop of the evening, the choir moved further up Mount Road. As they left, Graham's sister, Jane, came up to Phil and unexpectedly gave him a kiss on the cheek. The lads around him laughed and Phil blushed.

"Blast!" said Matt. 'That's two bob I owe Rachel. She bet me that you would get a kiss by the end of the evening. I didn't know that Jane would be in on it!"

"Expect they will share the bet between them," replied Phil. "Still, it could have been worse. It could've been Graham that kissed me!"

"Too right," said Matt. "Mind you if Rachel had organised that, I would have given her half a crown."

Phil landed a good-natured punch on his brother's arm as they gathered around the next prearranged streetlamp, near the junction of Mount Road and Muchall Road. 'See amid the winter's snow' and 'Angels from the realms of glory' could be heard in all their wonder at what was the top-most point of the choir's journey that evening.

At the end of the carol, Steven looked at the younger boys and realised they were flagging a bit, despite the excellent fare that had been laid before them, and devoured, that evening.

"Just a couple more to sing down Muchall Road before our final performance at Matt and Phil's house," he said and proceeded to lead them down the hill.

Phil had mixed emotions when they stopped bang outside the house of the girl on the bus. "Well, of course, we would," he muttered to himself. "It's where the streetlight is," which again he knew only too well having gazed up that road so many times.

Phil sang the bass parts to 'In Dulci Jubilo' and 'Ding dong! Merrily on high' but his thoughts were elsewhere.

"I don't even know her name. Our paths have only crossed once in over a year but why is it that when I think about her my mind becomes so befuddled," he wondered. "And what can I do about it? Talk to Matt I suppose. Definitely not Rachel! She would have a field day with that. But she might know who she is. There can't be much difference in their ages. Maybe she was in the same infants' class as her at Woodfield Avenue."

As the choir carefully crossed the Penn Road, still busy late into the evening, and onto the drive of Phil and Matt's house, the front door opened and their parents welcomed the choir, asking them to sing a couple of carols outside, for the neighbour's benefit, before coming inside. 'Good Christian men rejoice' was followed by 'I saw three ships' before Steven said they would round off the evening with the customary 'Silent night'.

Then they all piled into the warmth of the front room, for cocoa and biscuits, mostly chocolate, including Phil's favourites, Wagon Wheels and Tunnock's chocolate tea cakes. Again, there was very little left when Steven thanked Phil's parents for their kindness and said it was about time he saw the younger lads home.

"I will make sure Bill gets the remaining collecting tins to tot up the evening's offerings," said Dad. "Looks as if you have done even better than last year, Steven. Well done."

"Most people said they wanted to support the charity. I think the BBC Play 'Cathy Come Home', on TV earlier this year, made many more people aware of the homelessness problem and the work Shelter has started to do," explained Ian.

"No one should be homeless in this day and age," said Dad. "Especially at Christmas."

Mum agreed as she and Rachel began to say goodnight to everyone.

"You not giving Graham a kiss goodnight?" asked Phil, with a knowing grin.

"Certainly not," replied Rachel. "But I bet I'm two bob better off."

Chapter 8 - Surround yourself with Sorrow

Christmas 1968 was a white one, with heavy snow falling across a large part of the country overnight on Christmas Eve and into Christmas morning. Across the Black Country, between four and ten inches of snow had fallen, with the weather remaining icy cold well past the New Year, and the slushy white landscape lasting for days.

After the Christmas Day festivities, Phil decided he needed Matt's thoughts on his dilemma. They had both stayed up late on Boxing Day to watch 'Match of the Day' on TV, but the weather had put pay to pretty well all the day's fixtures, including the Wolves home game against Coventry. The rest of the family had gone to bed, full of chicken and ham leftovers, mince pies and yule log, so it seemed as good a time as any for a chat.

"I had pretty well the same problem with a girl who lived in Coalway Avenue," said Matt. "She went to the girls' high school and I was at the grammar. I saw her on the bus most days, to and from school, but she was always with a group of other girls. I had no reason to go to her house, or down her road, so I decided that I would just bide my time."

"And wait for what?" asked Phil impatiently. "What happened?"

"Not a lot for a while and then we were both waiting for a bus in town one day," replied Matt. "And I asked her if I could help her with her satchel as she was loaded down with books, and we began to chat on the bus."

"What happened after that?" enquired Phil.

"Well, we went to the pictures a few times and took a few walks over Penn Common, but then I went off to Oxford and we stopped seeing each other and that was that really," explained Matt.

"Not much of a romance then?" said Phil.

"I suppose I'm not much of the romantic type," remarked Matt. "Are you?"

"I haven't really had much chance to find out," said Phil as he slumped back in his chair in the lounge. "So, you think I should just wait and then the opportunity will arise?"

"If it's meant to, it will," said Matt. "It's known as kismet."

"What? Nowhere near kissing anyone yet, except Jane last weekend and that wasn't any of my doing," said Phil.

"Not kissing – kismet, you twerp," said Matt. "It means fate, fortune or destiny. Whatever will be, will be."

"You've come back from Oxford with a lot of new words and ideas, Bruv," said Phil. "Sometimes I wonder whether it's English you are studying, up at New College, rather than chemistry?"

"You'll find out that there's a heck of a lot more to life at uni than just studying, Phil. You'll find that out for yourself in a year or so, and, by then, this girl across the road will be just a distant memory," said Matt.

"Just a couple of things wrong with that," replied Phil. "As nothing has happened, there won't be anything to remember or forget, and secondly, the rate I am going at school, I'll be working in a bank, rather than going to university."

Matt stated the obvious. "Not going well then?"

"My end-of-term report wasn't as good as it should be and a lot was written about making steady improvement next term to have any chance of good grades, though I have been predicted a B in maths, same in chemistry and a C in physics," said Phil.

"Good enough to get into most red brick unis," replied Matt. "But you will need at least two As to do scholarship level for Oxbridge."

"I know – you got two As and a B didn't you," said Phil with a sigh.

"Well, if your youth club footie team can improve, then maybe so can you," said Matt encouragingly.

"With the exams, it will be just me and only me though. It ain't a team effort," said Phil. "Anyhow, St Aiden's aren't as bad as they were at the beginning of the season and we've started winning the occasional game."

"Any chance of me having a game for them before I go back?" asked Matt.

"Depends how long this cold weather lasts," replied Phil. "No problem fitting you into the team, but I can't see the Mount Road pitch being playable for a week or two. When do you go back down to New College?"

"Not until late in January, but Dad wants me to help him clear the coal bunkers at the back of the garage. Says they are redundant now we have central heating and, if we knock the low walls down, he will have more room for bicycles and the like, which means the garden shed won't be so cluttered," said Matt.

"I'll help with that!" said Phil. "Sounds like more fun than reading or revising."

"It might well be, but Mum and Dad will want to see you with your nose in those textbooks before you go back to school next week, so I would suggest you forget about this girl, the Wolves, St Aiden's next game and anything else at the moment," said Matt.

"Guess you're right," sighed Phil.

"Let's get off to bed now, ready for revision for you in the morning," continued Matt, although he knew that was about as likely as the recent snow disappearing overnight.

Matt was spot on about one thing though. St Aiden's Youth Club FC had improved. Mind you, from the start they had had, it would have been difficult to get any worse. Very few teams lose their very first competitive game by

14 goals, the score being 17-3, and many of the side were surprised they had actually scored three.

The idea of setting up their own football team had come about after a lengthy day's footie game at the back of the church in early September. Phil thought it was Wynn's idea. Wynn was sure that Rob had suggested it. Only John said that it was nothing to do with him.

They approached some of their dads about how to go about it and they offered to do the initial paperwork as long as the boys ran it themselves from then on. Paul's father, Jim Barnwell, worked for the town council and reckoned he could get them the Mount Road pitch as their home ground. John's dad, Bill Shakespeare, was an accountant and said he would look after any money matters. Phil's father, being a lay preacher in the parish, reckoned he could get it approved by the parish council as representing the church youth club.

So, before the local youth club league began in October, St Aiden's mission church had its first-ever youth club – in name only really – as it was just a device for the lads to meet after choir practice on a Friday evening and select a team to play the following afternoon. To make it look more plausible, an old table tennis table had been donated, without any bats, and Phil's dad seized the opportunity to get rid of the quarter-sized snooker table from home, with cues and snooker balls.

Subs were paid weekly so that records were kept correctly, and any new players, introduced to the team were told that the weekly subs also acted as their match fee, so everything was above board. Wynn was elected captain and Phil became the club secretary, attending league secretaries meeting once a month at the Youth Service HQ, at the town end of the Penn Road, next door to what was the Midland Counties Dairy, now owned by Unigate.

These meetings were rather daunting for Phil as he was by far the youngest to attend by many decades – most of those present had been involved with youth clubs and their football teams for donkey's years. This was all very new to Phil, so he sat at the back and said nothing, taking a few notes, and making sure he came away with any dates for extra fixtures such as the cup games.

St Aiden's Youth Club FC joined the lowest of the three leagues run across town. Some away games were over in Tettenhall or Wednesfield or even in Low Hill where Matt had done his Christmas student post stint, telling Phil it wasn't an experience he was keen to repeat. When they played there, they reckoned that coming away well beaten was maybe the safer option!

That first-ever game was deeply etched in their collective memory. When it came to picking their very first 11, they all thought they knew their best positions. John and Wynn were to play at full-back, Phil centre-half, Graham and Pete at right and left half respectively, and youngsters Paul and Mark as wingers. Slim said he wanted to play centre-forward, and Rob, with young William, made up the outfield 10 as inside forwards. However, they had no one to play in goal, a position that remained vacant until the morning of their first game. In hindsight, it perhaps should have stayed vacant!

It was Rob who brought Stuart along, saying he had told him he'd been asked to go for a trial with division 3 side, Walsall FC, as a goalkeeper. By half-time, St Aiden's were 9-1 down and it was obvious to all that Stuart hadn't had a great deal of success at his trial. He was next to useless.

It wasn't all his fault though, as many of the lads agreed afterwards on the journey home. As a team, they had misjudged the step up from playing on a small patch of grass behind a church to a full-sized football pitch. Some of them had played together in teams at school but never all 11 as a team before, so they were not always sure where teammates would be positioned or what to expect from each other.

Add to this the fact that the opposition – Ashmore Park Rangers – were bigger, better, and more organised, having been in the league for a few years, and the realisation that they had been hammered was possibly a tad easier to accept. They were encouraged by the fact they had scored three goals on their first outing, although they all agreed that Slim was maybe not quite of the same class as the Doog and maybe better at cricket than footie.

Over the coming autumn months, the team began to play better and, although they lost their first six games on the trot, and were rooted to the bottom of the league, by the end of November they had found a new goalkeeper who could actually catch a cross and then take a goal kick that went past the halfway line. Mates from school joined as new players – they never had to attend the youth club, just pay their subs – and finally, they managed a respectable 1-1 draw against St Chads in Tettenhall.

By the time the first half of the season had been completed, their first win at home, on a cold and wintry December afternoon, was celebrated as if they had won the actual FA Cup and, as they returned to their changing rooms at Manor Road Secondary Modern School, there was talk of greater success after Christmas. Much of this was down to introducing Dave, as goalkeeper, Pete, a stylish midfield player and Roy, at centre-forward, who really thought he was playing for the celebrated comic-strip team, Melchester Rovers.

Roy may have not been the most mobile of centre-forwards but he could really thump the ball, causing many slighter lads to move smartly out of the way if he cannoned a free kick goalward. Pete was a magnificent passer of the ball, often finding the young lads, Paul and Mark, out on the wing ready to cross for Roy to head goalward.

These new players made better players out of the Aiden's originals and the team began to play with more confidence. Soon, instead of dreading the next fixture, the players really began to look forward to it. Obviously, some only played when others were unavailable or injured, but many, like Slim, were quite happy with this as they just liked to be involved. After that first game, they never saw Stuart again and no one ever bothered to ask him to pay his subs!

Phil really enjoyed trying to be like his Wolves defensive heroes, David Woodfield and Frank Munro, his only regret being that he no longer accompanied Adrian, Joe and Brian to Molineux on many Saturday afternoons. Instead, he chose to be out in all weathers trying, with 10 other lads, to play for each other and get a win to move them up from the bottom rungs of the third division of the Wolverhampton and District Youth Club league.

The festive cold snap continued to cause games to be postponed well into the new year, with Wolves' supporters missing out on a trip to Everton. However, it then turned out to be the mildest January for many years. Councils pitches were pronounced fit to play and so both St Aiden's and Wolves got back into action, with mixed success in both instances.

Matt got his game, helping St Aiden's to a narrow 2-1 home win against Compton Youth Club before he returned to Oxford, and Wolves put Hull out of the FA Cup in early January. They followed this with a narrow 1-0 home win over struggling Nottingham Forest, before the wintry weather returned to London in mid-January, resulting in the West Ham game also being called off.

Wolves then had a string of away fixtures, with Spurs beating them in the fourth round of the Cup before the re-arranged Everton fixture ended up as a 4-0 away thrashing for the Wanderers at Goodison Park. Wolves managed to draw at home 1-1 with Burnley before the arctic weather closed in again in early February, resulting in even more games being postponed, both in division 1 and in the local youth club league.

So, on Saturday, 15th February, Phil awoke with little idea whether he would be either playing or watching football that day. The previous week had been typically uneventful with the exception of a mysterious postal delivery on the Friday, February 14th, Valentine's Day.

Phil was usually well out of the house before the postman arrived, by which time he would be cycling through Penn Fields, down Jeffcock Road to the corner of Bantock Park, before racing down Merridale Road to get to school on time. Even if the postman had been very early, Phil wouldn't have bothered to check as there was rarely any post for him.

That Friday was the exception to the rule when a pristine white envelope, with neat handwriting on it, showed clearly that this was addressed to him and only him. Later that day, Mum presented it to him over the tea table, as surprised as he was that he had received what seemed to be a card, especially as his birthday wasn't until June.

As Phil opened it his face immediately reddened. It was a Valentine's card. On the front were two teenagers, drawn cartoon style, drinking from straws placed in fizzy drink bottles with the message at the top of the card '*Just thought I would 'POP' the question*' and at the base '*Will you be my Valentine?*'. Inside, under the Happy Valentine's Day message, was simply written 'From J'.

Phil glared at Rachel across the tea table.

"Is this your idea of a joke?" stuttered Phil.

"What?" replied Rachel. "No idea what you're on about."

"Oh no," continued Phil, his face now even redder with annoyance than embarrassment. "So, if it wasn't enough for you and Jane to play that kissing trick on me before Christmas, and win your bet with Matt, the two of you have now gone and sent me a Valentine's Card as a wind-up!"

"No, we haven't!" exclaimed Rachel. "I wouldn't waste money on you. The cost of the card and the stamp wouldn't be worth it, even if it has obviously wound you up. I don't know anything about THAT card and neither does Jane, so belt up."

"That's enough from the both of you," said Mum. "Neither of you are too old to be sent to your rooms for the rest of the day, so eat your tea and let's hear no more about it. Put the card in your room Phil and calm down."

Phil did as he was told then returned to the kitchen with absolutely no appetite after being, as he thought, the butt of a prank perpetrated by his sister and her best friend. He would be off the choir practice in an hour or so and would grill Jane's brother, Graham, to see what he knew and ask him to let him know if Jane asked any unusual questions about him over the next few days.

Phil heard about 11 the next morning that their game against Codsall Youth Club had been called off because their pitch was frozen and unsafe. It was just over a week ago that a really strong cold front had covered the country with snow again, with severe frosts at night. Most of the heavy snow was confined to Scotland and the north of England, but the temperatures stayed well below freezing, bringing the coldest and severest winter weather to the Midlands, with temperatures sinking to minus 20°C in some places.

A quick round of telephone calls confirmed that the usual individuals would be at Molineux that afternoon. Regular meeting time and place agreed, Phil asked Mum if he could have a quick early lunch as he wanted to get into town as, he reckoned, the buses wouldn't be running to the normal timetable because of the weather and there would be a really large crowd with Wolves at home to Manchester United.

Bill McGarry, Wolves manager, had wanted the game postponed but the referee, John Homewood, had inspected the pitch at lunchtime and pronounced it fit to play. Phil got off the bus at Victoria Street, dashed straight into Beatties, and spent an hour in the warmth of their record department once again, listening to a few tracks from groups he had heard recently on Radio 1.

Phil's weekend habits had now become faithfully established around the radio shows on which he knew the latest and most remarkable singles and album tracks would be played. He wasn't particularly interested in the chart hits, which would get regular plays throughout the day, but more so on the tracks his favourite DJs played.

Ten till midday on Saturday morning was the usual lunacy with Kenny Everett 'with his Grannyphone', as advertised in the *Radio Times*. Then, as Phil was getting ready to go out on Saturday evenings, he could enjoy a new one-hour show, hosted by Pete Drummond, who featured an impressive progressive music playlist, similar to John Peel's *Top Gear*, which was another dedicated listen on a Sunday afternoon, whilst he was supposedly doing revision.

If Phil was minded to do his revision on a Sunday morning, then the radio would again be tuned to 247 metres medium wave to listen to Dave Symonds, from ten until midday, another radio presenter who went out of his way to find music that was more psychedelic and progressive than standard pop.

In fact, Phil was beginning to become somewhat spoilt for radio choices, with Radio 1 presenting more and more shows featuring the type of music he liked. The DJs introduced him to new bands, solo artists and pop music trends that would have passed him by if it wasn't for his ardent listening. Certainly, Radio Luxembourg never had such a variety of shows, and presenters, some of whom seemed to love to introduce their listeners to new music.

Many of these presenters began to mention that some bands were moving towards what was being described as 'concept' albums. These were LPs where the tracks would have a common narrative or theme. The Beatles had toyed with this idea with 'Sergeant Pepper's Lonely Hearts' Club Band', and the Beach Boys LP 'Pet Sounds' has also been called a concept album. The Moody Blues 'Days of future passed' LP may well have been the very first to have been recorded with orchestral accompaniment, but Phil didn't really think it was a concept album.

Bands who had enjoyed enormous chart success, like the Who, the Kinks and the Bee Gees, were working on similar projects; and one side of the experimental album, 'Ogden's Nut Gone Flake', by the Small Faces, was a modern fairy tale based on a character called 'Happiness Stan' and narrated by the comedian, Stanley Unwin. It was all very new, often very strange but to Phil very interesting and exciting.

The one concept album that caught Phil's ear was by the Pretty Things, not a band that had been one of his favourites up till then. Their initial heavy R&B style had changed fundamentally from the 'long-haired upstarts' band that had earned them a couple of top 20 hits in the mid-sixties to a more psychedelic and experimental sound.

Phil had become aware of this new sound from a couple of singles Martin had added to his treasured collection of psychedelic 45s. The first, released in 1967, was called 'Defecting Grey' and mirrored what many groups were doing at that time – using the psychedelia craze to write songs which had a variety of unusual sounds, tempos and styles. The second, in the spring of 1968, was called 'Talkin' about the Good Times', a zany mix of rock guitar, heavy drumming, mellotron backing, sitar solos and a brilliant harmony chorus. Phil loved both, and neither he nor Martin could understand why they hadn't been massive hits.

Then, from November 1968, many of his favourite radio shows began to play their new double A-side single, 'Private Sorrow/Balloon Burning' which had been promoted in the music press as 'Two sides of Sorrow'. This single was a taster for their forthcoming album, entitled 'S.F. Sorrow', made up of 13 tracks, chronicling the life of Sebastian F. Sorrow – born around the end of the 19th century, who went to work in a 'small town just eight miles from everywhere', then off to war, before emigrating to America, losing the love of his life and finally enduring total madness and the loneliness of old age.

Phil was not so struck by the story more by the style of the songs, the melodies and the harmonies, which involved all the band, together with the diverse approaches that each song seemed to have. He thought that this was definitely psychedelic rock. Or was it progressive rock? He didn't really care as the more tracks he heard, the more he wanted to hear.

The LP didn't have the smooth harmonies of the Zombies, or the jingle-jangle of the Byrds, or the sunshine of the Beach Boys. There was a grittiness to the sound that Phil really enjoyed. The band were experimenting with different sound effects and techniques, using these to create soundscapes like backward guitar sections, not dissimilar to the Beatles on 'Strawberry Fields Forever', possibly Phil's favourite single of the past decade.

The LP, as a whole, had a massive impact on him. It had harmonies and melodies which were often mixed with savage lead vocals and heavy rock guitar riffs, but it worked. There was a really dark nature to the songs – about death, depression, loneliness – but the overall sound had a beauty, a resonance, a charm.

Phil thought it was a brilliant album which included some folkish elements, whilst exploring a path from their blues roots to new psychedelia and intermingling hard rock guitar riffs with strange but delightful vocal arrangements. Compared with the sharp three-minute bursts of pop vagueness that filled the charts, it was exuberant, ambitious and innovative – and Phil considered it a masterpiece.

He discussed the album with Martin, 'the fountain of all pop music knowledge', who pointed out that the producer was Norman Smith. Phil had never heard of him. Martin said he was responsible for the clever sound of the recent Pink Floyd singles, and their first album 'The Piper at the Gates of Dawn' and had supposedly played bongos with the Beatles once! Phil had no idea where all this knowledge came from, but those specific nuggets of pop trivia explained the exceptional sound on this record.

So, from its release in mid-December, Phil was back infuriating the sales assistants in any record department he could find, including the recently opened HMV Records in the new Mander Centre, to listen to as many tracks on this LP as possible. Each track persuaded him that this was the next record to buy and include in his small but eclectic album collection so that he could enjoy listening to it over and over again.

It wasn't until he had actually had the gatefold LP cover to read that he was able to see the full story of the hero unfolding, as the band included short informative narrative paragraphs between the songs in the liner notes. "If this is what a concept album is", he mused, "I hope there will be plenty more like it."

When Phil had thawed out, happily listening to music in Beatties basement, he knew that the other lads would be assembling in Queen Square ready to slip and slide down to the Molineux for today's game. He walked up to the statue to find no one there. Glancing at his watch, he was surprised that he was first to get there and annoyed that he could have heard another track from the debut LP from Robert Plant's new band.

Soon enough though, Joe sauntered up Lichfield Street; Brian appeared from Darlington Street, and Adrian from Dudley Street and they were ready to cross St Peter's Market car park to join the long queues to get into the game, with Brian taking his seat in the Molineux Street stand as usual.

The visit of Manchester United could always guarantee a big crowd and, even though their form had taken a dip this season, there was still a certain anticipation of an exciting game to come.

"Any predictions for today?" asked Joe.

"Size of the crowd or the score?" answered Phil.

"They'll be over 40,000 here today, they reckon, and as usual half of them will be in the South Bank with us," replied Joe. "Still a full crowd will keep us warm. I reckon Wolves to win, 2-0."

"Think it might be tighter than that," Phil replied. "2-1 to the Wanderers with new boy Hughie Curran getting the winner, I reckon."

"Yeh, could be," said Joe. "Really not sure why Wolves got rid of Frank Wignall to Derby, but Curran looks like a similar player and was Norwich's player of the season last year. Is he playing with the Doog up front, Ade?"

"Looks like it in the programme," said Adrian. "Doog at nine, Curran at ten, with Waggy and Mike Kenning putting the crosses in for them, whilst Knowles and Bailey will pull the strings in midfield."

"Still, David Woodfield's back in defence That's a real bonus but I don't understand why McGarry has Frank Munro down as sub – he's real class!" said Phil.

"Yeh, but Woodfield and Holsgrove are so used to playing together at the back," said Joe. "McGarry's always going to go for that."

As the first half got under way, it was obvious that the cold and icy pitch made it difficult to play sweeping passes without falling on your backside, although both teams adjusted to the conditions fairly quickly.

Peter Knowles dominated the midfield – not easy when you are playing against international legends such as Bobby Charlton and George Best – and seemed to play with much more composure than his opposition counterparts. Wolves were soon on top, forcing United into unaccustomed errors, resulting in the Wolves first goal just before the half-hour mark.

Wolves skipper, Mike Bailey, pressured United into losing the ball, then crossed the ball for Hugh Curran to hook it towards goal. Their goalkeeper, Alex Stepney, could only parry it and there was Derek Dougan to head back into the empty net. The crowd erupted and the lads were glad to cheer and energetically jump up and down in celebration, on the cold, icy terraces.

Wolves continued to dominate the play in the remainder of the first half and got their deserved reward just before half-time, as Curran scored on his home debut, tapping in to make it 2-0. The Wanderers went in at the interval with their heads held high, with the Wolves supporters as happy as Larry, chanting 'We want six', somewhat optimistically as Wolves had rarely scored more than two all season.

"Don't suppose you told your dad what games to choose on his pools coupon for today, Joe?" asked Phil with a grin, knowing he couldn't have done that at home where, in his parents' eyes, even doing a pools coupon was regarded as gambling. "You're spot on with the score and I said the new boy would score today. Not bad, eh?"

"Them really playing well," replied Joe. "Wolves have adjusted to the pitch and the conditions much better than United. Mind you, it's only half-time. We can't have a repeat of last season, can we?"

"You never can tell," chipped in Adrian, with his usual pessimism.

And he was disappointingly right as within two minutes of the restart, three Wolves defenders had every opportunity to clear the ball. All failed and Bobby Charlton took the opportunity to nip in and clip it into the Wolves net just inside the post giving Phil Parkes no chance. Joe was livid.

"That's exactly what happened last time out," he railed. "We are so slow after the break. What was happening in our defence? They just left it to each other and Charlton's far too capable and experienced to pass up such a gift. Another like that and we might lose to them AGAIN!"

The goal gave United belief and it really became a game of two distinct halves, with the visitors now very much on top. Twenty-three minutes into the second half, it was Best who scored the equaliser, with a skimming header from a Brian Kidd cross, after the Wolves midfield had given the ball away.

"We'll be lucky to come away with a point," said Joe. "Yow've put the 'fluence on them, Ade! How can they play so well in the first half and then be so poor in the second?"

Wolves held on to a draw and surprisingly nearly got the winner in the final minutes when Hugh Curran controlled the ball brilliantly and then beat Stepney with a terrific shot, only to be given offside.

"Curran's fitted in really well," said Phil, but Joe was already in one of his sulks.

"I can't believe we let them back into the game like that," he grumbled. "That's the third time we have been ahead against United in three years and we've never won."

"At least we came away with a point today," replied Adrian. "And we nearly won it at the end."

Joe glowered at Adrian and stomped off up the terraces with the other supporters.

"Doubt if he'll be coming over to Venturers this evening whilst he's got a cob on like that," continued Adrian. "Who have they got on, anyway?"

"Brian said it was The Montanas. They've been trying to book them for yonks," replied Phil. "They're reckoned to be one of the best local bands around. Better than the Calis, N' Betweens or Finders Keepers but not up your street, Ade. They won't be doing the bluesy stuff you like."

"Doubt they'll play the psychedelic stuff you and Martin are into either. Still, it should be a good evening," said Adrian as they parted company at the end of North Street to catch their buses home. Although not quite as dispirited as Joe, both were glad to get home as quickly as possible, stand in front of a cosy fire, have a bite of tea and a long warm bath before getting ready for the club that evening.

Joe didn't make it to the youth club that evening. Neither did Spud, Angie, Coops or any of the usual Wednesfield contingent. The weather, and hence the unpredictable bus timetable, meant that getting across town might be achievable but getting home less likely. Phil had walked gingerly down Wells Road and Pinfold Lane, suitably attired with anorak, scarf and gloves on this very cold February evening.

He met Adrian outside the Penn Cinema, as arranged, before joining the queue at Springdale Methodist Church to enter the youth centre for yet another Saturday evening's enjoyment.

"Is it just me getting older or is the queue full of young 'uns?" asked Phil.

"Seems like it," replied Adrian. "Maybe they're all Monts fans?"

"Could be," said Phil. "They've been one of the most popular bands in the Midlands for some years now. Brian was chuffed to book them tonight."

They paid their two-bob entrance fee and were pleased to find that the caretaker had put the heating on full blast earlier that evening. They both offloaded their coats onto Janice in the cloakroom.

"You're going to be busy this evening, Janice," said Phil. "Big crowd and everyone's wrapped up well tonight. You OK?"

"Yes thanks, Phil," Janice replied. "Save me a dance later, will ya?"

"Might well do that," smiled Phil, and he and Adrian went off to find Martin.

As always, he had collared one of the band to talk about music. This time it was the Montanas' lead singer Johnny Jones who, like Martin, was an avid reader of the music press, mainly the *Melody Maker* and the *New Musical*

Express. They were deep in discussion as the two lads approached.

"Evening Mart," said Phil. "All good?" Adrian nodded and said nothing.

"Yeh," replied Martin, "Just catching up with Johnny before the band get on stage. He's been telling me that some of their singles reached the charts in some areas of the States and had done pretty well – better than over here – but no one got that information back to their management or they wouldn't have been here tonight – they would've been touring America!"

"Our gain then," said Phil although Johnny agreed to differ and went off to get ready with the rest of the band. The roadies, Micky and Keith, had set up the instruments, microphones and amplifiers on the raised rostrum at the far end of the hall, and ten minutes later the band members began to amble across to test out their kit.

The Montanas had been around since 1964, quickly establishing themselves as one of the best local live bands, performing remarkably accurate versions of the chart hits of the day whilst releasing close harmony singles of their own which were on a par with the Fortunes or the Searchers. Their ability to do close harmonies so well meant they could faithfully cover American hits from the Beach Boys, the Four Seasons or the Association.

They had done some live radio appearances on 'Saturday Club', 'Easybeat' and the 'Radio One Club', where their singles were often championed by DJs such as Brian Matthew.

A youth club like Venturers wasn't their usual venue, their regular residency being at the Cleveland Arms in Willenhall, as well as often playing the Civic Hall and many nightclubs across the northern cabaret circuit. But then they were managed by the legendary Roger Allen, known as the Black Country's Brian Epstein, who had also arranged overseas tours for the band in Holland, France and Germany.

In 1966, they did a UK tour with the Walker Brothers, like the Californians, and also with the Troggs. It was after this tour that the line-up changed, with a new drummer and bass player joining from other local bands, to become a five-piece band. Johnny was still their lead singer, together with all five harmonising on most songs. Bill Hayward played lead guitar and was an original band member, along with Johnny and Terry Rowley, who had begun as their bass player.

Terry had moved to keyboards and become the group's musical arranger when Roger Allen brought in Jake Elcock on bass. By far the youngest group member, at 18, was Graham Hollis who had replaced Graham Crew on drums. By now, they had developed into one of the most proficient bands in the local area, both in the studio and performing live although somehow that hit record kept eluding them.

Their performance that evening showed their undoubted professional talent and experience. They impressively rattled through covers of current chart hits such as 'Listen to me' by the Hollies, 'Ob-la-di, Ob-la-da' by Marmalade, and 'Elenore' from the Turtles, before turning to one of their favourite artists, the Beach Boys to play 'Do it again'. The crowd at the club adored them, applauding each song and appreciating how they could replicate each chart success so faithfully, giving members the chance to dance throughout the evening.

"That was a number one last August," said Johnny. "Remember when it was really hot and sunny! Hope these songs are warming you up on this winter's evening. The next one was a single we released in 1967. Hope you like it."

The band played 'You've got to be loved' perfectly and followed it with more cover versions of the Love Affair's 'A day without love' and Manfred Mann's 'Fox on the run'. Phil, Martin and Adrian had been listening at the back of the hall.

"They're really good. Very professional but they don't seem to have much passion in their playing. It's all a bit cold, if that's the right word, on a day like today," said Phil.

"It is for this evening. You're not wrong. Johnny said that he was a bit fed up of just being thought of as a great covers band," replied Martin.

"Not my bag," said Adrian.

"Bag!?" replied Phil and Martin together.

"When did you start becoming hip, Ade?" asked Phil.

Johnny was up at the microphone again explaining that the group had written the next track and they performed 'Someday you'll be breaking my heart'. Again, the audience showed their appreciation and didn't seem to share the lads' thoughts on the evening's performance. To these teenagers, it was great music to dance and sing along to, as they all knew the words to the latest chart hits.

"This next song was a hit for the Dave Clark Five recently and was written by our Brummidgen mate, Raymond Froggatt," said Johnny. "Wish he'd write a hit for us."

'Red Balloon' was followed by another of the Monts' singles, 'Step in the right direction', and then they took a break. Martin, Adrian and Phil were already in the kitchen drinking a cuppa.

"You look as if you're about to say summat, Phil?" said Martin.

"I was just thinkin'. We've been coming here for over two years now," replied Phil.

"So what?" asked Martin.

"Joe and Ade are already 17 and I will be in June," continued Phil.

"Me, too, in May," said Martin. "But what's that got to do with the price of fish?"

"Haven't you noticed the crowd in tonight?" said Phil. "They're mostly the age we were when we first came here back in late 1966, 14 or 15 years old. Some of them younger. We've become the old men of the club!"

"Blimey, you're a cheery soul this evening," countered Martin. "And you're wrong. It's not about age, it's about the music. We haven't outgrown the club. It's just that our music tastes have changed."

"Yeh. Reckon you're right. Sorry to be a bit mardy," said Phil. "The Monts have started playing again and I did say I would have a dance with Janice."

"I reckon you're ok with her," said Adrian. "Why don't you ask her out? The way she looks at you, you're on to a cert there, mate."

"Nah, she's just a mate," replied Phil, slightly embarrassed.

"She could be the J in your Valentine's card," said Adrian, with a mischievous grin.

"Who told you about that?" asked Phil rather annoyed. Martin looked away sheepish.

"Anyway, Janice isn't her real name. She got called that once cos she sounds like the girl on 'Thank Your Lucky Stars' and she told me it just stuck. And a fine friend you turned out to be, Mart," said Phil, as he went back to the hall whilst the other lads enjoyed their wind-up.

Phil listened to the Monts remarkable versions of the Four Seasons 'C'mon Marianne', the Five American's 'Western Union' and the Association's 'Time for Livin'' as he danced with Janice, before taking her and his ticket back to the cloakroom. The Montanas might be one of the best local bands around but it just wasn't Phil's sort of music anymore.

"I'm off home, Ade," he said. "You'll have to find someone else to upset. I reckon the Monts are going to start playing the slow numbers pretty soon, for the young lovers to dance to. Good luck smooching on your tod!"

As he left, he heard the band sing the acapella first line of the Casuals' hit 'Jesamine'.

"Well, it's a nice name and it starts with a J, but I don't know any girls called that," he thought as he began his long walk home, with his feet crunching on the grit that had been spread along the pavements on that bitterly cold evening.

Chapter 9 - Tears in the wind

For the next seven weeks, up to Easter, the weather was not dissimilar to how Phil felt. Gloomy, overcast and a chilly cold front seemingly hanging over the whole of the Black Country. With high pressure in the north-east and low pressure in the south-east, the whole area had what seemed to be uninterrupted rain throughout March, with skies only brightening over the Easter weekend in early April.

Martin had been right. It wasn't the youth club that was the problem, it was the music. Saturday evenings, down on Warstones Road, were still worth looking forward to. Good company, meeting friends, making new ones, having lots of laughs and a pleasing feeling of belonging. The club still booked some of the best bands around, like Varsity Rag, Cats Eyes and Sight and Sound, all very professional and all able to replicate the hits currently in the chart. They just didn't play the sort of music that Phil, Martin or even Adrian now listened out for on Radio 1.

They had chatted about trying some of the newer clubs, such as The Catacombs and The Lafayette, that had opened in the centre of town last year, and which seemed to book bands who played more progressive or psychedelic music. However, those outings would have to wait for a while as, for all the lads, their main focus at the moment was revision for the A-level exams, starting in just six weeks after their return to school.

The atmosphere at home wasn't helping Phil either although it really wasn't anything to do with him. Phil's mum's father was very ill and unlikely to see out the summer. He had been suffering for some time and Phil had hardly spoken to him for quite a while, save for the standard greeting on visits to Grandad's home in Chesterfield.

Not that there was anything unusual in this as, from their very existence, grandchildren were neither to be seen nor heard, if Grandad had anything to do with it. It was never a warm, friendly or welcoming household. With Grandad's deterioration, visits were becoming more frequent, disturbing Phil's weekend plans and often resulting in Mum being even more tight-lipped in response to any enquiry about her father's health.

The gloom that accompanied such visits was difficult to lift, even though there were some happier memories for Phil to recall. Grandad always had an avid interest in sport and had taken both Phil and Matt, as youngsters, to Saltergate, the home of Chesterfield Football Club where, together with other long-standing supporters, known as Spireites, he would loudly inform the referee, in his broad Derbyshire brogue, as to how useless he was.

Neither Matt nor Phil would ever repeat the new words and phrases they learned on those terraces or say whether Grandad had uttered them. Even more happily, maybe a decade before, Easter trips sometimes included sunshine days spent at Queens Park in Chesterfield, watching Derbyshire County Cricket Club entertain, customarily, their local rivals, Yorkshire. Grandad would have a brown ale or two whilst the family enjoyed their picnic spread out on the car rug, by the boundary, at the lunchtime interval.

Although Phil's father championed Hampshire and, for some unexplained reason, Matt had decided to support Surrey, the cricket conversation was always good-natured, and the boys often found time to play either French cricket in the park, or, during spring showers, Owzthat, played in the back of Grandad's large Austin Cambridge, which both entertained and passed the time.

In past years, there had been fewer and fewer outings as Grandad's health, as well as his disposition, worsened. However, Phil hadn't forgotten that his own obsession with the wireless had also started during those Derbyshire family stopovers. When required to become unseen and unheard, he had found sanctuary in their staid and soulless front room where he had come across the wonders of a valve radio.

There he had all the time in the world to tune the wavelength dial to Hilversum, Budapest, Helsinki and, of course, Luxembourg. The radio was still there and so, on these protracted, despondent weekend visits before Easter, he would attempt to revise in that same sombre sanctuary, with Radio 1 playing music – quietly, of course.

Phil's mother had never grown up in an atmosphere where affection was evident or emotions openly discussed, so she dealt with the impending loss of her father in very much the same way. Her father had championed her at Chesterfield Girls' Grammar School, where she became head girl, and then she was the very first pupil from that town to gain entry to Cambridge University, something her father was immensely proud of.

Maybe Phil's dad could have shown her more support, but he had his own issues to deal with as, just over a year back, he had taken on his first headship at Graiseley Secondary Modern School. There could be no doubt that it was an important position, in terms of both career and salary, and to become a headmaster before he reached 40 had been a real achievement, although it also meant that he seemed to be at work a lot more than at home.

The school was situated in Penn Fields, which suggests a pleasing rural district of Wolverhampton. Not so. It was situated adjacent to the centre of town, close to many small factories and offices of major businesses, such as Tarmac and Unigate, which employed many of his pupils' parents. In the few years since it had opened, it had become the most multi-cultural school in the town, with a third of the students from Asian families, a third of Afro-Caribbean descent and the rest from England, Ireland and the Far East.

To say that dealing with all the different religions, languages, traditions and, unfortunately, differences in accepted behavioural norms was a challenge, would be something of an understatement. Phil's dad had got through those demanding early terms and, whilst things had settled down, it was still a daunting undertaking, especially from someone who passionately believed in the opportunities of comprehensive, rather than selective, education.

So, with Matt – known as 'number-one-son' in the family – being away at Oxford and Rachel out of the house most of the week, immersed in her various sporting activities, it wouldn't have taken the worst observer in the world to spot that, in the early part of 1969, there was something not quite right at home. And it wasn't the best environment to help Phil, at a time when he was going through such scholastic uncertainty and apprehension.

Phil wasn't sleeping well either. It could have been the anxiety of the approaching examinations or maybe it might be that life just wasn't happening the way he wanted it to. He dreamt more than usual and none of these dreams were heartening. There were dreams where he repeatedly turned over the exam paper to find that it was written in a language, he didn't recognise at all. It wasn't French, Latin or English, or even Gornalese.

Then, he would be standing on the terraces at a football match in just his swimming trunks. It wasn't cold and no one seemed to notice that he had practically nothing on. Conversations took place as normal, goals were scored, crowds cheered, whistles were blown, and it was very, very sunny. Warmth, like that, was rare at Molineux on Saturday afternoons.

Then he would be fully clothed again and walking along the far side of Penn Road towards home. The girl from up Muchall Road would be walking on the other side. If he tried to cross to her there was an endless stream of traffic to prevent him from doing so. If he ran to keep up with her, she always seemed the same distance away from him. And he still didn't have a clue as to her name!

It wasn't that these dreams unsettled Phil but they always left him with the same sensation – of hopelessness, feeling unable to change anything. What was more unsettling in Phil's life was what was happening to his music. To Phil, it was HIS music. It had become his passion and more.

It occupied a massive part of his life, whether it was reading the music press, or round at Martin's listening to new singles or his favourite Radio 1 shows and presenters, or in record stores, either browsing through album racks or asking the assistants, who all now knew him by his first name, to play certain tracks in the shop itself, as the audio booths had been removed to make room for the growing number of LPs that were being released.

There had also been a shift in the mood of his music. It had become more inward-looking, mellower and nowhere near as optimistic as the 'Summer of Love' two years earlier. Then it had all been so hopeful and carefree, so bright and colourful, so inventive and new. The Beach

Boys had 'Good Vibrations', the Small Faces enjoyed time in 'Itchycoo Park' and all you needed was love and flowers in your hair.

Matt had returned from Oxford for the Easter break, with a handful of albums – some bought, some borrowed. Bob Dylan's 'Blonde on Blonde' double LP, from 1966, included a track called 'Sad Eyed Lady of the Lowlands', well over 11 minutes long, covering the whole of the album's fourth side. It was one of Matt's favourites and he would play it repeatedly. To Phil, it was completely lacking in melody and just went on and on and on.

Similarly, tracks such as 'Meet on the ledge', from Fairport Convention's album 'What we did on our holidays', introduced Phil to music known as folk-rock, although even the brilliant voices of Ian Matthews and Sandy Denny did nothing to lift his spirits. Matt also liked songs by the Canadian songwriter, Leonard Cohen, which made Phil somewhat concerned regarding Matt's mental state. He began to wonder whether this apparent trend towards morose songsters would lead to mass depression if that was all university students were listening to these days.

He had heard some of these tracks on the second sampler album from CBS he had bought just after Christmas. This one was called 'Rock Machine, I love you', on which Mr Cohen would emote 'Hey that's no way to say goodbye'. Phil reckoned that, in terms of making relationships, he hadn't even said 'hello' yet but there were some upbeat tracks to listen to, from artists such as Laura Nyro, Blood Sweat and Tears and Taj Mahal.

One of Phil's real favourites was Simon & Garfunkel's 'America' opening with the line "Let us be lovers…". Matt also had their album 'Bookends' but that appeared to be seeped in melancholia too.

The compilation seemed to be a mish-mash of blues, jazz or soul tracks, all good songs but with too many brooding tracks by artists such as Dino Valente who Phil reckoned may or may not have been in the San Francisco psychedelic rock group Quicksilver Messenger Service. Martin said he had been, but at this time, as many groups were breaking up or changing line-up, it was difficult to keep up with all these personnel changes each week in the *NME*.

The Animals and the Yardbirds had disbanded. Steve Marriott had left the Small Faces and Peter Tork was no longer a Monkee. No loss there, thought Phil, although it had been over a year since their manic feel-good series had come to an end and even Phil was missing the madcap antics of this 'made-for-TV' band on Saturday evenings.

Cream had played their farewell performance, last November, at the Royal Albert Hall and it was rumoured that Ginger Baker and Eric Clapton might become part of a supergroup, called Blind Faith, with Stevie Winwood, who had reportedly disbanded his group Traffic in early 1969. There was rumour after rumour circulating that the Beatles were about to break up.

Of course, bands breaking up was nothing new to Phil. Two of his favourite groups, Buffalo Springfield and the Zombies, were no more, both having broken up last year, but he knew that the first was down to musical differences and the second to a lack of commercial success, to the dismay of both Kenny Everett and Phil.

This musical unease didn't help Phil feel any more certain about the future. He hoped, week in week out, that he would be free of unwanted distractions, whether musical, or at home, or even from the weather, which might then allow him to concentrate on his examination revision.

It never really happened though and then a very unusual track, first heard on John Peel's 'Top Gear', started Phil on yet another search to find out more about one particular artist. This time it was a Canadian singer-songwriter called David Ackles.

Last year 'Top of the Pops' had featured a single by a new group, Julie Driscoll, Brian Auger and the Trinity. The song was called 'This wheel's on fire', and it was written by Bob Dylan. It was recognised as one of the foremost songs of the psychedelic music genre, with the instrumental backing swirling around Julie Driscoll's sensuous vocals. Phil loved it but couldn't find any more songs recorded by the band until he heard their follow-up single on the wireless.

It was called 'Road to Cairo' and had a hypnotic organ intro, not unlike the sound of another of Phil's favourites, Procol Harum, followed by another superb vocal from Julie

Driscoll. Her appearances on TV had had a massive effect with the music press giving her the nickname of 'The Face'. Her very short, feathered cropped hair and long black eyelashes with dark eye shadow, like Dusty Springfield, began to be copied by girls across the country, especially those who had been mods but were now embracing the latest fad, skinheads.

Phil thought she looked totally gorgeous and his crush on her was part looks, part voice. Her voice was new, different and hard to label. To Phil, it was so much raunchier than those female artists who had won the *NME* Poll Winners Concert in the past – from Helen Shapiro to Cilla Black – and the way she interpreted a song was similar to some of the American singers, such as Nina Simone, who used their voice more like an instrument.

Like the band's previous top-five hit, Phil thought that the production of 'Road to Cairo' was utterly brilliant, mixing brass and keyboards with lyrics delivered with every note rich and lavish, whilst the song's story played out through David Ackles' expressive words. It was this introduction to his work that started Phil on as difficult a path as he had encountered with Buffalo Springfield. Ackles was a complete unknown in the West Midlands or even throughout England and there had been very little publicity regarding his songs or recordings.

Then Phil heard John Peel and Pete Drummond both feature his single, called 'Down River', suggesting that there was probably an album from which it came. Hearing his own version of 'Road to Cairo', played live by David

Ackles in September on 'Colour Me Pop', a new music show which was shown late in the evening on BBC2, convinced Phil that he should keep plugging away to try to find out what this album was called.

Unsurprisingly, it was just called 'David Ackles' so once again his order was placed with Beatties' record department and then he waited. Further visits were often met with disappointment as first the album was renamed 'Road to Cairo', to cash in on the Driscoll/Auger minor hit single. Secondly, the label on which the record was released, Elektra, was comparatively new and didn't have the same distribution network, in England, as the bigger labels such as EMI, Decca or PYE records. Eventually, the good news came through and Phil was told that the record should be in the store in the first week of April.

Phil's dad was busy with parish duties over the Easter weekend, conducting services at St Aiden's on both Good Friday and Easter Sunday. He had dropped Mum off at the train station, early on Thursday afternoon, to go to Chesterfield to be with her father over that weekend and so, with the exception of attending church and helping with meals and household chores, Matt, Phil and Rachel had the weekend very much to themselves.

Wolves were away to Liverpool on Easter Saturday, so Phil had joined Brian, Adrian and Joe at Molineux for the reserve game against Blackpool. For reserve games, entrance was a heck of a lot cheaper, so they went and sat in the Molineux St Stand where most seats were for season-ticket holders for first-team games, but few went to reserve games. A pity, as the second string were currently third in the Central League, with only the mighty Liverpool and Manchester United above them, and forwards Derek Clarke and Jimmy Seal scoring freely.

And, of course, they could watch one of their very own, Wolverhampton Grammar School's ex-head boy Stewart Ross, playing. Reserve games never had the same thrills and excitement as watching the first team, but Wolves reserves were in good form and many of the players were playing well enough, hoping to play division 1 football next August. Also, at reserve games, any goals at the first team away games were announced as soon as they were scored.

That afternoon, after 20 minutes, World Cup hero Roger Hunt put Liverpool ahead and by 5 o'clock both games had gone to form, the reserves beating out-of-form Blackpool and Liverpool winning 1-0 at Anfield.

As the lads filed out of the ground at full time, Joe seemed pretty chipper and Adrian was also beaming.

"What's brought these smiles on?" asked Phil.

"Not sure about Ade, but only losing 1-0 to the 'Pool, with them chasing Leeds for the title, ain't a bad result," said Joe. "They hammered us 6-0 here, at the end of last September, so today's result has to be a real improvement. We'll see on Tuesday evening against the champions, Man City. Everyone coming?"

"Hope so, if I can," said Phil. "What's tickled you, Ade?"

"I reckon I know," said Brian. "Martin has managed to book another brilliant band tonight, called Chicken Shack and they play great blues stuff – just what Ade likes."

"Really looking forward to seeing them this evening," confirmed Adrian. "Love their stuff. Already bought both of their albums. The new one's called 'OK Ken' and the first was called '40 Blue Fingers, Freshly Packed and Ready to Serve'."

"Yow must be having a laff," said Joe. "No one calls an album that! And you've forked out on two albums – last of the big spenders, eh! Where yow off to, Phil?"

"Just remembered that I have to collect an LP I'd ordered from Beatties before they close," he replied.

"I bet we've never heard of the band," said Joe, correctly, which made them all laugh as they parted company in Queens Square to go their separate ways home for tea before meeting up again that evening at Venturers.

The youth centre was buzzing when Phil got there. In the hall, the roadies were setting up the equipment which looked pretty awesome compared with other local bands. Chicken Shack were still seen as quite a local band though, as their members came from Stourbridge and Kidderminster.

They were previously known as 'Shades Five' and played many gigs for a few years on the renowned Ma Regan circuit of venues across Birmingham and the Midlands area. Over the past two years, they had become acknowledged as one of the pioneers of the British blues boom, along with Fleetwood Mac, Savoy Brown, Ten Years After and Free.

To see them playing at a small youth club on the outskirts of Wolverhampton was somewhat amazing for most of the club regulars. The band was now based in London but somehow Martin had managed to contact their agent and, having explained how well Savoy Brown had gone down at the club, secured this gig.

Martin was looking decidedly smug when Phil found him in the club kitchen, cradling a warming cuppa.

"You must be chuffed," said Phil.

"Pretty good, eh," replied Martin. "Just one down side. Christine Perfect isn't with the band tonight. They've got Paul Raymond in on keyboards from Plastic Penny. You remember them? They had a hit with 'Everything I am'. You really liked the single as it sounded like Procol's stuff."

"Oh yeh. Should be terrific blues music though," said Phil. "Ade is a big fan. Says he has bought both their albums."

"He's already up front by the stage having a gander at the guitars the roadies have set out," said Martin. "You won't get much out of him this evening. He'll be all in but clippetts."

Just then the sound of the roadies testing the mics interrupted their conversation. "One-two, one-two." The two mics, next to the guitar and keyboards, seemed to be satisfactory so the drummer, Dave Bidwell, and bass player, Andy Silvester, took their places on the rostra stage, followed by Paul Raymond.

The hall was full and expectant. The enigmatic Stan Webb, tall, skinny with a shock of curly hair, ambled through the throng and climbed on stage, plugged in his guitar, called out three, four then hit a chord to start an instrumental called 'Webbed Feet'. Bass and drums providing the typical blues tempo, leaving Stan to feature his virtuoso style of guitar playing.

The end of the song drew staunch but restrained applause as most youngsters weren't sure how this evening was going to go. Those who knew were waiting fervently for more of the same and Stan thanked them.

"Cheers," he said. "Great to be back in the Black Country, home of British blues."

"And the gold and black," came a reply from the crowd, alluding to the traditional Wolves' club strip.

"Yeh that too," smiled Stan. "Here's a number written by the great Rudolph Toombs, called 'Lonesome Whistle Blues'." Again, it rolled along brilliantly with the rhythm section predominant, enabling Stan to match his vocals with the guitar licks, whilst Paul supported with solid 12-bar shuffle piano.

That really got the crowd going and many of them were now on their feet dancing.

"That last song was covered by the great Freddie King," said Stan. "Both of those first two tracks are from our first album called '40 Blue Fingers'," and before he could finish, some of the devotees at the front shouted back 'Freshly Packed and Ready to Serve'.

There was a surprised look on Stan's face which turned into a broad grin.

"Amazing. So, some of you know our stuff," he continued. "Well, here's a track that will be on our new LP, hopefully going to be released later this year."

They played 'Midnight hour', followed by 'Tell me' and then another new song.

"That's called 'Road of love' – another song I've written for the new album. We are going back into the studio later this month to record it in London but it's great to try it out live here for you. Love playing live," explained Stan.

And that was the predominant theme of the evening – how much the group enjoyed playing the blues live. It didn't matter whether they were written by Stan or covers of well-known blues artists such as Chester Burnette, or Stan's hero – Freddie King – the joy of performing, from all four band members, just permeated right across the hall.

There was a minority who obviously didn't groove to the blues, looking for more mainstream pop that evening, but many found they could dance to tracks such as 'See see baby' or 'Baby's got me crying' or 'The right way is my way' so the floor remained crowded with dancers right through to when Stan announced they would take a break after the next song.

It was another of his own instrumentals called 'Pony and Trap', again giving him full licence to dominate the stage with his virtuosic guitar playing. When the rest of the band retired for a break, he picked up an acoustic guitar to play his own awesome version of the folk classic, 'Anji' – written by Davey Graham – the tune all guitarists would try to master to see if they were any good. Stan was good, very good, leaving the crowd in awe of his instrumental brilliance.

Phil found Adrian standing by the counter, waiting for a cuppa and looking into the distance, somewhat dazed.

"You enjoying it?" asked Phil.

"Oh yeh," replied Adrian. "I reckon they are better live than in the studio, but I think they miss Christine Perfect on lead vocals. Stan Webb's a fantastic guitar player but not the greatest singer. Great choice of songs. Some of his own and a few blues classics."

"Martin and I haven't heard of many of the artists Stan mentioned," said Phil.

"Well, it ain't your bag, is it?" stated Adrian. "You like bands who have good harmonies and melodies. Not really the blues, is it?"

Their conversation was halted by the sound of a guitar being tuned and chords strummed from the stage. Adrian said nothing. He was gone, back to his place in the hall, seated cross-legged gazing towards the front on the stage. Phil smiled as Joe came up to him.

"Never seen Ade so animated," he said.

"It's his 'bag', as he says these days," replied Joe. "You staying till the end or getting back home for 'Match of the

Day'. Coops says that today's game at Anfield is the main game on telly tonight."

"Might do," said Phil. "Like the band and blues music is OK but I could do with something to lift my spirits. Our choirmaster, Steven, really likes Fleetwood Mac and has lent me their first two LPS. I like their up-tempo 12-bar blues stuff like 'Shake your money maker' and 'Dust my broom' but I don't reckon their slower numbers are as good. 'Albatross' was a brilliant instrumental but it's not really the blues."

Just then a single guitar rift began to be repeated in the hall and attention once again focused on Chicken Shack. The drums and bass laid down a recurring rhythm, so recognisable from all blues tracks, and Paul's keyboards added an extra slow boogie-woogie dimension to the song, again allowing Stan to enjoy dazzling solo guitar segments. No vocals just solid 12-bar blues. The young crowd loved it. Good playing by a good band just playing genuine blues. At the end of the song, the applause was deafening.

"Thank you," said Stan. "We are going to drop the tempo now to do our versions of songs by a couple of great blues songwriters, Lowell Fulson and Little Brother Montgomery. Enjoy."

'Reconsider Baby' with Paul playing organ, sounding very much like Georgie Fame or the Peddlers, and the plaintive 'First time I met the blues' was followed by the even more soulful 'You ain't no good'.

"That was a song written by the wonderful Christine Perfect," announced Stan. "And last time we were all in the studio, she recorded the next track which will be our new single. We're going to play it for you now and I will have a stab at the vocals. It's called 'I'd rather go blind'".

Ade was right, thought Phil. Stan Webb wasn't a patch on Ms Perfect when it came to singing but it was a great version of the Etta James' hit – one that Phil had heard played on Radio 1 last year.

"We're going to follow that with another new track called 'Tears in the wind', which will definitely be on our next album," announced Stan and the song began with Andy Silvester's two-note bass riff, shadowed by Stan's guitar. This time Stan's vocals fitted the song perfectly.

As Phil listened, he somehow knew he should go home. It was a song of heartbreak but so beautifully structured with a simple melody over an equally simple arrangement. Best thing he had heard all evening and best to leave on a high, even if it made him feel just as low as when he had set out earlier that evening.

When he reached home 20 minutes later, the house seemed very, very silent.

Phil had expected to hear the television on in the rear living room, as Matt was home and should be watching the football, but through the glass in the front door, Phil could only see just a single light on in the kitchen. Phil turned the key in the door and then saw Dad, sitting at the kitchen table. He looked up from his newspaper and motioned Phil to come in to join him.

"Mum's back," he said quietly. "Grandad passed away this morning. No TV tonight, Phillip. Matt and Rachel are in their rooms. Can you do the same and I will close down?"

"Yes, of course, Dad," said Phil. "How's Mum?"

"She's not said much since I picked her up from the station," said Dad. "I guess it must be a relief to her as Grandad had been really ill for quite a while. The funeral is next Friday so don't make any plans for the end of the week."

"OK, Dad," said Phil. "Can I still go to the Wolves match on Tuesday evening? It's the champions, Man City. Grandad liked his sport so I guess he would want me to go."

Dad smiled. "You could be right, and you'd probably be better out of Mum's way this week, so you best get your head down on your revision before you go back to school a week on Monday," he said. "It's probably the most important term for your education."

Phil went up the stairs to his bedroom but instead of his usual routine of putting his radio on quietly, he went to bed in silence. As he was trying to make sense of all that had happened and get some sleep, he remembered the last song he heard at the club that evening and the lyrics came back to him.

"Oh, what's the point
Now you've gone away
Crying my eyes out
Wishing my life away
It's just that you're leaving
Has made me cry

Tears in the wind
Tears I will never dry."

And he wondered whether his passion for this music would ever be shared with either of his parents.

The rest of the weekend went decidedly slowly, not just because the family was subdued and mournful, but because Phil finally had time to sit down and listen in full to the latest addition to his LP collection – the David Ackles album – in accompaniment to his essential exam revision.

Phil had heard both 'Down River' and 'Road to Cairo' before. They were the kind of story songs of loss and longing that he really liked. The first was about a prisoner returning home to find that his lover hadn't waited around for him and the second about a traveller who didn't fancy returning to his family. Neither was a barrel of laughs but both so interesting in a lyrical way and the songs were so brilliantly constructed, with Ackles backed by some fantastic musicians, not just on guitar and keyboards, but also complicated bass lines and percussion that helped his songs to grow in intensity along with the storyline.

Phil hadn't had the opportunity to hear any of the other eight tracks on either side of the LP with the audio booths now gone. All of the new songs showed that Ackles was a really strong songwriter although maybe he wasn't the greatest singer, having a dour, growling vocal style not dissimilar to two other popular troubadours of the time, Tim Buckley and Leonard Cohen.

There were only two up-beat tracks – 'Laissez-faire' and 'What a happy day'. The first an elaborate protest song which could have been written for a theatrical production and the second the total opposite, extolling the happiness that comes from singing and just existing. Other tracks ranged from the gentle, sentimental mood of 'Lotus man' to the downright misery of 'My name is Andrew'.

However, the final track was a revelation to Phil. 'Be my friend' was a song of stunning beauty and spoke to him as very little had before. Phil had friends but not the friend that this song spoke about. Someone who is there for all the things you love to do and share the times you have together, good and bad – as the song says – 'the simple gift, the words that lift, be my friend'.

He listened to all six minutes plus of that track over and over again, re-setting the stylus so many times on his Dad's radiogram that he thought he might have to replace it with a new one. He soon knew the lyrics and melody by heart, but he couldn't come anywhere near the wonderful musical arrangement, with Ackles playing brilliant piano, supplemented by a rousing heavenly organ solo which nudged the song to an uplifting crescendo.

Phil knew the song wouldn't get played on the radio. It was far too long and dour, even with its heartening and uplifting words, but he knew that if it was played, he knew who he would dedicate it to.

Unfortunately, all Phil's concentration was being focused on listening when he should have been concentrating on his A-level revision. His maths for science revision was pretty well done with questions on past papers easily completed in the required time.

His physics revision still had a long way to go. Phil struggled with the different definitions of energy – kinetic, latent and potential – feeling that he would never find enough energy himself to finish his revision before the exams. He may well be able to remember Hooke's law, and both of Newton's laws, but applying them, under examination conditions, still perplexed him.

Phil knew that carbon-based compounds constituted much of organic chemistry but the textbook might as well have been written in Greek for all the sense it made to him and, as for the periodic table, it didn't seem to generate the same memory building blocks that were stimulated by listening to Alan Freeman on 'Pick of the Pops' every Sunday evening at five.

How was it on Monday mornings, at school, he could recall all the new chart entries, and what number they had entered the chart, but when asked which elements were inert or which were halogens and could they be both, he hadn't a clue. And why were some gases designated noble? Still, it was somewhat belated, in early April 1969, to realise that science was not your chosen specialism!

Phil's had no feelings of either confidence nor expectation, but he remained in that front living room for hours, the music on low volume, with words that spun before his eyes from textbooks and revision crammers, hoping it would all slot into place over the next few weeks.

On Tuesday evening that week, Phil enjoyed a rare evening out at Molineux. Weekday games were infrequent and games under floodlights even more so, although Wolverhampton Wanderers had been trailblazers, over a decade earlier, when they became one of the very first English clubs to install floodlights at their ground.

Wolves had then played a succession of evening friendlies against the best foreign sides of the day, including Glasgow Celtic, Racing Club Avellaneda from Argentina, Maccabi Tel Aviv and Spartak Moscow, who they beat 4-0, resulting in the newspaper headline stating that the Russians had been "hammered and sickled".

It was the last floodlit fixture of 1954 that was best remembered by most Wolves fans when the visitors were the Hungarian champions, Honved, a gifted side that included six internationals who, a year previous, had humbled England's national team not once, but twice, 6-3 and 7-1. The 'Mighty Magyars' were thought to be invincible and, quite early in the game, were 2-0 up and seemingly coasting to victory.

Stan Cullis, Wolves manager then, had other ideas and made the ground staff water the pitch heavily at half time which, adding to four days of persistent rain, turned the pitch into a quagmire. That certainly slowed the fleet-footed Hungarians down and Wolves came away 3-2 winners after 90 minutes, much to the delight of the 60,000 fans present and the many more who watched on their television, as the BBC broadcast the second half live that evening, again something that didn't happen every day of the week.

It was unlikely that the television cameras would be at Molineux on a Tuesday evening in early April, 15 years later, but all three lads – Joe, Adrian and Phil – were happy as Larry, Curly and Moe to be standing on the South Bank that evening, all taking a much-needed break from their scholastic endeavours.

"Don't fancy our chances much tonight," said Adrian, with his usual glumness.

"Neither do I," replied Joe. "We've only won once since the start of February and that was against QPR, who look bound to be in division 2 next season. And we've picked up just one point from the last five games, letting in 11 goals and only scoring 3."

"I read in the paper this morning that the reason City aren't doing so well is their away form," chipped in Phil. "And that's why they won't win the league this year. Anyhow, our last three games have been against the top three – Leeds, Liverpool and Arsenal – so give the team a break. I'm looking for summat to cheer me up this evening so less of the niggles, fellas."

The match announcer then read out the players' names for each side and there was astonishment around the ground.

"No Waggy, and skipper Bailey's not playing," said Joe. "Who's Bertie Lutton? We might as well go home now!"

"And City have put out a really strong side," said Adrian "Nearly all of them will be playing in the Cup Final, later this month, against Leicester."

"Thanks, lads. That's really cheered me up," growled Phil.

The start of the game made their mood even gloomier. In the first 30 seconds, England forward Francis Lee lost his marker, John Holsgrove, who had slipped having received the ball from a throw-in and Lee was in on goal, making no mistake and scoring past a stranded Phil Parkes. There was no need for words – the looks between the three lads said it all. 1-0 down and Wolves had hardly touched the ball.

City's goal had put the crowd of over 28,000 in the ground into stunned silence, except for the small group of City fans, bouncing up and down at the centre of the South Bank, singing and chanting. After the remainder of an uninspiring first half with very few chances for either side, the half-time whistle went with boos ringing out from all four stands. This was not a game to gladden anyone's heart.

"Can't see us getting back in this one," stated Adrian, spreading the gloom a little more than usual. Joe and Phil decided to ignore him and voice more positive advice.

"We need some experience out there," said Joe. "Someone's got to take a lead. The Doog is skipper tonight so he needs to step up to the plate. He only had one good chance in the first 45 minutes. You can't expect a young-un like Lutton to be brilliant on his debut."

"Peter Knowles seems lost without Bailey there," said Phil. "Munro needs to play just in front of the defence so that Knowles can get forward more and supply the wingers."

The second half commenced and within two minutes it was as if the lads' advice had been passed on to the players. Dougan raced to the byline, put over a great cross and there was Knowles to score a tremendous bullet header, giving the City keeper, Dowd, no chance.

It was as if someone had turned a switch on for the Wolves team as they mounted attack after attack and the crowd sensed that this game was far from over. Knowles had woken up and was running the game, spreading passes out to John Farringdon and young Bertie Lutton on the right and left wings respectively. They would then dash past the full-backs and get crosses over into the City penalty area.

Midway through the second half, Dougan met one of these crosses superbly, thrashing the ball into the roof of the net to put Wolves into the lead. The once-silent crowd was now cheering and singing about Dougan's smiles – always the chant reserved for his goal celebrations.

A third goal was needed to finish the game off and, with just seven minutes to go, Lutton dribbled the ball from defence, found Knowles with an inch-perfect pass who then matched the pass to Munro, running through the City defence to score with a stunning shot.

"Sometimes football just needs to be played simply," said Joe, when the celebrations had died down. "A bit of skill, two great passes and a precise shot and we're 3-1 up. Now we can go home happy."

And they did, even Adrian.

Phil's earlier gloom had lifted as he sat on the top deck of the bus on his way home. It would return as the week plodded slowly on, with hours of irksome and ineffective revision and then the sombre trip to Chesterfield dressed smartly for Grandad's funeral. A few years back, Grandad may well have appreciated that second half of football but now – thankfully Phil thought – he had been relieved of all the wretchedness that had incapacitated him in recent times.

"Better make the best of it," thought Phil, as the Hillman estate followed the A38 through Litchfield, Burton-on-Trent and Belper before the sight of the town's crooked spire announced their arrival at the house on the hill in Tapton where his grandparents had retired to just a few years ago.

No radio on this journey but if he needed to withdraw, maybe at the wake later, then his customary sanctuary would still be where he knew it would be – exactly the right place to be unseen and unheard on an occasion such as this.

Chapter 10 − She is still a mystery

Ever since Phil had entered the sixth form, it had been drummed into him that A-level examinations would be the most difficult he would ever have to take. He didn't agree. To Phil, it was a lot more challenging to learn, understand and retain sufficient knowledge to get through nine O-level subjects, especially if you had a boffin of an older brother to live up to.

Sitting A-levels or any examinations had really never worried Phil. It was the content of the examination papers that produced fear and anxiety, particularly with physics and chemistry, two subjects that seem to cover such a myriad of topics that he had no idea which ones to concentrate on to give him any chance of decent grades, or at least the grades that had been predicted for him, as a requirement for university acceptance.

As June approached, Phil was now completely sure that miracles would be required in both these subjects to get either A or B grades, which were essential for Oxbridge scholarship tutoring in September, in the extra year in the sixth form that followed skipping the second year in the alpha stream. And, when the exams arrived, Phil got off to the worst possible start.

He was sure that the start time for his two-hour chemistry practical exam was 1:30 in the afternoon, and so, just after midday, he was contentedly eating an early lunch at home, ready to go off to school within the next half hour, which would give him plenty of time to get there with all the other hesitant examinees.

However, a glance at his exam schedule resulted in complete panic. Phil had read 12:30 as 1:30 p.m. which meant he had less than 30 minutes to don his uniform, get all his examination paraphernalia together and cycle, like the wind, the couple of miles to school, lock his bike and finally get to the chemistry labs. The only fortunate aspect of this calamity was that his parents were not at home.

Traffic lights were ignored, gears crashed and, with school tie still in his pocket, Phil arrived at the chemistry laboratory well after the examination had begun. No words were spoken, just a gesticulation from the examination invigilator as to an empty place he should have taken up around 25 minutes before.

Phil looked at the exam paper. Some of it seemed to resonate from lessons where the chemistry teacher had been present, which had often been sporadic rather than customary, and practical sessions had often been relegated to the tail-end of lessons only to be curtailed by the bell for break or lunch. Phil knew though that blaming others was not an option. After all, there was no one to blame but himself for misreading the exam schedule.

Looking around the laboratory, everyone else was absorbed in their academic efforts. There were a couple of grins at his tardiness, but he knew he was already at a massive disadvantage, starting the exam nearly half an hour after everyone else. And everyone else probably knew what they were doing. Phil didn't but he would have to give it a go, knowing that his written papers were going to have to be more than brilliant to make up this lost ground.

They weren't. In fact, his worse fears were realised as many of the exam questions focused on organic chemistry or atomic structure and bonding. He could remember Boyle's law and Dalton's law, but Hess' law was beyond him and he wasn't sure what the difference was between the words enthalpy or entropy. As to the question on the ionisation of krypton, that only resulted in a distracted smile because he knew that his fifth form classmate Bobby, now studying classics, was an avid collector of the ever-entertaining DC comics in which Superman featured.

Phil had similar experiences with the physics papers, although he was slightly more confident of gaining a better grade there as surprisingly some of the questions were actually on topics he had covered in his revision. All the mathematics for science papers had been a breeze, solving the required number of questions well within the three hours on both papers.

However, Phil knew that, by the end of all the exams, it was unlikely that he would be returning to school in September, to join Martin, Joe and Adrian for a third year in the sixth form and the opportunity to go on to university, maybe even to join Matt in Oxford. No chance now, he thought.

All the exams had been completed by the start of July and, with three weeks left until the summer school holidays, Phil felt mightily relieved that it was all over. He didn't let on to his parents about how he thought he had done, telling them that he found some questions difficult but that was to be expected. After all, these were A-levels, weren't they, and he assured them that he had done his best. He never mentioned the chemistry practical, although he suspected his late arrival may have got a mention in the staffroom

The pressure was off. There was no point in doing any further revision or any need to do any studying at all. The examination papers would have been sent off for marking and checking and it was now just a matter of waiting for the results to come out, around the middle of the summer holiday. Phil felt that was that. Since there was no point in worrying his parents, he began to enjoy life again.

Many of the lads were not required to be at school for those final few weeks of term, although Adrian and Joe had been told they would definitely need to attend, as next year they would be head boy and head of junior school respectively. No such dizzy heights for Phil so he spent a great deal of time around at Martin's house, or Chris's, listening to music.

However, there were just a couple of days in mid-July when he donned his school uniform and cycled into school, voluntarily, to talk to one particular member of staff. The sole reason behind this was that Apollo 11 was about to be launched from the Kennedy Space Centre on July 16th and, because of the examinations, he hadn't had any opportunity over the past few weeks to discuss this momentous event with Taff Williams.

Phil knew that Taff would be now free from teaching on Tuesday and Thursday afternoons as that was when, earlier in the term, he would have been teaching physics to upper six science, including Phil. He found Taff in the physics laboratory prep room as expected.

"Afternoon, Minor," said Taff with a grin. "I assume you haven't come to just pass the time of day. I wonder what could be on your mind?"

"Is the launch still on schedule?" asked Phil.

"As far as I know, all systems are go for an early afternoon launch," confirmed Taff. "That means that it should take three days to reach the moon and they could be landing on the surface the next day. My colleague at NASA tells me it's all very hopeful. They have learnt so much from the previous missions, especially Apollo 10. You excited?"

"You bet. More than that – really can't wait," said Phil. "So, the landing should be late on Sunday evening then. Both the BBC and ITV are covering it. I will be glued to the telly straight after church on Sunday evening and can stay up as long as I like, Dad says."

"Well lucky you," replied Taff. "Last staff meeting of the term for me, first thing on Monday morning, so I will have to catch up with all the TV coverage later in the day.

The BBC Home Service will suit me on Monday morning. Fancy being on the mission, Minor?"

"That would be really fab," said Phil. "Aren't all the crew ex-fighter pilots? I suppose I would have to join the RAF first. I'm not sure I will ever have anywhere near their experience. All three have already been in space – Armstrong, Aldrin and Collins – so they should know what it's all about, shouldn't they."

"But no one has ever stepped on the surface of the moon before," said Taff. "They've done simulations in the American deserts, but this will be the real thing. I wouldn't mind being at Mission Control at NASA rather than at our staff meeting on Monday."

They talked for half an hour or more about the space mission, Phil making sure they kept to that topic rather than go anywhere near how he had done in the examinations. Then the bell went, and Taff said he was on duty in big school. He asked Phil to let him know as soon as he got his results.

Phil wasn't looking forward to that difficult conversation, but he knew he owed it to Taff to let him know what his grades were when they came through. He wended his way home, looking forward to the coming weekend's events, especially those in outer space.

On Sunday, 20th July 1969, Phil spent a great deal of the afternoon and evening in front of the television in the sitting room. In fact, he seemed to have been there for most of the week, as on Monday and Tuesday he watched the last two days of the third cricket test match against the West Indies at Headingly in Leeds. Just when the tourists looked to be taking control of the match, England contrived to win by 30 runs, mainly down to Derek Underwood's brilliant spin bowling and Alan Knott's wicket-keeping, and that meant they had also won the series.

Just before 2 o'clock on Wednesday afternoon, saw the start of the week's Apollo 11 coverage by the BBC, introduced by Cliff Michelmore, with the 'Sky at Night' presenter, Patrick Moore, on hand to give scientific and technical explanations as well as an analysis of the mission's progress. Throughout the next few days, there would be regular short bulletins, and after midnight, BBC1 broadcast pictures of the approach to the moon beamed back live from the spacecraft.

In the *Radio Times* that week, there had been an eight-page pull-out section entitled 'Man on the Moon'. It gave all the information about the three-man flight crew, the spacecraft – the rocket, the command and lunar modules – and how the mission would pan out, from lift-off to the moon landing, telling readers how long they were expected to spend on the moon's surface.

There were artist's sketches of the landing, together with a full page on developments over the past decade, under the heading 'Race you to the moon', detailing the steps both the Americans and Russians had taken to reach this point. There were pictures of NASA mission control and the special Apollo 11 studio the BBC had created.

Everything was meant to encourage viewers and listeners to keep up with every single element of this 'journey into space', even providing a list of all the 'space talk' so that everyone could follow the 'language of the moon men'.

They described it as a historic adventure but to Phil, it was so much more. He excitedly read every section thoroughly over and over again so that he could memorise all the diagrams and keep descriptions of each mission feature in his head, often wondering why organic chemistry textbooks had never had the same appeal.

To him, the leading light of these programmes was a presenter called James Burke who seemed as passionate about the mission as he himself was. As the BBC's main science reporter, Phil had seen him on 'Tomorrow's World' although he hadn't been aware that Burke had covered the space missions since Apollo 8, making him the font of all knowledge when it came to describing what was on the TV screen. Phil hung on his every word as he presented each bulletin with so much enthusiasm and insight.

Church on Sunday meant that Phil missed the 6:45 evening bulletin, which covered the lunar module separating from the main spacecraft before beginning its descent to the moon's surface. However, he was settled comfortably into an armchair at 8:45 for the main evening Apollo 11 programme of 'Man on the Moon'.

"How long is this on for?" asked Rachel.

"Up to the news, around 10," replied Phil. "You ought to watch it. This is real history – happening right now. They reckon that they will land on the moon at around 9:20."

"And then what will they do?" continued Rachel, displeased that she couldn't watch what she wanted that evening. "Can't we switch channels? On BBC2 they've got the Supremes singing live. I love them," she said.

"Not a hope. I've been wanting to watch this for ages. ITV are covering it as well," informed Phil. "And to answer your first question, they will actually be the first men ever to walk on the moon."

As Mum came in Phil said, "You want to watch this, don't you, Mum?"

"Not really," she replied. "But I know you have been looking forward to it all week, so you can watch it, Phillip, as long as you watch the BBC coverage."

When it came to watching television, Mum and Dad were a tad snobbish as regards programmes on ITV, although Mum rarely missed an episode of 'Coronation Street', and more recently 'Crossroads' had become her new obsession.

"The moon landing's tonight, isn't it? Are they going to actually step on to the moon's surface?" she enquired. "Well at least that will be it, after today, and I can prise you from your armchair and outside into the sunshine. With all this space coverage, as well as the cricket, I doubt you have noticed that the temperatures nearly hit 90 degrees this week, Phillip."

"I thought you would be interested in this, Mum, with you teaching physics and studying engineering," said Phil.

"I might find the rocket design and the mathematics behind the journey a little interesting, but I've no fascination for space travel. The moon could be made of cheese as far as I'm concerned," Mum replied.

"That's the title of the debate on after the news," said Phil, but by then Mum was on her way out of the room muttering about getting ready for school tomorrow, closely followed by Rachel, still sulking. It was gone 9 o'clock when Matt joined him.

"Have they landed yet?" he asked.

"They're on the descent. Should land within the next half hour," replied Phil.

"A real slice of history this," said Matt. "No one has ever gone so far from Earth before."

"And then they've got to lift off the surface and re-join the command module, Columbia, and get back home," said Phil. "It's an amazing journey."

Both the brothers were transfixed by the pictures on the screen as the landing module, Eagle, descended towards the moon's surface, accompanied by Burke giving a running commentary. At 9:19, on that unexceptional Sunday evening, the world heard Neil Armstrong's say "Houston, Tranquillity Base here. The Eagle has landed."

The lads leapt from their chairs with joy, as if they had just witnessed a goal scored by the Wolves. Neither of them spoke as they continued to watch in complete wonder as photographs were being sent back from the mission.

They were actually just photographs of some soil but soil that was over 240,000 miles away, on the moon that would appear in the night sky each and every night, and these pictures were coming from a spacecraft that had actually landed on its very surface.

Finally, they heard Burke say that the EVA wasn't going to happen for quite a few hours, probably not until after 3 am.

"Who's Eva?" said Phil.

"It's not who, you bonehead," said Matt. "It stands for extra-vehicular activity which, in plain English, means any activity done outside the spacecraft."

"Ah that'll be the moonwalk then," said Phil. "When did they say it might be?"

"Not till the early hours of the morning, by the looks of things," said Matt. "I've got to be up earlyish for my holiday job in the morning so I'm off to bed."

"Think I will stay up and watch a bit more," said Phil. "Night, night."

"Sleep well. Reckon you might well be drifting in space in your dreams tonight, Bruv," replied Matt. "When do you expect your exam results? Still not too confident?"

"Middle of August, they reckon, and no, not filled with much hope. I think I had better start looking for a permanent job soon, but I am going to enjoy this for now. Night."

Phil watched up to the news before making his supper and returning to see a strange programme called 'So what if it's just green cheese?' which featured actors Judy Dench and Ian McKellen, reading prose and poetry about the moon, as well as musicians Dudley Moore and Marion Montgomery. Phil wasn't really taken with Mr Moore or Miss Montgomery's jazz renditions but loved David Bowie's recent single 'Space Oddity' and listened intently to the Pink Floyd playing a seven-minute instrumental piece called 'Moonhead', which he thought was somewhat self-indulgent and definitely lacking in melody.

By 11 o'clock that historic evening everyone else in the family was tucked up in their beds, struggling to get to sleep on what was an unusually temperate July night. Conversely, Phil was straining to stay awake after all the excitement of the evening's events so, having failed to be enthused by the next programme, which was an Alistair Sim comedy film, he decided to turn the TV off and go to bed.

Earlier in the day, he had consulted the *Radio Times*, spotting that the BBC1 coverage would continue through the night which meant he could catch up on events the following morning.

For the first time since that opening day of Radio 1, Phil set his alarm for a bright and early start. He was not disappointed as, although Neil Armstrong had made his the very first footprint on the moon at a few minutes before 4 am, the TV coverage continued to repeat this historic event, with Armstrong's words "One small step for man, one giant leap for mankind", unsurprisingly becoming the main newspaper headline that day.

Phil watched the Apollo 11 coverage, live and repeats, for most of Monday morning. He was both weary and euphoric. "This is going to be the start of man's exciting journey into space, discovering planets, moons and asteroids and maybe, as so many science-fiction books, comics and films had imagined, aliens," he reflected. "Not space monsters, like the Martians in H. G. Wells 'War of the Worlds', but different species like Spock, the Vulcan in the new 'Star Trek' series", which had just started showing on Saturday evenings, replacing 'Dr Who'.

Everyone else had left the house by 8 a.m., either off to school or, in Matt's case, to work. Phil knew that he would also need to find some work soon, either a holiday job to raise some money to increase his small but, in his eyes, select record collection or, if his worse fears were realised, something more permanent.

Maybe, in September, he could enrol on a further education course or start an apprenticeship at the Wulfrun College or at Wolverhampton Polytechnic. He knew that such options might be just about acceptable to his parents, who were still thinking that he could, and should, go to university. Should he think about doing a teacher training course? Now they would approve of that!

And, if Phil had to find a job, how should he go about it? He hadn't thought about this at all. His mind had been so focused on the examinations that he hadn't considered his future much. He'd been so anxious about how he would do that he hadn't contemplated what failure would mean to his hopes and dreams.

One thing was pretty certain, he couldn't see his parents welcoming the prospect of him becoming a radio presenter, like his current Radio 1 heroes John Peel, Kenny Everett or his new favourite, Johnnie Walker, even if it was with the BBC rather than out at sea on a pirate radio station. Phil just loved the zaniness and musical passion of Everett's shows on Saturday morning and the steadfastness of Peel, now on Sunday evenings, introducing listeners to new groups and musicians, but Walker's shows eclipsed them all.

Johnnie Walker had continued to broadcast with the last pirate radio station Radio Caroline, even though being involved with such stations became a criminal offence around two years ago. He then lived, in broadcasting exile, in Holland before returning to England in 1968, fearful of arrest. Luckily that never happened and, in April the following year, he was offered a new show by the BBC on a Saturday afternoon, starting at 2 o'clock.

His very first Radio 1 show was actually on Cup Final day when Manchester City were up against Leicester at Wembley. With the game being shown live on both BBC and ITV, there weren't very many listening and consequently there were probably very few who noticed that the rebel from Radio Caroline had retracted somewhat on those defiant on-air anti-establishment pledges he had made as a pirate radio DJ.

Phil didn't care about that. Walker was just so relaxed and succinct. He obviously loved the music he was playing and, whilst the BBC restricted the number of records he could play as they were still under pressure to include a great deal of live music, any frustrations never came across. He always sounded as if he was having fun. Phil thought that, if he ever got the chance to be a radio DJ, then he would try to sound like him.

He just really loved these shows and, with no football to play or watch in May and June, Saturday afternoons with Walker had become another 'must-listen' time for Phil's radio obsession. Together with Dave Symonds on Sunday mornings, it was no surprise that his parents had been content, over those early summer weekends, to see Phil ensconced in either the front living room or his bedroom, with textbooks open. Rarely, if ever, did they notice the wire of the earpiece coming from the transistor radio in his pocket.

However, that was many weeks back and now the pressing issue was Phil's future. He knew that Mr Stewart would welcome him back as a paperboy but, at 17, he thought that he should, and could, earn a lot more. Paper rounds also meant very early mornings and, if he was looking for more permanent work, the evening round wouldn't fit in. Phil needed help but he couldn't talk to his parents about this. A holiday job would be the best option for now, at least until that examination results envelope dropped on to the porch doormat.

Phil's salvation came from an unlikely source. It was after choir practice the next Friday that Paul Barnwell mentioned that his father was looking for students to work in various departments at the Town Hall, throughout the summer school holidays, and wondered whether Phil would ask Matt if he was interested.

"Matt's already been back from Oxford for a few weeks", explained Phil, "and he's started a summer job. I'm looking for a holiday job, though. Can you put in a word for me instead, Paul?"

"I'll see what I can do," replied Paul. "I expect my Dad will give you a call over the weekend. Any preference? Out in the parks, on the bins or an office job?"

"Don't mind," said Phil. "I just need some cash over the summer."

Mr Barnwell called the next day and Phil began work, early the following Monday morning in the Rates Office in the Accounts Department for Wolverhampton Town Council, as an office junior. And he would be earning more than doing around four paper deliveries every day. Maybe going to work had benefits he hadn't really thought of!

To Phil, one of the novel aspects of going to work every day was the absence of uniform. For over a decade, he had had little or no choice in the clothes he would climb into every weekday morning and wear all day. They were laid out for him and that was that. Now there was a choice. Not much, but a choice. Yes, it was shirt and tie still, but the shirt didn't have to be plain white and the tie wasn't a school tie.

"No, you cannot wear your jeans, Phillip," decreed Mum. "They are for evenings and weekends. Not cords either. It will be plain dark grey or black trousers. Yes, your school ones will do for now."

A jumper wasn't necessary at that time of year, but some sort of jacket was required, rather than the blazer with the school crest on the front pocket. Phil wanted either a denim or a leather one, but Mum had other ideas. As soon as she heard that Mr Barnwell had offered him a summer job, Phil was on the bus, with Mum, into town to visit John Collier, to her the only men's clothes shop that would have the correct attire. They came away with a plain tweed sports jacket with a fine herringbone pattern and a pair of equally uninspiring slate-grey trousers.

On the Monday, though, Phil felt that he fitted in at the Town Hall, clothes-wise. Most male employees were dressed in a suit, shirt and tie with well-polished shoes. Mum had made sure his shoes were buffed to perfection on Sunday evening. Phil's jacket and trousers made him stand out a little but, as a teenager, it was more than acceptable. Phil knew he wasn't going to become the council's fashion rebel!

As always, he compromised. The jacket, the trousers, the shirt – all said conformity. Shoes and socks likewise. But a tie could speak volumes, he thought. His current favourites were the kipper-style ties favoured by Mods, bringing back a style of broad tie that had been popular in the late 40s.

Some had geometric designs, others diagonal stripes; some had floral paisley patterns, others with motifs of birds or animals; some small, some large. Phil had bought one he felt was not too outlandish. It was a red and white pattern on a navy-blue background, the pattern made to look like a strand of chain-link fencing. Not too striking although it was noticed by the rather attractive blonde in the typing pool, her eyes meeting Phil's as she smiled – beautifully.

Phil never got on the bus wearing that tie. It would be tucked away in his jacket pocket to replace the steady-Eddie boring plain tie Mum had chosen for him, on the journey both to and from work.

The work at the town hall didn't really stretch him much. Most of the tasks he was asked to do were pretty straightforward. Totalling up columns of figures using a wonderful Olivetti add-listing machine, filling in bank paying-in books and adding up cheques, taking hand-written memos or letters to the typing pool, or just dealing with the post. None of it was on a par with organic chemistry and you didn't need to know Newton's laws of motion to carry out what was required.

Phil enjoyed these early weeks at work. His favourite day was Friday when, during the morning, he was one of a group whose job it was to make up pay packets for the hundreds of council workers who were paid in cash every week on a Friday afternoon. This entailed being locked in on the top floor of the town hall – basically the council attic – with other accounts staff, mainly female, and an extraordinary amount of cash, all of which had to be divided into smaller amounts and then put into small brown envelopes for each employee on the weekly payroll.

Phil had never seen so many five-pound, one-pound and ten-bob notes. There were florins, half-crowns, shillings, sixpences, pennies and halfpennies in small bags which bulged like potato sacks. Phil was dying to write '*Loot*' on these sacks once they had been emptied. The whole process took all morning and there was a lot of trouble if either of two things occurred.

First, all the money, down to the last halfpenny, had to be accounted for. If there was anything left over or if there wasn't enough to make up the last packet, then one employee's pay packet was wrong and, with hundreds processed every Friday, then each and every packet would need to be checked. Everyone wanted to avoid that.

Secondly, under no circumstances could you ever leave the room, even if you were caught short. All the group were asked "if they had been" before the room was locked and, if there was an emergency, it would be an accompanied toilet visit which, as Phil was the only male in the group – except for the wages supervisor, who never left the room – would prove a tad embarrassing. He always had just a single small cuppa at breakfast on a Friday.

Phil found that working in an office was much better than he had expected mainly because most of the employees – at least those who would pass the time of day with him – were young and female and many were happy to share their lunch sandwiches with a grammar school lad.

Most of them had left school at 14 to follow a clerical or secretarial career. Phil was surprised how many were married by their mid to late teens or had had steady boyfriends for years. Lunchtime conversations centred mainly around what their husbands or boyfriends did, whether workwise or how they would tell them where to go, what to wear or how to behave. When Phil suggested that times were changing and that they could have their own careers and live out their dreams, he was quickly put right. "Might happen for them high school girls but not us" came the usual response.

Still, it became a most pleasant routine, and, at the end of each week, he would also be the recipient of a light-brown pay envelope, containing at least a fiver, a couple more pound notes and a ten-bob note, his weekly pay. To Phil, this was more money than birthdays and Christmas put together and initially meant he had to make some rather significant decisions.

First, he needed to open a bank account. He was sure that Dad would arrange that. His second important decision concerned what he would do with his newfound affluence. With clothes sorted by Mum, Phil was torn between saving and spending. His savings had grown in the past year, when so much focus had been on scholarly matters, effective or otherwise. He had his eye on a Grundig reel-to-reel tape recorder, spotted in the front window of Waltons Electrics in Worcester Street. It wasn't cheap and would absorb both savings and earnings.

Phil hadn't ventured into either the Beatties basement or the new HMV music store on the upper level of the Mander Centre for quite a while. When he did, he was most surprised to see many recent additions to their record racks, thus muddling his thoughts on where his accumulated riches would be best spent.

The break-up of one of Phil's early favourite bands, Buffalo Springfield, more than a year previous, had generated new music from the band's three main songwriters. Richey Furay had formed a country-rock band called Poco and their debut album 'Pickin' up the pieces', featuring Jim Messina, who had produced and played bass on the final Springfield album, was released back in May.

In the same week, Neil Young also released his second solo album, 'Everyone knows this is nowhere', a heavily guitar-laden LP, with some songs over 10 minutes long. Stephen Stills had joined forces with David Crosby, from the Byrds, together with Graham Nash, from the Hollies, to form the supergroup Crosby, Stills & Nash. They released their eponymous first album just 10 days later.

Phil had heard tracks from all three LPs on the radio and loved all of them. However, there was also the added distraction of the availability of Procol Harum's third album called 'A Salty Dog' which had a truly brilliant title track. Purchasing all four albums would set him back nearly two weeks' wages. The acquisition of the tape recorder, which he dearly wanted to record tracks and programmes from Radio 1, would have to wait for quite a while.

Whilst he was mulling this over, trying to find a way of getting all the records he wanted, as well as the tape machine, he continued to browse through the record racks and noticed that, whilst the price of LPs had now increased to well over two pounds in many cases, record companies had begun to issue albums on what the record assistants were calling 'budget record labels'.

These labels had been around for a while but usually featured studio or session musicians performing versions of hit songs by top artists, or they were albums from more easy-listening artists, such as choral groups or orchestras playing the hits of the time, very similar to the Embassy label sold by Woolworths.

This recent change meant that many mainstream recording labels had set up their own budget labels. Columbia had Harmony Records, Capital had Pickwick, RCA Victor had RCA Camden, Decca had Vocalion, and EMI had Music for Pleasure or Classics for Pleasure, depending on what type of music you wanted. And all these budget albums were often less than half the full price of an LP.

Phil had taken a shine to Marble Arch Records, the budget label for Pye, which released cut-priced albums by the Searchers, the Foundations, the Ivy League and the Kinks, as well as many of the American bubble-gum groups from the Buddah Label. They also featured West-coast bands, on the Kama Sutra label, such as Sopwith Camel and one of Phil's favourites, the Lovin' Spoonful.

So, the deal was that their two albums 'The Best of the Lovin' Spoonful, Volumes I and 2' could be purchased for less than the price of any of the other albums on Phil's list. No contest, so throughout those late-July, early-August, evenings he would wallow in the good-time music of this melodic New York group, whose leading light, John Sebastian, was, in Phil's opinion, just as brilliant a songwriter as Lennon and McCartney or Ray Davies.

These albums included the two UK hits – 'Daydream' and 'Summer in the City' – as well as many of the hits the band had had in the States – 'Do you believe in magic', 'Rain on the roof', 'Darlin' be home soon', 'Younger girl' and 'Six o'clock' – and Phil's two absolute faves, 'You didn't have to be so nice' and 'She's still a mystery'.

All were upbeat, cheery songs with strong choruses and harmonies, lifting his spirits on those warm summer days, despite a few nagging thoughts at the back of his mind. When were the exam results going to arrive and what on earth would he do if they were even worse than he thought?

Thursday, 14th August confirmed Phil's worst fears. He and Matt were having their breakfast, before getting the bus to work, when the post hit the doormat in the outer porch. Phil went to look and there it was, a very official-looking envelope, with the Oxford and Cambridge Examinations Board logo by the postmark and the address, written in his own handwriting, just as the school had requested him to do earlier in the year.

His first thought was to hide it and read it himself at work before confronting Mum and Dad with the results.

"Any post for me?" called Matt from the kitchen.

"Haven't looked yet," replied Phil, with trepidation.

"You OK?" said Matt. "Is that what I think it is? It is the middle of August."

"Yep, it is," replied Phil. "Haven't opened it yet."

"Bring it here," said Matt. "Let's do it together."

Matt found Dad's letter opener and passed it to Phil who slowly opened the envelope and unfolded the letter.

"Well, I got the same grade as you in maths for science," announced Phil.

"That's good, but what about the other two?" asked Matt, although by then he noticed that the tears in Phil's eyes. "That bad, eh. Go and tell Mum and Dad. It's best to get it over with right now and then go to work."

Phil had no fight in him to do otherwise. He went upstairs and knocked on his parents' bedroom door. He went in, passed the letter to Mum who read it before passing it to Dad. Neither of them said a word. Phil said he was sorry. He hadn't worked hard enough.

"Don't expect being late for your chemistry practical helped," said Dad.

"Oh, you know about that!" said Phil.

"Always taught you that parents know everything," Dad said. "But now's not the time to look at what went wrong. Get ready to go to work and we will talk about it this evening."

"Go on, Phillip," said Mum. "Get on that bus and don't worry. We're not annoyed. We know you tried your best. Let's talk about this later."

Phil sat on the bus all the way into town in shock. Grade B for the maths paper was good, really good, but an E for physics – meaning that he hadn't even got over half the questions right – was lower than he'd thought. He hoped he might get a C. And as for chemistry, he was only awarded an O level pass – practically a complete failure. One out of three wasn't great.

As the day progressed, ordinary office errands became a real welcome distraction and whilst he had a pit in his stomach all day, no one at work had any real interest in his A-level results and so the day seemed to improve as it went along. It was only on the bus home that he wondered what the reception party would be when he got in. Opening the front door, he found Mum in the kitchen preparing tea.

"Good day at the town hall, Phillip?" she asked.

"Yes thanks, Mum," replied Phil. "You been busy?"

"I have actually and I hope you will be pleased with my endeavours," she continued. "I want to talk to your Dad when he gets in and then we can talk about things. Go and get changed. Tea will be on the table in around 20 minutes."

Nobody mentioned anything to do with exam results over tea. There was little conversation, mostly polite and succinct. Rachel was at Jane's house that evening and Matt already knew all about it, so there wasn't any need to raise the subject. Tea finished; Mum spoke first.

"Matthew will clear away whilst we talk to Phillip in the front room," she said.

Matt nodded. Phil followed his parents up the hall and into a room usually reserved for formal occasions. He felt as if he had been summoned to the headmaster's office. But suddenly he remembered that it was often a happy room, where, every Christmas, presents would be laid out for all the family. This was going to be the complete opposite, he thought!

He wasn't sure whether he should sit down. Certainly not next to the radiogram that was probably one of the main reasons for his present predicament.

"Relax," said Dad. "Mum's come up with a plan that you might like."

"How do you feel about going back to school in September, Phillip?" she asked.

"There's little chance of me doing Oxbridge entrance with those grades," Phil replied. "Or do you mean college, to do an accountancy course or even teacher training? I've thought about those options."

"No, not college. Back to the grammar school," Mum continued. "Working there means I can easily talk to other teachers and Mr Wrigley has said that he would be happy to have you in six maths next year and you could have a go at the two mathematics A-level subjects – pure and applied. You've done a lot of the syllabus for both in maths for science. What do you think?"

Phil didn't know what to think. "Will they allow that after those results?" he asked.

"They wouldn't have said so if they didn't," said Dad. "There are a couple of conditions though. You probably need to redo physics, to improve that low grade, and we may also look at you doing entrance exams to some of the other top universities, such as Durham or St Andrews in Scotland. We both think you can do better if you do the right subjects."

"You better think about it over the weekend, Phillip," said Mum. "I need to let the school know first thing Monday morning."

"Okay, will do," said Phil, in shock for the second time that day. "Thanks, Mum, and you too, Dad."

"It's all your Mum's doing," he said. "She just asked me if I thought it was a good idea and I knew you wouldn't want to redo chemistry. Never really taken to it have you, so this is a much better solution. As long as it's what you want to do. After all, it's your future, not ours."

It didn't take Phil the whole of the weekend to decide. He enjoyed the usual Friday routine at work and, in a way, was slightly relieved that office work didn't have to be his chosen career, although job prospects with the local town council were not to be sniffed at. After a few weeks, the office staff had got used to him, particularly his mannerism of always humming some piece of pop music they had probably never heard of.

On Friday evening, after choir practice, he went round to see Martin to catch up on all his recent music acquisitions, as always in admiration not only of the number of singles in his collection but also the diversity of his choices, ranging from the poptimism of the Love Affair's 'Bringing on back the good times' and Amen Corner's 'Hello Susie', to the progressive releases by Jethro Tull's 'Living in the past' and Juicy Lucy's version of 'Who do you love?'.

In amongst these singles was an instrumental masterpiece, 'Time is tight' by Booker T and the MG's, sitting next to Bob Dylan's latest release 'Lay, lady, lay'. Martin's devotion to finding obscure gems was illustrated by inclusions from bands called Three Dog Night, Classics IV and the wonderfully named Thunderclap Newman. Phil was never bored delving through Martin's box of singles. There was always something new and often quite unexpected.

Chris was there when Phil arrived. Throughout the six years they had been at school together it would have been easy to label some classmates as swots. There was no doubt that Chris, like Martin, was well above average when it came to intelligence although he just looked and acted pretty normal.

There was Bobby, Simon and Carter G – not Carter A – all of whom were geniuses or should that be genii. Phil wasn't sure about that. He was sure though that they all looked like professors even in their teens. But Chris didn't. He didn't wear glasses as the others did, starting with the NHS prescription kind in the first year before moving on to the John Lennon style by the fifth form. Nor did Chris wear short-sleeve V-necked jumpers or odd socks.

He would take part in the same things as everyone else although this was where his brilliance rather evaporated. There can never have been a teenage lad who lacked co-ordination to the degree that Chris did. In basketball, he struggled to run and bounce the ball at the same time, with umpires' whistles constantly blowing for what was known as 'travelling'.

If he was chosen for his house cricket team, the captain would always position him as close to the boundary when fielding so that he was as far away from the ball as possible, and he would always bat last if at all. In school house team games, he was the reserve, but he was always there. He never seemed to mind. Chris was part of the team. He was with the others. He was happy.

"Hi, Chris. You good?" enquired Phil.

"Yeh. Pretty well," replied Chris. "How were your results?"

"Not great," said Phil. "What about you?"

"A's in all three subjects," said Chris. "Same as Martin, but we both failed the general paper!"

"Blimey!" replied Phil. "I got a B in that. I wrote a long essay on the effects of popular music on the changes in contemporary media."

"Were your grades good enough to stay on at school?" asked Chris.

"Not really," replied Phil and went on to explain what his Mum had sorted out for him before asking them if they thought he should go back into six maths.

"No question," said Martin. "A year at school rather than going to work every day has got to be better. I'm fed up with working in the Beatties' book department over the summer hols. Good money for buying records, especially as I get staff discount, but boredom city!"

A similar conversation took place on Saturday afternoon when Phil sat with Joe and Adrian watching Wolves reserves lose 2-1 to Notts Forest at Molineux, the first team being away at Sheffield Wednesday. Joe had done well enough, getting B grades in physics and maths for science and a C in chemistry. He would still be entered for Oxbridge entrance exams as many at the school thought his sporting prowess would count for a great deal when it came to gaining a place at one of the colleges where they valued sport above academic ability.

Adrian had done as expected – brilliantly. He had matched his athletic brilliance, breaking long-standing school records in both the long and triple jump and representing the county in the latter discipline. He would return to school as head boy in September and with two A grades in biology and chemistry, and a B in physics, many thought he would be a shoo-in at any college at either Oxford or Cambridge.

Everybody seemed to be going back to school in September. No one was off to train at college or start working full time. By late Saturday, Phil was certain that he would join his school friends for another year and would inform Mum and Dad that he would spend the next

12 months studying more diligently and attempting to improve his A-level grades.

A week later he found himself in a very, very long queue at the turnstiles of the South Bank stand to go into Molineux.

"Can't wait for this game," Phil said to Joe.

"Yep, we haven't had such a brilliant start to the season for yonks," Joe replied. "United have yet to win a game, scoring only three times in four games. Should be an easy win."

"Can't see this run carrying on though, can you?" said Adrian with his usual pessimism.

"Why not?" asked Joe. "Four games so far in August and four wins. Okay, we have let in more goals than Everton and the `Pool but that's why we aren't top of the league. It's only on goal difference. And we are joint top scorers with the `Pool."

"Mind you, if we don't get a move on, we won't get to see the game at all," said Phil. "Never seen the queues this long before."

The queue snaked from the turnstiles, up the Molineux Fold, round the front of the Molineux Hotel and spilt on to the road around the junction of North Street and Wadham's Hill. Construction on the town's brand-new ring road had just started, adding to the congestion with so many supporters keen to get to the match.

Many of them were less than happy with this new transport development which would cut the football ground off from the city centre. This gave rise to an oft-repeated comment "Wolvo must be the only town in Britain to have a ring road that goes through the middle", revealing that many Wulfrunians had little regard for their town planners.

The lads got in just after the kick-off and made their way to their usual vantage point, at the side of the stand.

"See the Red Devils are here in force, as usual," said Phil, looking across to the centre of the vast South Bank where the Manchester United supporters had congregated and were in full voice with their usual gusto and bravado,

"Hopefully they will be more subdued by 5 o'clock," said Joe. But he was wrong as the game was played out in a very guarded manner, both teams showing maybe too much respect to sides of such history as Wolves and Man United. Neither of the two talented forward lines seemed to want to 'have a go' at getting just the one goal that would have meant so much to both sets of supporters.

A win for United would be their first of the season and Wolves hadn't registered five wins to start a season since the 1950s. And if both the Toffees and the 'Pool dropped points, Wolves would be top!

Wolves were missing wonder-winger Dave Wagstaffe but still had Dougan and Curran up front, together with Peter Knowles, who was scoring freely this season, and they had signed Jim McCalliog from Sheffield Wednesday, who had made his debut at the start of August. United had an equally strong forward line with Denis Law, Bobby Charlton and George Best all playing alongside a debutant in defender Ian Ure who they had just bought from Arsenal.

It should have been a goal-fest but with both goalkeepers – Phil Parkes and Alex Stepney – making some great saves, from Best and Dougan respectively, the game ended goalless and supporters left the ground a tad disappointed.

"Did you hear the size of the crowd? Over 50,000 today. Not bad for a 0-0 draw," said Joe. "You were right, Ade. United were better than their league position suggested. See you later this evening? Expect you've got enough dosh to stand us all a cuppa after working at your brother-in-law's chippy these hols? What's it called again?"

"Fred's Plaice!" said Adrian. "Yes, I know it's a bit corny but it's always really busy. He's given me tonight off as he knows I go to Venturers on Saturdays. Who's on tonight, Phil?"

"Not sure," replied Phil, as they strolled back to Queens Square in the sunshine. "There's Brian. I'll run and ask him."

Phil wasn't gone long and came back with Brian.

"It's a local band. They've been around quite a while. Since '65 I think. They've had a few names – they're now known as Lady Jane and the Royaltee," explained Brian. "Martin says they're good."

"That's good enough for me," said Phil. "There's me bus. See you later, fellas."

As he stepped on to the bus, he was staggered how full it was. Every seat was occupied, and a few people were standing downstairs. He thought he would try his luck upstairs where there was just one seat left, next to the girl who lived up Muchall Road.

Phil sat down and just looked vacantly straight in front of him. He took his Wolves match programme from his anorak pocket and started to read it.

"Been to the game, then?" asked the girl.

"Yeh," replied Phil.

"Good game?" she continued.

"Yeh. A good match but no goals," said Phil.

"My Dad won't let me go," she said. "Says it's not a place for a young lady."

"I'd take you," said Phil unexpectedly. "What was he thinking, saying that," he thought.

"That'd be really nice of you, but he probably still wouldn't approve, knowing my Dad," said the girl. "Here's our stop."

Phil stood up and let her go before him. She thanked him with a smile. He could feel he was blushing, and his legs felt as if they didn't belong to him. He followed her along the bus aisle. He wanted to act like Joe Cool, but his heart was beating faster than ever. As he walked down the stairs, he noticed how brown and shiny her hair was. They got off the bus and walked to the corner of Penn Road and Muchall Road, together.

"I live over there," said Phil. "Number 330."

"What a daft thing to say," he thought.

"I know," she replied.

As the traffic cleared, Phil crossed the road, and she began to walk up Muchall Road.

Reaching the other side, he turned and shouted: "My name's Phil."

The girl turned. "I know. My name's Judy," she called out before disappearing into her drive.

Chapter 11 – Suite: Judy Blue Eyes

If Phil had been asked what he had for tea that evening or which way he had walked to Venturers later, he would have had real trouble remembering any of the facts at all. Since his eventful bus trip home, his mind had been scrambled. He had eaten. He had walked just over a mile to the youth club, down Pennhouse Avenue and Wells Road – or was it Pinfold Lane or Hollybush Lane? He hadn't a clue.

His thoughts were befuddled. Why had he said that to her when what he should have said was so obvious. Why hadn't he walked up Muchall Road with her instead of crossing the main road? Why had he been so tongue-tied? Judy wasn't. What a lovely name. It wasn't until he was standing in the queue for the youth club, that it registered that her name began with a J! Not Jane, not Janice, but Judy. The Valentine's card? Really? It couldn't have been, could it?

"You coming in or what?" Brian's question broke his train of thought.

"Yeh. Of course," said Phil. "Sorry, miles away."

"You were light-years away, on a different planet," said Brian. "If this is the effect a goalless draw has on you Phil, I don't want to be around when Wolves lose for the first time this season or score a hat full! And have I heard right? You and I will be back in the same form in September."

"Yeh, me Mum's wangled it so that I can have another go at my A-levels in six maths," replied Phil. "Lucky to get a second chance, really. Is the band here yet?"

"Oi yow two. Pack up nattering. We wo get a chance to see 'em if yow don't shut your cake 'ole and go in," came a shout from further down the queue and Phil nodded to Brian and went in.

Uncharacteristically, Phil had arrived at the youth club a lot later than he usually did. Over tea, and whilst having the requisite Saturday evening bath before getting ready to go out, he had dithered. No one seemed bothered if he was early or late that evening. At home, everyone else was going about their own business. Whether he got there before the band had started simply wasn't on his mind. It just wasn't important.

Most of the regulars were at the club that evening. The Wednesfield contingent had made it across town yet again although Coops was still on holiday. Joe said hello, spoke to Phil about the game, whether Wolves could continue their impressive early-season form and how long did he think we could stay unbeaten. Phil's replies were brief and disinterested. It just wasn't important.

The band had already set up and the four of them strolled casually through the crowd to the rostra blocks,

Lady Jane attracting plenty of wolf whistles from the lads. She was an absolute stunner with beautiful long dark hair, a gorgeous smile and legs that went on forever. Her real name was Anna Terrana. Her brother Phil played bass and sang harmonies, together with the guitarist Geoff Hill. The quartet was completed by drummer Graham Nock.

As a band, they had been on the local music scene for over four years, winning many of the regional talent contests. Both Phil and Anna were really good looking, which certainly helped with publicity shots, and they took a great deal of care to dress the part, keeping up with all the latest fashions. Their dual vocal talents set them apart from the other local bands and, back in 1967, the Astra Agency had taken over their management. Now great things were predicted for Lady Jane and the Royaltee.

They began with a fabulous version of the Mamas & Papas' hit 'I saw her again', followed by Mama Cass' recent solo hit 'It's getting better'. Phil and Anna switched lead vocals and their harmonies were just perfect.

Local music journalist John Ogden had recently written, in one of his review columns for the *Express & Star,* that "Anna's style is the nearest I have heard to that of Mama Cass of the Mamas and Papas". Musically, it was a terrific start to the evening and the crowd adored it. Songs they all knew, performed really well, and great to dance to.

"Right up your street this," said Martin to Phil.

Before he could reply, Phil Terrana stepped up to introduce the next song. It was a cover of the current chart hit 'Ragamuffin Man' by Manfred Mann, on which he sang lead vocal. The next song involved the whole band harmonising on this year's Beach Boys summer hit 'Breakaway', again going down a storm with the ever-enthusiastic crowd.

As the applause died down, Phil Terrana continued as the band's frontman. "This was our very first single which was released on the CBS label earlier this year. It's called 'That kind of girl'," he said. Once again, the vocals were switched back and forth, with Anna taking over on lead to sing the B side, called 'Will you be staying after Sunday', a more easy-going track but just as good.

"Bet you have that in your collection," Phil said to Martin, who nodded.

"Great song," he replied. "That should have been the A-side. It would have been a hit, I reckon."

The band continued with perfect cover versions of recent top 20 hits – Tommy Roe's 'Dizzy' and Family Dogg's 'A way of life'– and then finished the first half of their set with both sides of their new single, 'Let's ride' and 'I need your love', which Radio 1 breakfast presenter, Tony Blackburn, had championed but to no avail as it disappointingly failed to chart.

"Yow with us now then, Phil?" asked Joe, as the lads sauntered off for a cuppa at the break. "He wasn't when he got here, so Brian said," he continued. "What's up with yow?"

"It's not important. I'm over it now," said Phil. "That wasn't a very long first set. It's not even 8.45 yet," he continued, quickly changing the subject.

"Ah, then you don't know about the roadie," chipped in Spud. "He's Phil and Anna's dad and he always makes sure they're home by 11, so it'll be an early finish for all of us tonight. He was an Italian POW who stayed over here after the war, like a load of `em did. Good news for us though 'cos they're one of the best bands around, I reckon."

Spud knew his stuff and, like Martin, was rarely wrong on music matters. Lady Jane and the Royaltee were all back on stage again before the lads had finished their drinks and straight into a cover of Marmalade's 'Baby make it soon' followed by the Troggs 'With a girl like you' but, with Anna singing lead, they had changed the lead lyric to 'With a boy like you'.

Phil Terrana then introduced the next track by the Lovin Spoonful and Geoff Hill kicked in with the guitar intro before Phil and Anna traded vocals on the song. 'Lovin you' was one of Phil's favourites on the recent 'Best of' LPs he had bought. He quietly sang along to the song, once again off into his own world, seated on the top deck of the bus, earlier that day.

The song finished and Anna began the next one, bringing him back to earth, as she sang the first line of 'I'd like to get to know you', which had been a hit in the States for vocal harmony band, Spanky and Our Gang. It was a most beautiful song and they did a great version, with fabulous harmonies, although it simply made Phil think that this wasn't the place he wanted to be tonight.

He turned to go just as Martin pulled on his arm.

"This is really good. Your sort of stuff," he said.

"I'm off home," said Phil. "Just not feeling too clever tonight, I reckon. Need a good walk to clear my head."

"I was going to ask you about next weekend," said Martin.

"What about it?" asked Phil.

"It's the Isle of Wight Festival," continued Martin. "Chris and I fancy going. You wanna come with us?"

"I'll call round on Monday, after work," replied Phil. "Not sure my folks are very happy with me still this summer and there's another week's work at the town hall to go. Really need to sort a few things out. See ya."

Phil spent that final week of the summer holidays, the last week of August, dithering. Should he go to the Isle of Wight Festival at the weekend? It was rumoured that Bob Dylan was going to play, having been in semi-retirement for the past three years following his motorcycle accident in 1966, but then, unlike Matt, Phil wasn't really a Dylan fan.

Other bands on the festival bill included Free, Family and the Moody Blues, all of whom Phil would have gone to see if they had been playing locally but the real draw was one of his favourite bands, the Pretty Things, whose album, from last year, 'S.F. Sorrow', was still getting regular plays on the home radiogram. The Who were also going to be there, topping the bill, and featuring some tracks from their new 'Tommy' double LP. To see both bands play tracks from their respective rock operas would be brilliant.

Maybe his parents would approve of him going if he told them he was going to listen to opera or a symphony orchestra or a choir! But even if they all hitchhiked to Portsmouth, and then stayed with Grandma in Emsworth, the cost of the ferry to the island would make a large dent in his savings. And they would have to leave on Friday which would mean him missing his last day at the town hall but, more importantly, a day's pay and that would mean the purchase of that tape recorder would have to wait, maybe until well after Christmas.

So, by Tuesday, Phil had decided not to go. Mum certainly wouldn't approve, he reasoned, and maybe he had given them both enough to worry about over the summer. Perhaps he should knuckle down to his last week at work and get ready to return to school. It was the right thing to do, he reckoned.

By Wednesday afternoon he had changed his mind again and now he really wanted to go. So, after tea, he was on his bike to Martin's house to find out about the arrangements. An hour later he was back home, despondent as neither Chris nor Martin had gained parental approval, their reasoning being that such a trip so close to the beginning of what was likely be a really important term for them, with both applying to go to Cambridge University, was just not on the cards.

Mentally, Phil was all over the place throughout the week. He had spent more time than usual gazing up

Muchall Road, not so much hoping to catch sight of Judy but just wondering what on earth he should do. Maybe staying at home this weekend, rather than on the Isle of Wight, meant they might bump into each other again.

He hadn't seen her all week but then again, he'd been at work so maybe there might be more chance to see her over the weekend. But then it was Judy who had started the conversation on the bus, so wasn't it now down to him to make the next move? Of course, it was, but what should he do?

Saturday came and went, with Phil spending most of the day in town, checking the tape recorder was still in Walton's shop window, then meeting Joe and Brian to watch Wolves reserve side win 2-1 at Molineux against their local arch-rivals West Bromwich Albion, before dropping by Beatties to collect the latest addition to his LP collection, the eponymous album from Crosby, Stills and Nash.

He spent Sunday listening to the album, enjoying it as much as he had 'Buffalo Springfield Again' twenty months earlier. Phil's mum made every effort to distract him, encouraging him to sort out his school uniform, clean his shoes, and basically be ready to return to school on Monday. To her, it was very important that he was in the right frame of mind to re-start school, although she hadn't a clue as to why he seemed so distant and distracted.

Phil lost himself in his new album. It was a real gem. One press review described it as "warm, inviting, homely and cosy", and another as an "eminently playable record". Seriously understated on both counts, reckoned Phil

Each and every track was beautifully written and whilst many thought it was too perfect and over-produced, it was right on the mark for Phil, full of exceptional harmonies, glorious melodies, and beautifully crafted songs.

The lyrical and musical amalgamation of the three members of this supergroup had led to ten very different and contrasting tracks on the album. Three were written by Graham Nash: 'Marrakesh Express', so obviously a single release, 'Lady of the Island', a beautifully sensual vocal and guitar love song, and 'Pre-road Downs', probably a song left over from his Hollies days, but here brilliantly augmented by Stills reverse-recorded guitar.

David Crosby's three contributions were again as diverse as they were brilliant. The angst of 'Long time gone', a song written on the night that Senator Robert Kennedy was assassinated, together with the overtly anti-war song 'Wooden Ships', were in stark contrast to the beauty of the subtle harmonies on his love song 'Guinevere', written about some of the ladies in his close circle, and accompanied by his guitar which was tuned differently to produce a hypnotic refrain, set beneath deliciously concordant vocals. It soon became one of Phil's favourites.

Stephen Stills actually had four tracks to his name. The final one '49 Bye-byes' was a combination of two songs left over from his Buffalo Springfield days, and 'You don't have to cry' was actually the very first song this trio had ever sung together. Both tracks emphasised the vocal chemistry between them which was also evident in Stills words for 'Helplessly hoping', a song that was a clever exercise in alliteration from start to finish, with the final refrain of "They are three together; They are for each other" perfectly summing up the group.

And then there was the opening track, 'Suite: Judy Blue Eyes', written by Stills and performed as four distinct sections in which he played every instrument – guitars, bass and drums – as well as taking lead vocals, with Crosby and Nash adding harmonies. Phil loved the arrangement of the whole track, which was as complicated as some of the Buffalo Springfield records but simple in some parts to accentuate the importance of their three-part harmonies evident throughout the record.

Phil had first heard this track, albeit an abridged version released as a single, on the radio earlier in the year. He thought the title was 'Sweet Judy Blue Eyes', unaware that Stills was again playing with words, as the song was about his then-lover, the singer Judy Collins.

The song's lyrics seemed to bring together so much that had happened over the past week and Phil hoped that it may well become more meaningful to him in the coming weeks. The song title had become so significant to Phil, although he had absolutely no idea what colour Judy's eyes were!

The first day of September dawned warm and bright. It was a new month, a new week, a new start. At the breakfast table, Phil thought how different it might have been. Would he still have been at the town hall or enrolling on some course at Wolverhampton Polytechnic or Wulfrun College? Maybe he would have decided accountancy was a safe bet or possibly embarking on some completely different journey working in a factory.

"Stop daydreaming and get your tie and jacket on, Phillip, if you want a lift to school," said Mum.

"Thank goodness she had had the gumption to speak to the maths staff," he thought.

As he took his jacket from the wardrobe, he glanced down at the bus stop outside his house. There was Judy, standing towards the back of the bus queue.

Tie stuffed in pocket, jacket quickly slung over his shoulders, Phil was downstairs in a trice, checking he had enough change for the bus fare, and opening the front door.

"Thanks for the offer of a lift, Mum. I'm getting the bus," Phil shouted as he closed the front door and ran to join the queue.

Phil followed Judy up to the top deck of the bus where she sat down squarely in the middle of the double seat near the back, moving across to the window as he approached, so he knew she had saved the seat for him.

"Hi. Where are you off to?" he asked.

"I've finished school and I am starting at college in town, carrying on studying languages," she replied. "I can see you are back at the grammar school."

They chatted throughout the journey into town, Phil explaining how badly he had done in his A-levels and how he had been given a second chance to maybe get grades which would be sufficient to go to university. Judy explained that her O-level results had been good enough to get on to the languages course at Wulfrun College, as she wanted to be an air stewardess. Phil thought that she would easily be the most glamorous air stewardess ever.

That week, each and every day, they caught the bus together and came home together, Phil always waiting for her outside Joan's outfitters in Queen's Square in the afternoons. They chatted about their days, how different things were at college for Judy, and how things were very much the same for Phil, although he was already happier to be studying subjects that he found much more to his liking.

At the end of each journey home, Phil didn't make the same mistake as on that first occasion and always walked Judy to the drive of her home. By Friday, they had become a regular sight to other bus commuters, just two teenagers chatting and laughing. On the last home journey of the week though, Phil was surprisingly quiet. He was summoning up the courage to do something he had never done before.

"Fancy going to the pictures tomorrow evening?" asked Phil, as they approached Judy's house.

"With you?" replied Judy.

"Of course, with me. Unless you would rather go with someone else?" said Phil.

"No silly. I'd love to go with you," said Judy. "What's on?"

"Well. I've looked and there's a Burt Lancaster film about skydiving called 'Gypsy Moths', or Elvis's latest called 'The Trouble with Girls'," explained Phil.

Judy pulled a face. Still a beautiful face, Phil thought, but obviously neither film was the right choice, certainly not for her.

"The Odeon still has 'Goodbye, Columbus' on. It's a romantic comedy and the music is done by one of my favourite bands, the Association," said Phil.

"Then that's the one," agreed Judy. "Romance for me and music for you. Sounds just right. What time shall we meet at the bus stop?"

"Film starts at 7. So, we can get the 6:15 bus. OK?" replied Phil.

"Great. It's a date then. See you tomorrow," said Judy, and she gave Phil a kiss on the cheek.

"What was that f-f-f-for?" Phil stuttered.

"No reason really. Just thank you for making my first week at college so nice," said Judy.

Phil blushed, smiled and began to walk back down the road, turning just the once to see if she was still at the foot of her drive. She was and she smiled back before going in.

Over the coming weeks, this weekly pattern was maintained. Keeping each other company on the way to college and school, finding films to go and see, and just getting to know each other more and more every day.
Some weeks it would be Phil's choice of films and predictably he chose a couple of films more for the music

than the storyline. Neither of them enjoyed the drugs and violence of 'Easy Rider' but Phil enjoyed the "groundbreaking" soundtrack which included songs from bands such as the Byrds, Steppenwolf, the Band and Jimi Hendrix. The film 'Alice's Restaurant' wasn't quite what he'd expected, as it was a comedy based on an 18-minute song recorded by Arlo Guthrie, but it was still quite good.

Judy's choices were more mainstream, historical films or Westerns, such as 'The Madwoman of Chaillot' which had a cast list of well-established stars like Katherine Hepburn, or 'Mackenna's Gold' in which a whole raft of 40s and 50s film legends starred. They enjoyed each other's choices but most of all they just liked going to the cinema together.

Sometimes there wouldn't be any film that either of them wanted to see but they would choose to go, just to be together. At other times, there were movies they both enjoyed such as 'Paint Your Wagon' or the film they went to see in late October, the splendid 'Butch Cassidy and the Sundance Kid', after which Judy was undecided whether Paul Newman was more handsome than Robert Redford, comments which lead to Phil's first bout of jealousy.

Occasionally, after school and college, they would stay in town for a while and have a coffee. They wouldn't go to Milano's in Darlington Street as it still had parental forbidden status from its bikers reputation from the late 50s, and Phil knew that some sixth formers from both the girls high school and the boys grammar would frequent The Kleeber Café in Queens Street so that was maybe not the right place for a private tête-à-tête. Certainly, they never went into the café in Beatties as they would have lowered the average age by around fifty years!

Their favoured venue became The Golden Egg, recently opened by the entrance to the new Mander Centre on Queens Square. With its brightly coloured décor, modern furniture and melamine crockery, it was different, brash, and fun which was maybe why it suited them. Moreover, the frothy coffee was cheap but very good.

Some evenings in late September and into early October, when the weather was still very unseasonably warm and pleasant, they would take walks, sometimes after school around West Park, or later in the evening over Penn Common. They talked, held hands and laughed. That seemed to be all that was needed to enjoy each other's company, whilst each goodnight kiss was becoming more intense, as the weeks went by.

Slowly, both of them became aware that their parents, or more specifically mothers, were acting differently towards them. Simple statements would become questions, not necessarily embarrassing, such as one from Phil's mum.

"When are you going to bring this young lady you have been stepping out with back home for tea, Phillip? I would like to meet her."

This would be met with a shake of the head from Phil but he knew that such an event would have to take place sooner rather than later so he asked Judy if she would like to come in, on their way home one evening.

"That's exactly what I was going to ask you!" she replied. "My mum has been on at me to ask you in for the last two weeks."

The deeds were done in both houses on consecutive evenings, as Phil and Judy thought it was best to get these potentially embarrassing occasions over and done with as soon as possible. It was only then that they would both feel that all parties were satisfied that neither of their offspring was 'stepping out' with a wrong 'un!

These icebreakers actually had an unexpected benefit. Now, rather than during long walks or sitting on park benches, or the back seats in the cinema, they could instead enjoy the comforts of home, as they were now welcome to use the respective front rooms at home – to sit, chat and listen to music.

Phil introduced Judy to the wonders of the Zombies, Buffalo Springfield and Procol Harum, never quite knowing whether she enjoyed any of their music. Her tastes were more towards the Beach Boys, Simon & Garfunkel, Cat Stevens and the Beatles, a little different from Phil's fascination with more obscure bands and singers, but little that he disliked.

Most of the time they felt like they were being chaperoned, rarely without another adult in the house, but this didn't worry or frustrate them. They just enjoyed being together and doing something neither of them had done before – starting a relationship with someone who wasn't family, who hadn't sat next to you in class, or sang in the choir with you. And it was someone you had chosen to want to be with.

They talked about what they hoped they might do in life, never quite saying whether they wanted to do it together. Of course, Phil would love to be involved with either radio, music or both but it was likely he would end up at university this time next year. Judy had her heart set on becoming an air stewardess with an airline that travelled all over the world, going to as many new countries as possible, speaking different languages and seeing places that she had only read about or seen on TV.

Phil and Judy knew that the here and now was just as important as their future hopes and dreams and that this new friendship was just one of the many changes that they were both experiencing in a strangely uncertain but enjoyable manner.

Phil's surprise return to school then occasioned a series of unexpected pleasurable episodes. He was now in six maths, with many classmates that had come up in the A stream, rather than the Alpha stream, at the grammar school, many of whom he had lost touch with since junior school – not so much Brian, but certainly John and Roy.

Studying mathematics, whether pure or applied, seemed to Phil infinitely more pleasurable than chemistry or physics, although he was timetabled to be in the physics laboratories for many periods each week in a necessary effort to improve on that lowly E grade attained last summer.

His excellent progress in mathematics, in just a short space of time, had been observed by all his teachers and this apparently effortless proficiency led them to suggest that he might be considered good enough to sit scholarship examinations for the University of St Andrews in the spring term, something that certainly pleased his parents after missing out on the possibility of following Matt to Oxford.

In sport, Phil was back representing the school at football after a gap of five years. He had been captain of the under-13 team in his very first year at the school, not realising again that this was down to favouritism rather than ability, as the team was coached by that same teacher, who a year later would teach him history, and was at that time again eager to impress Phil's father.

Playing right-back in the school's second eleven, with Joe in goal and Coops the other full-back, was not only thought to be worthy of representing your school but was also a lot of fun. The second eleven was made up of good, proficient players, many in their final year at school although often those who didn't volunteer to take part in the weekly training that was decreed by the PE staff.

And anyway, the first team was full of youngsters, 15 and 16-year-olds who had risen to the pinnacle of sporting excellence quicker than those at the end of their time at school. It was also a golden era for the school, winning many leagues and trophies. The second eleven just tagged along, for the home and away games to other grammar and independent schools, intent on enjoying the occasion rather than worrying about the scoreline. They were happy outings.

A year previous, the school had finally decided that the Combined Cadet Corps should no longer be compulsory on Thursdays, so the awful experience of travelling there and back again in the dreaded – and very itchy – khaki army uniform became a thing of the past.

In its place was the school's Music Appreciation Society, which now met on Thursday afternoons and of which Phil was one of the founder members. So, instead of army square bashing, rifle cleaning and learning semaphore signals, he, and other like-minded lads, listened to and discussed a wide range of music genres, from light or baroque classical to the bizarre repertoire of modern artists such as John Cage, Miles Davis, Captain Beefheart or Tyrannosaurus Rex.

Something for everyone's taste was very much the group's creed and, as music had remained just as important in his life as sport, Phil still enjoyed being involved in both school and house choirs. He also continued to play E-flat horn in the brass band, and, as with many of his hobbies, it was just as much for the group bonhomie as it was for the performances – rarely practised but thoroughly enjoyed.

As September and October passed, Phil seemed to be experiencing so many enjoyable aspects in his life. Was it all down to the fact that he now had a girlfriend? If so, then he wasn't complaining. He was playing a lot of football, sometimes three times a week, often twice on a Saturday – for the school in the morning and for St Aiden's Youth

Club in the afternoon. He had left the church choir as Friday evenings, previously reserved for choir practice, had now become film nights with Judy.

With playing so much of the 'beautiful game', attending Wolves home games had become a bit of a rarity, especially as on occasions Judy would stroll up to the Mount Road recreation ground to watch him playing for St Aiden's. Phil wasn't certain she found the experience a thing of beauty even though they were now a much more skilful and successful side. However, much to the surprise of both of them, they became involved in a particular activity – albeit in different places – studying Italian.

Students in their third year in the sixth form at the grammar school were 'encouraged' to study for an extra O-level as, according to some of the staff, they might have too much time on their hands after scholarship studies. Economics was an option, or you could plump for religious studies, classical music, or languages, such as Spanish, Italian and German, not options found lower down the school.

It would have made more sense for Phil to have opted for either music or economics but there were two reasons why, for two periods a week, he began to attempt to learn Italian. The first reason was to do with the school's Italian teacher.

She came from the country itself and had become the wife of the Italian consulate in Wolverhampton, something that had been established when so many Italian POWs, held in camps in Shropshire and Staffordshire, had decided to stay after the Second World War.

Not only was Mrs Frereton a tad eccentric as a teacher but she had promised that, when she returned to her home in Bologna, in northern Italy, at Easter, she would take a handful of students with her, to help them 'speaka' the language.

Adrian and Phil thought this was too good an opportunity to miss and so elected to study Italian. The fact that Phil found out, after just a couple of weeks back at school, that Judy was also studying Italian, was simply an added bonus which helped him to endure studying a language that was as foreign to him as the country itself.

The final week of October was half-term and, after an unusually warm and dry month, Phil was looking forward to having much more time to spend with Judy in the coming week. That was until his mother issued a three-line whip to say that the whole family was to visit Chesterfield over the first weekend, leaving early Saturday morning and not returning until late Monday afternoon.

The disappointment was written all over Phil's face, knowing that there would be very little to do in the Derbyshire market town, other than maybe a kick-about on Tapton Park with Matt, who was down from Oxford and, along with Rachel, had been similarly compelled into this family visitation.

If Phil had bothered to find out any pertinent details behind Mum's desire to go home then maybe he shouldn't have been so crestfallen and certainly a lot more understanding. His grandmother had struggled in the past six months since Grandad passed away, added to which both of Phil's uncles were now living away from home. She missed Grandad terribly and had found the loneliness of living alone very hard to come to terms with.

To Phil, the conflict of his emotions was equally tough. Here he was, perhaps the happiest he had ever been in his life, being dragged away for a long weekend to a dour and unhappy environment with very little in the way of escape or light relief. After failing to get parental agreement to go to watch Chesterfield FC on the Saturday afternoon, he settled into his usual armchair, by the radio in the front room, just catching the end of Johnnie Walker's show before John Peel's monotones became a welcome distraction.

It was whilst he was listening that Phil began to devise a plan that could well brighten up the remainder of the half-term holiday. He hoped that, by the time next Saturday had come and gone, he may well have succeeded in achieving two aims that he had been working on for a while – first, taking Judy to Molineux and then to Venturers.

Judy's father was a director for one of the town's largest employers at the time, the construction company, Tarmac. In the few weeks that Phil had known Judy, he hadn't really spoken more than a few words to her father but he was aware that Tarmac had a very sophisticated computer at their factory.

The school had also arranged that Phil and other six maths classmates would go on a short weekend course at Loughborough University, in the next spring term, in an attempt to learn the intricacies of computer programming languages, such as Cobol, Fortran and Algol, words which had as much resonance with Phil as the Italian he was struggling with.

The opportunity to go to Tarmac, to look at their computer, and ask the computer operators questions, seemed not only to be a good grounding for this course but might also ingratiate him with Judy's father. Phil was quite surprised that he was most impressed at this request and said that he would make some immediate arrangements for a visit to Tarmac's computer section and a chat with the staff working there.

Later in the week, Phil asked Judy if she would like to go to the Molineux on Saturday afternoon to see Wolves play their arch-rivals, West Bromwich Albion.

"Dad will never agree to that," she replied.

"No harm in asking," said Phil. "You never know, he might surprise you!"

The next day an astonished Judy met up with Phil to say that not only had her father agreed that he would be happy with Phil taking, and looking after, his daughter at Molineux on Saturday afternoon but that he had also expressed opinions implying that he thought Phil was an earnest and thoughtful young lad.

"That was his description, not mine!" laughed Judy.

"And whilst you're about it, ask your mum if it's alright for me to take you out on Saturday evening, as well?" said Phil "The band on at Venturers is one of the best around. You'll love `em."

Saturday came around and they met at the bus stop as usual in the early afternoon. The look on the faces of Joe, Adrian and Brian, standing by the 'man on the `oss', as Phil strolled up, holding hands with Judy, was priceless.

"Yow not going to the game, mate?" asked Joe. "It's the Baggies!!"

"Course I'm going to the game," replied Phil. "And so is Judy. Judy, this is Joe. That's Adrian and he's Brian."

"Phil's told me loads about you lot," she said.

"All bostin, I hope," said Brian.

"Doubt it," said Adrian.

"I'm under parental instructions to ensure Judy's safety," said Phil. "So, is it the South Bank or the Enclosure?"

"The Enclosure's for kids," replied Joe. "Yow'll be alright with us in the South Bank. There won't be much trouble with that Albion lot after we've stuffed `em 4-0. We'll look after yow. Good thing yow ain't relying on just Phil to keep yow safe!!"

Phil grinned as he knew he was in for an afternoon of having his leg pulled and there would be many more comments at his expense whilst Judy was in their company. They made their way into the South Bank and headed for their usual vantage spot, by the side of the stand. None of the lads needed to perch on the stanchions now, but Judy shinned up there and leant on Phil to get a better view.

The crowd was bigger than the lads had expected, with just under 40,000 in the ground, all keen as mustard for kick-off at 3 o'clock, in this local fierce Black Country derby. Most of the Wolves fans had only one thing on their minds though. Where was Peter Knowles? Was he coming back? When the stadium announcer read out the teams, there was a mass sigh when, like the past four home games, his name wasn't in the line-up.

"I'd heard a rumour that McGarry had persuaded him to play this week," said Joe.

"I'd heard he was now a milkman," commented Adrian.

"I'd just love to see him in our side," said Phil.

"You and 30,000 others," agreed Joe.

"Why isn't he playing?" asked Judy. "Is he really that good?"

"He's got religion, so they say," said Adrian. "He became a Jehovah's Witness when Wolves were on tour in America last summer and now he reckons that playing football isn't what God wants him to do. Doesn't make sense to me."

"He really is that good. He's our George Best and he's our best player, I reckon. Better than the Doog or Waggy," said Joe. "He should be playing for England but he won't now. It's all a bit lampy if yow ask me."

When Knowles began that season, he had made it clear that he was uncertain about his future as a professional footballer, after his religious conversion, but Wolves began the season unbeaten for six games, with Knowles scoring three wonderful goals. His last appearance had been in early September, against Nottingham Forest at home, after which he just gave up playing. Everyone hoped he would come back but now it seemed most unlikely.

The start of the game matched the respective league positions of the two rivals. Wolves, still near the top of the league, whilst Albion were closer to the relegation places, attacked for a great deal of the first half with West Brom defending resolutely, especially their goalkeeper, John Osborne, who made two brilliant one-handed saves to deny both Hughie Curran and Jim McCalliog.

By the time the half-time whistle went, most Wolves fans were wondering when, and not if, their side would score, as they had scuffed several chances in the first 45 minutes. With the clubs being only just over ten miles apart in the Black Country, the Baggies fans were there in force, right in the middle of the South Bank, chanting and singing the usual tribal banter, offensive or otherwise, engendered by this intense encounter.

It was one of the oldest football rivalries anywhere in the world, having started over 80 years ago, although it wasn't until the 1950s, when both clubs were in division 1 and Wolves were often enjoying the upper hand, that the rivalry had become a lot more fanatical. Hearing those fans made Phil wonder whether he had done the right thing in bringing Judy to this game for her very first experience of Molineux.

"You ok?" he asked, at half-time.

"Yes, fine," she replied. "Not sure I understand all the rules and no idea who each player is, but it's a really exciting atmosphere. Thanks for bringing me." She kissed Phil on the cheek which made him go red and raised a snigger from Adrian. Judy leant over and gave him a kiss, too.

"And that's for looking after me as well, Adrian," she laughed, as Adrian looked away embarrassed. "There can't be many girls in the crowd today that have three knights in shining armour looking out for her!"

"We could do with some wizardry on the pitch in the second half," said Joe quickly, moving the subject back to football and hoping to sidestep his kiss.

The Albion began the second half going forward a lot more and both Mike Bailey and Gerry Taylor had to clear shots off the line, with Parkes well beaten, to keep the game goalless. With a quarter of the game to go and just when both sets of fans were thinking the game would end goalless, Wagstaffe crossed from deep on the left-wing, Dougan rose to head the ball invitingly into the Albion penalty area and new boy, Mike O'Grady, in just his sixth game since joining from Leeds, hit his second goal for Wolves, with a rasping shot into the roof of the net. It was a belter of a goal!

The crowd went berserk, with the exception of the Baggies fans who became ominously quiet, looking around them in a menacing manner. Phil, Joe and Adrian knew never to celebrate too openly in the South Bank as that would often attract attention from the visiting supporters. The smiles on all their faces said it all. Winning was always good but beating the Albion was the best.

Judy picked that up quickly and just hugged Phil tightly, staying close to him for the rest of the game. As they left the ground, he asked her if she had really enjoyed it and wasn't just saying that to please him.

"No, silly," she replied. "I'm not sure I would want to go to every game like you do, but it's been a really exciting experience and sharing it with you is a bit special."

"And today isn't finished yet," said Phil. "The Light Fantastic are on at Venturers tonight. They're a really great live band. So, what time shall I call for you? Do you want me to ask my Dad to drive us there?"

"You usually walk there, don't you?" replied Judy.

"Yeh, but Dad won't mind," said Phil.

"No, walking there would be nicer. You can keep me warm going there and hopefully coming back," Judy replied, with her usual comely smile. It was a smile that would suffice for Phil until he went to call for her, later that evening.

Life had become one new experience after another for Judy since she and Phil had begun seeing each other. She was unaware of course that Phil was thinking exactly the same as they walked, hand in hand, along Warstones Road, as they approached the youth centre at Springdale Methodist Church.

For nearly three years, this Saturday evening journey had been a solitary one for Phil, usually accompanied by thoughts of the afternoon's sport mingled with the anticipation of the musical treats to come. Most of his concerns then had been about whether there would be any parental problems if he stayed out too late or kept his dad waiting for his lift home. Now his only concern was whether Judy would enjoy an evening that he had suggested would promise so much.

On the music side, he needn't have worried. The band booked that evening, the Light Fantastic, lived up to their well-earned reputation of being one of the most hard-working and one of the best, if not THE best, local live bands around. This was unusual for a group that had only been around for just over a year, and moreover whose line-up wasn't entirely made up of lads from the Black Country.

The drummer, Tony Harrison, came from Hampshire. Lead guitarist, Richard Brown, grew up in Brechin, and rhythm guitarist, Keith Locke, was from Liverpool. The local boys were Birmingham boy Ron Dickson, on bass guitar, and, the latest to join the band, Roy 'Dripper' Kent, on lead vocals, who had left Finders Keepers at the end of 1967.

As a group, it wasn't just their ability to play different types of pop music really, really well, it was also their enthusiasm to entertain that came across to their audience, whether it was at a working men's club, the Civic Hall or a youth centre, like tonight. They played as if they were going to enjoy the evening more than you were and they probably did.

They started off with covers of recent hits, 'Bad Moon Rising' from Creedence Clearwater Revival and 'Viva Bobbie Joe' from the Equals, two great upbeat songs resulting in most of the teenagers dancing right from the start. Phil was mightily impressed by Judy not being at all shy about dragging him straight on to the dance floor. Not surprisingly, Joe, Brian, Martin and Adrian remained static, at the back of the hall, mainly watching Phil with a sense of disbelief and maybe just a little admiration.

The group's next choices – covers from what the music press had termed 'bubble-gum music' – smashes from groups such as the Archies, the Cuff Links and Crazy Elephant – maintained the high energy of the band's performance. Their rhythm was spot on from Ron on bass and Tony on drums, and they all contributed to a great vocal sound, with Dripper taking the lead, both on the songs and with the amusing chat in between each number. That's not to say that the other band members weren't shy at chipping in with comments and jokes throughout.

There probably wasn't a better sound from a local band around at that time and it didn't seem to faze them if they had to be a bit different when covering current chart hits. It was obvious that, to them, it was all about enjoyment. The Light Fantastic just enjoyed playing. They loved entertaining and they had become very good at it.

Dripper sauntered leisurely up to the microphone.

"Yow all have a bostin time?" he enquired, already knowing the answer. "These next two are by our Brummie mate, Roy. Anyone here called Susie? Or maybe Curly? This one's for yow."

'Curly' had been The Move's most recent top-20 hit and Amen Corner had made it to the top-10 with 'Hello Susie', both penned by the charismatic Roy Wood. The Light Fantastic versions were true to, and as good as, the originals but seemed to be more fun that evening, as was their version of the Love Affair's latest hit, 'Bringing on back the good times'. The first half of their set was completed by the Beatles 'Ticket to ride' and Humble Pie's 'Natural born bugie' which had everyone – including Adrian, Joe and Brian – on the dance floor. Only Martin was unmoved.

At the break, Judy said she needed to 'powder her nose' and left Phil with his mates.

"Didn't think this was your sort of stuff," said Martin. "Not very progressive, is it?"

"Never mind `im. Yow got a brahma there, mate," Joe said. "She's a real looker and a great mover on the floor. So, what on earth is she doing with yow?"

Phil really didn't actually have an answer but before he could speak Brian piped up.

"Has she got any sisters?" he asked

"Ger away with you," said Phil. "Only a younger brother!!"

"Yow'll be alright when the Fantastic get on to their slow numbers and, of course, we all know about their big finale," smirked Joe.

Just as Judy was walking back towards the lads, they grinned at Phil and then the band were back on stage, playing the first few notes of the Monkees' hit 'I'm a believer' and drawing the audience back on to the dance floor. The lads were right as the band's repertoire continued to become slower and more romantic, starting with current hits, 'Listen to me' from the Hollies and 'Sweet Caroline' by Neil Diamond, followed by Vanity Fare's 'Early in the morning' and 'Hooked on a feeling' by B J Thomas.

After covers of 'My Sentimental Friend' by Herman's Hermits and 'Frozen Orange Juice' by Peter Sarstedt, Dripper said that they would play two more songs and that would be it, although everyone knew it wouldn't be. Two smoochy pop ballads – 'Soul Deep' by the Box Tops and a brilliant version of Jackie de Shannon's song 'Put a little love in your heart' – were followed by rapturous applause from the crowd with plenty of foot stomping and whistles.

The band trooped off to their dressing room as the applause continued and the crowd became aware that something special was about to happen. After a couple of minutes, the door at the side of the club opened and in walked four of the band – Dripper, Richard, Keith and Tony – carrying a large coffin on to the stage. They placed it in the middle as smoke and dry ice started to come from the rear of the rostra stage.

Tony sat down at his drum set, a funereal look on his face and began a well-known rhythm beat. Dripper began to sing in a cartoonish fashion "I was working in the lab late one night, when my eyes beheld an eerie sight" and then the rest of the band began to play, no one noticing that Keith was playing bass, with Ron nowhere to be seen.

Just as they all sang with Dripper on the 'Monster Mash' chorus, there was a loud creak and the lid of the coffin began to slowly open. The form of a giant fiend – Ron was way over six foot tall – slowly sat up, looking like a cross between Frankenstein and Dracula, and just smiled, as blood began to drip down from the fangs in his mouth.

Stepping out of the coffin, Ron 'the Monster' staggered around the stage as the band continued to play their extended version of Bobby 'Boris' Pickett's hit from 1962. The crowd loved it, especially the boys as, when Ron lurched towards any of the girls, they would seek refuge and safety in the arms of the nearest lad, whether boyfriend or not.

After a few verses, the Monster made his way into the crowd, walking seemingly blind but knowing that he was scaring many of the fairer sex as he loomed towards them and the crowd parted, like Moses splitting the Red Sea. He continued his path towards the dressing room as the band continued to encourage everyone to "do the mash, do the monster mash", finally finishing with a wonderful noisy flourish. The crowd went crazy again, as they all took their bows and left the stage. It was a brilliantly staged ending.

Phil and Judy walked home, arm in arm, slowly and quietly. As they reached the junction of Pinfold Lane and the Penn Road, Phil asked Judy if she was okay.

"Yes fine," she replied reservedly.

"Well, you've hardly spoken a word since we left the youth club. You're not still frightened by the monster, are you?" said Phil.

"No silly, that was great fun," replied Judy.

"Blimey, you were hugging me pretty tight when he came down into the crowd," said Phil. "I thought I wouldn't be able to breathe!"

"Didn't hear you complain," said Judy, trying to smile.

"No complaints but who's got your tongue now or have I done something wrong?" Phil enquired.

"No. Quite the opposite," said Judy.

"What do you mean?" asked Phil. "I thought you really enjoyed yourself this evening?"

Judy stopped and looked straight at Phil, with tears in her eyes.

"And I loved this afternoon," she said. "And that's the problem. I have enjoyed myself so much today. Going to the football and then to the youth club, all the time being with you, and I don't want it to end."

"And why should it?" replied Phil.

"Because you will go off to university and I will want to train as an air stewardess and so we won't be together," said Judy with the tears now falling down her cheeks.

"But that's yonks from now and we just don't know what will happen between now and next September," said

Phil. "The past couple of months have been the first time I have stopped worrying about what is to come and I have just seen what each day brings. I never knew there would be only one seat left for me to sit on the bus, next to you. I didn't know that you had noticed me. I thought it was just one way, that I wanted to ask you out, never ever thinking that you might want to go out with me. If you want to know how I feel then I want to carry on seeing you each and every day."

"Me too," said Judy and she hugged Phil as tightly as she had at Molineux and at Venturers, and then gave him a passionately long kiss, getting toots from the horns of a couple of passing cars on the Penn Road.

"What was that f-f-for?" stammered Phil

"For being you and for a lovely day, you daft ha'peth," said Judy. "Now you'd better walk me home or we will be so late Dad will forbid me from seeing you again and I don't ever want that to happen."

They continued their walk home, a bit quicker now, and at the top of the drive to Judy's house, Phil received the second most passionate kiss of his life, a smile, a wave and Judy was safely home, just as Phil had promised her dad. A tad late but Phil was sure Judy's smile would win her father round. Who wouldn't be forgiving with that smile, he thought?

As Phil walked the short distance home, he wondered whether there would ever be days as good as this one: seeing the Wolves beat the Albion, a great night at Venturers, spending pretty well the whole day with Judy. If someone had told him two months ago that November 1st 1969 was going to be like this, he would never have believed them.

As he walked round to the back door and unlocked it, he wondered where he really would be in a year's time? It would be the start of a new decade, no longer the swinging sixties but the some-sort-of seventies and maybe he would be on a degree course at some university.

Would it be at Aberystwyth, Sheffield or St Andrews – his first three preferred choices on his UCCA form? Wales, Yorkshire or Scotland? All foreign parts as far as most folks from the Black Country were concerned. He had heard that they all had flourishing student unions putting on great concerts so he would still be seeing cracking live bands.

As he climbed the stairs to bed, he wondered how many more LPs he might acquire to take with him. Not just the eight, like on 'Desert Island Discs', but all his collection which was now well into double figures and would easily be the most eclectic amongst his fellow students, he thought. There would be one important matter to attend to however and that was to save up for his own record player to take to university. No way was Dad going to part with the family radiogram, even if Phil used it more than most.

Climbing into bed, he remembered Judy's tears at being so upset if they were to part. He had no clue what the situation would be with Judy in a year's time and he really didn't want to think about it. They had had today and it had been great. They could have tomorrow and the day after and the day after that. Why not?

But as he drifted off to sleep a contented smile crept across his face. Phil knew that if there was one thing that would be an absolute certainty this time next year, then he knew that he would be, and always would be, a Wolves supporter!

ACKNOWLEDGEMENTS

Thanks go to many people for helping me to get this project completed – never easy for an expert procrastinator like me!

The information on 1960s Wolves games comes from a variety of sources. It is amazing how much can be sourced from the internet. Particular thanks to David Instone's excellent website – www.wolvesheroes.com – where you can find information on players who have proudly worn the black and gold over the past century – he lists over 1,000 of them, together with details on managers and Wolves legends. It's an absolute goldmine especially when a player's name comes up in an old programme and you can't recall them.

And talking of programmes, thanks to internet sellers where you can now fill in those gaps in your collection. I had excellent service from www.footy-progs.com who were able to find good annotated copies of programmes for the 11 games covered in this tome – much appreciated, Bob, Frank and Elvis.

And then there's YouTube. With several games featured in this book, you might think I was actually watching the game on TV from the detailed description given, and I was. There are now highlights of some 1960s games, mainly from BBC Match of the Day, available to enjoy all over again.

And for the ones that weren't on video, I have to give immense praise to Lisa at Wolverhampton City Archives for digging deep and finding the required match reports from the legendary '*Express & Star*' reporter, Phil Morgan.

When it comes to the music of the time, and particularly the albums that I have featured, I would hope that my research, using too many books and internet sources to mention, has been accurate and thorough. If not, I am sure there will be someone out there who will put me right!

Two sources need very special mention. First, John at www.brumbeat.net. If this tome has made you want to know more about the music scene in the West Midlands area in the 1960s, then look no further than this fantastic website.

Second, the late great Keith Farley author of the definitive work on music from this era in the Black Country entitled *'N Between Times – An Oral History of the Wolverhampton Group Scene of the 1960s* which can now be read on the Wolverhampton History & Heritage Website – www.historywebsite.co.uk – where you can also find a multitude of articles on the area, including many about Penn. Many thanks to all the contributors for their splendid pieces on this site.

In 2009, Keith revised his work and it was then published as *'They Rocked, We Rolled'* a year later, shortly after Keith's death and now a much sought-after publication, containing details of the various interviews that Keith did with many of the group members who feature in this work. The custodian of Keith's works is his life-long friend, Dave Cant, and I must thank Dave for his valued advice, support and friendship throughout this project.

In quoting certain lyrics from songs of the time, many thanks for the kind permission granted by the legendary Stan Webb, guitarist with Chicken Shack, who are still touring – details can be found on www.stanwebb.co.uk. In other instances, permissions have been requested.

There are many friends who have become very welcome 'critical readers' as chapters developed and were completed. Massive thanks to Coral, Linda and Paul, Will, Graham, Carys, George, and Jo in New Zealand. You all know how much I have valued your comments, suggestions and corrections, especially those to do with Black Country expressions and dialect!

Thank you to my fellow creative writing students who have so persuasively encouraged me to keep going with this venture. Penny, Sue and Lynne, for 'staying the course' with each chapter as well as Tam, Andre, Roisin and Jos.

The four most important people who have been instrumental in getting me to the point of publication are tutor, proof-reader, editor and cover artist.

The cover collage, mainly of the bands and the Wolverhampton landmarks that feature in this book, has been created by David Augustin, a brilliant artist, musician and composer. In fact, he is the most talented person I know. To see his stunning art, then find his work on Facebook – just search DAART. To hear some of his music search for Dreamlogic or you can find his compositions and arrangements on Soundcloud. Wonderful cover, Dave.

A big thank you to Cherry for putting her recent recuperation time to good use, as well as her master's degree in English, by proof-reading this tome. Editing of the book – and there was a heck of a lot to correct and improve on – has been fastidiously carried out by Cecilia. Both of you have little or no interest in football or the music of the time or knowledge of either the bands I saw or the places in Wolverhampton so important to me in my formative years. Thank you both for your patience, skill and expertise.

For any budding authors, you might consider joining a Creative Writing class in your area and you may possibly come across a tutor who encourages your work, points you in the right direction on matters relating to dialogue, layout, formatting and punctuation. I did and I thank you, Caroline, for your guidance together with constant support and encouragement over the past two years.

And finally, I am more than obliged to my wife, Sharon, who has been urging/encouraging/nagging me to write this book over the past few years and for then leaving me alone in my man-shed to just get on with it. Often the best way! So, if you haven't enjoyed reading this book, it's her fault!

Printed in Poland
by Amazon Fulfillment
Poland Sp. z o.o., Wrocław